Y0-BZT-464

Contents

Guilt Payment

by Ty Pak

Library of Congress Catalog Card Number: 83-71242
ISBN 0-910043-01-9

Guest editor: James Harstad
Cover and book design: Phyllis Y. Miyamoto

"A Fire" was first published in *Bamboo Ridge, The Hawaii Writers'
Quarterly*, No. 7 (June-August 1980): 28-36. It was reprinted in *Asian
and Pacific Literature*, Vol. I (1982: Hawaii State Department of
Education), 443-450.
"Steady Hands" was first published in *Bamboo Ridge, The Hawaii
Writers' Quarterly*, No. 13 (December 1981-February 1982): 27-34.

This project was supported by a grant from the National Endowment
for the Arts (NEA) in Washington, D.C., a federal agency. It was also
supported, in part, by a grant from the State Foundation on Culture and
the Arts (SFCA). The SFCA is funded by grants from the Hawaii State
Legislature and by grants from the NEA.

Bamboo Ridge Press
P.O. Box 61781
Honolulu, Hawaii 96839-1781
(808) 599-4823

10 9 8 7 6 5 4 3 2   91 92 93 94 95

Introduction

It is not the mission of that most civilized of American institutions, the National Geographic Society, to document conflict between peoples. Usually, as in the October 1952 edition of its familiar journal, it seems to go far out of its way to avoid the suggestion that human beings are ever anything but charitable toward and harmonious with one another and with all things of peaceful disposition whenever they are given a legitimate and informed choice. All its years of reassuring optimism have made that attitude and its extension, which is that with just a little more effort to understand one another we can indeed all get along amicably, seem plausible, even possible. This entirely admirable policy of promoting humankind's most virtuous impulses is reflected no more readily by the *National Geographic Magazine's* articles than by its advertising.

Thus, in that same October 1952 edition, a full-page Chevrolet ad depicts Mr. and Mrs. America and cherubic ten-year-old daughter Cindy returning home from church in their beautiful new Bel Air Chevy. Mr. America is of course driving, and Cindy is in the back seat, hair unruffled though the windows are down. They all wear hats and smiles and are being open-mouth and wide-eye admired by a young pair of clean-cut Jack Armstrong/Bob Steele boys who have successfully pleaded the fresh spring day as an excuse for innocent ecclesiastical truancy. The curiously half-mowed lawn across the redwood fence from them was perhaps left that way by a belatedly conscience-stricken Sunday morning worshipper, or perhaps by the boys themselves. A perfectly symmetrical row of poplars or junipers fades to softly rolling hills and gauzy skies.

All seems right in this ideal American world, yet the no-

1

tion that God is comfortably in His place is undercut by small, parenthetical italics of ominously veiled warning: *(Continuation of standard equipment and trim illustrated is dependent on availability of material.)* The warning does not specifically say what standard equipment or trim might be discontinued or what might cause it to be unavailable, but it happens to be true that buyers of 1952 Chevrolets (and 1952 Fords) were acquiring a product whose bumpers and grill were likely to be so thinly chromium-plated as to be unusually susceptible to oxidation. It does not say that should Mr. and Mrs. America equip their new Chevy with a radio (not standard equipment), they would gain the option to be personally addressed not only by the strident discourses of Walter Winchell: "Good evening, Mr. and Mrs. America and all the ships at sea," but also by those of Drew Pearson: "Captured Red prisoners carry leaflets that say...the Communists are sure to win the war because they have developed a bomb that kills only non-Communists." Or that daughter Cindy might find her emotions vicariously twinged by the poignancy of a song apparently directed at her own tender heart: "Cindy, oh Cindy, Cindy don't let me down. Write me a letter soon, and I'll be homeward bound..." and by the plaintive response: "Dear John, oh how I hate to write. Dear John, I must let you know tonight...."

The warning also does not say that should the Jack Armstrong/Bob Steele boys have an idolized father, uncle, cousin, or older brother currently performing his duty in the military service of his country, he might well return to them ahead of schedule as one of the pitifully patched-together and nerve-shattered Washing Machine Charlies occasionally seen talking to themselves on park benches or staring into empty beer pitchers at local taverns—if he returns to them at all. It does not say, in short, that there is a war going on in Korea, nor that the United States is up to its skivvies in that war. Nor does it say that one of the results of that war might be future generations of Chevrolets carrying future generations of Mr. and Mrs. Americas, themselves perhaps Asian-featured, past admiring boys whose family names are as likely to be Kim or Pak as Armstrong or Steele.

The 1952 Chevrolet ad may be extremely circumspect in its mention of the Korean War and its consequences, but the stories of Ty Pak, thirty years later, suffer from no such indirectness. Things happen head-on, fast, and chaotic in Pak's stories, as things must happen in wartime. And in Pak's stories it is always wartime, whether he is flashing back to early 1950's Seoul, or flashing ahead to contemporary Honolulu. Pak's stories not only give the war a sense of

2

personal immediacy missing from the writing of most of its journalistic correspondents—and from endless M*A*S*H reruns—but they also portray the war as a sort of ongoing social altercation still being fought in one form or another by its indigenous survivors in Korea, Hawaii, and across the U.S. mainland. And, in fact, around the world.

Expatriation under almost any circumstances must be an unusually soul-burdening experience. The circumstance of civil war could well be expected to add to the expatriate's burden so full a complement of guilt and trauma that an entire lifetime of amends and rationalizations would not give it dispatch. That is at least part of the message of Ty Pak's vigorous prose, and it is the part from which the sons and daughters of expatriate Kims and Paks might find important clues to their American identity.

Perhaps as relevant to them and probably more relevant to the sons and daughters of Cindy America, Jack Armstrong, and Bob Steele, however, are the decidedly unglamorous scenes of "limited" (meaning non-nuclear) armed conflict—of flame-reddened skies, of hills rolling with artillery—from which crippled trees and besieged cathedrals offer at best imperfect shelter during any day of the week or season of the year. And in which there are no lawns, half-mowed or otherwise, and no families of happy churchgoers in beautiful new 1952 Bel Air Chevrolets whose chrome will unexpectedly rust before its time. And of which not one of the witnesses is admiring. And beside which the prospect of nuclear adventure must loom like the desert sun to a grain of sand or a speck of dust.

In its March 1983 edition, the *National Geographic Magazine* continues to promote its optimistic world view. The world view of Ty Pak's stories is certainly less obvious in its optimism. It is, however, a good deal more forthright in its fictional representation of a tragic reality that can most properly be felt only through the experiences of its individual victims, both those who survive and those who do not. That the survivors are willing to continue their struggle for a life already proven to be considerably less than ideal must be seen as optimistic. And that a writer of Ty Pak's caliber should have chosen to record that struggle is itself reassuring.

James Harstad
Honolulu
April 3, 1983

Guilt Payment

"If I'd had the right teacher, I wouldn't have failed in the Western Regionals," says Mira bitterly.

"But you've won the Hawaii audition," I point out. "Look how many competitors you had to put behind to get that far. John Singleton's daughter, Mary, who everybody said had a heavenly voice, placed only third. You hold the crown here."

"I'm no tractable Polynesian lass to be content with an island title. I want to go all the way to the top. I want to sing at the Metropolitan. I want to show the whole world what a Korean-American girl can do."

"There is always next year, and besides you have to learn to be content..."

"With a thousand-dollar cash prize? And end up salesgirling or teaching a bunch of tone-deaf kids, occasionally singing on the side at churches and ceremonies for a pittance? I don't want any part of it. I must go to Florence and study under Maestro Vincenti."

"Isn't Florence where he comes from, that Italian snob hanging around you all the time, Peter, Petro, or whatever his blasted name is?"

"Piero. I haven't seen a man with a worse memory for names. I really don't see how you could have become a professor of English, which presumably takes a lot of memorizing. Well, after all, it's only the University of Hawaii you are a professor at."

"Young lady, we are discussing this Piero fellow and your fantastic scheme of going to his native town at a great cost for no purpose at all..."

"What've you got against him? Anyway, Piero has nothing to do with it. It's just a coincidence that the world-renowned maestro happens to reside now at the place where Piero was born."

"Where his parents and relatives live, no doubt."

"Will you or will you not make this little sacrifice? When I get the big roles, the money you are investing now will seem like nothing. I will pay you back every cent with interest. I simply have to go to Italy."

"But what have the Italians got that this great country of ours hasn't? Go back to Julliard and take graduate courses or private lessons from Professor Bertram whom you used to think so highly of."

"He is old fashioned. Passe. Played out. He is old. Period. I have to breathe fresh air, learn new styles and techniques, receive new inspirations, get out of this old country."

"Since when has the U.S. become an old country?"

"Father, I respect your knowledge of English, but you know very little about musicianship, especially operatic singing and the training and discipline that go with it."

Haven't I paid full tuition for all her special lessons ever since she was three? But of course I hold my tongue.

"Trust my judgment, father. If it was avoidable, I wouldn't ask. This is the only way. I know Mother would see it my way if she were alive."

That vanquishes me for good. Oh, the burden of remorse and self-recrimination! It was quite by accident that Mira came by this infallible formula for neutralizing my resistance. She was about seven and wanted to go to a carnival at the other end of the island. She had been to a dozen already, and they were of course all such dreadful bores to me. Besides, I had an important paper to finish for a journal. I couldn't spare the time. Pettishly she remarked that her friend Joyce's mother was taking her children, adding that if she had a mother like everybody else, she would not be left at the mercy of a selfish father who did nothing for others and just read and read all day long. Life was no fun at this house of ours, she said. Her mother, whom she had never known, would see it her way, she was sure.

Silently, like a sleep-walker, I drove her 50 miles to the Haleiwa Beach Park carnival grounds. I had been her slave ever since. Not that she was reckless in the exercise of her power. Like a discerning monarch she let me, her subject, enjoy a degree of independence—even an illusion of sovereignty—in small things, but when it came to things that really mattered, matters of money and time, out came the mighty club to beat me flat. She must wonder at the efficacy of this weapon, for invariably she asked me, a smile twinkling in her eyes, what wicked thing I had done to her mother. But she never really gave me a chance to tell her, as she bolted away humming or singing merrily over the fresh reaffirmation of her supremacy. After all, when you have it good, why jinx it by looking into the whence and wherefore? But would I have told her if she really wanted to know? Not in a million years.

* * *

We had been married only eight months, Yoomi and I, when the war broke out, on Sunday, June 25, 1950. On Monday I went to the university as usual. We were to carry on our business as usual, Syngman Rhee told us over and over on the radio. The whole affair was nothing but a border skirmish, for which the provokers, rash North Korean communists, would be soundly thrashed by the South Korean army, backed by the U.S. with its atom bombs. The spring semester was winding to a close, and the finals were not too far off. The monsoon had started early and it rained dismally, incessantly. Neither the faculty nor the students could keep their minds on their books. I called on my class to translate some passages from Hardy but could not get their attention. When I called a student's name, he would look briefly at me with indifference, then turn away to resume his talk with his friends. There was no point in dragging on. When I came out of the classroom, I noticed the same restiveness had possessed all the other classes: students had poured out into the school yard, milling around like lost ants. The general assembly bell rang and the dean mounted the rostrum. The school was to go into recess indefinitely until further notice. I left for home, wondering whether the indefiniteness included the end of the month, pay day.

Hayhwa Avenue was filled with trucks of khaki-clad troops in netted helmets heading north up Miyari Pass. There was an intermittent distant boom like suppressed thunder, which got louder and more insistent by the minute. At nightfall cannon shells whirred overhead, freezing the blood. Shrapnel tore the rain-drenched, blacked-out air. Machine guns and rifles rattled. Grenades exploded. The terror-stricken populace, caught in the crossfire, ran blindly for shelter, getting maimed and mauled in the process. They had to get away, to run, no matter where. The artillery shells seemed to be aimed directly at their homes, the places they had known so long and well, and they sought refuge by running right into the hills where the shells pelted like hailstones. The next morning the sky opened and the indifferent sun shone, disclaiming all responsibility for the nightmare of the previous night. Russian tanks were already in town. Rhee had fled south after destroying the Han bridge,

7

making sure that nobody, neither the invading army nor his trusting people, followed him.

A wave of mass arrests swept through the city. All those who had managed to make a decent living were counter-revolutionaries, enemies of the people. Their houses, their jobs were proof enough of their treachery. The dregs of society rose to the top and banded themselves into Youth Leagues, Women's Leagues, People's Leagues. Armed with fixed bayonets, the gift of the victors, these upstart self-decreed legislators and justices, flaunting their red headbands and armbands of authority, ferreted out the enemies of the people who had committed the colossal crime of supporting their families with all the diligence their training and aptitude afforded. The Soosong Elementary School, packed full to bursting with such undesirables, was posted with armed guards. Other public places also served as collection and detention points. A percentage of the prisoners were taken out at regular intervals and shot at public squares, where their bodies were left to be spat on and kicked at, to rot for days. First to go were all government employees, however lowly: office clerks, guards, even custodians. But top priority was given to the so-called power sectors, policemen, tax officials, and soldiers. There was a whole division of Rhee's soldiers, stragglers and wounded, who hadn't gotten away before the bridge fell.

I went into hiding and managed to elude the first searches. We had just moved to the house a few months before, and nobody in the neighborhood knew about my teaching position at the university. But they caught on soon enough, and Yoomi, nearing her time and anemic from malnutrition, had to go to the district office to account with browbeatings and threats for my absence. With the intensifying American air raids, which did not distinguish between military and civilian targets, it wasn't too uncommon to be reported missing, unless there were witnesses to the contrary. There was no food in the house, and Yoomi had to drag her heavy body laden with clothes, utensils, and other valuables for barter at the nearest open market, until we had nothing left. Even the bedding was gone, and we shivered at night.

The only news we had of the war was what the communists gave out. The fall of the Pusan perimeter was imminent, the last holdout of the American running dogs. They would be driven into the sea to drown, and the fatherland would at last be one. As the days lengthened into weeks, I wondered whether there was any point in my continued hiding, which meant overworking Yoomi to death. I contemplated seriously

8

giving myself up, but Yoomi wouldn't have it. Sangjo Kim, the historian, Wongyong Chay, the criminologist, and all those we knew had been coralled and marched away God knew where.

One day after carrying home a sack of barley for the last of my winter clothing, she collapsed at the gate. Since I could not go out and help lest the neighbors should see, she crawled on all fours, undid the latch, and came into the house. Her labor had started. The placenta had burst. It was our first birth, but I had heard that this was an emergency. Her life was at stake, but when I made ready to run for the midwife who resided in the neighborhood, Yoomi clutched my ankles with an unbreakable grip. She would not let me go. I watched helplessly, biting my lip as the pangs tortured and twisted her. Mira was eventually born. Yoomi, delirious with fever, lay unconscious for days. I hated the bawling lump of flesh, the cause of the impending death of my beloved.

I made barley broth and fed it to the baby, but she rejected the food after a few sips. She raised hell, her face turning red and blotchy. In spite of her delirium Yoomi heard the child, hugged it close and fumbled about her breast. I offered no assistance; either the baby had to survive on barley broth or perish. It would not further endanger its mother's health by leeching. With an uncanny homing instinct the little brute deftly sought out the teats. Then, gathering her lips into a snout, she cupped them over one with a flopping sound and sucked away voraciously, draining her mother's life blood. She sucked and sucked, until the previously swollen sacs sagged and shriveled. Then she bawled for more.

I was furious and could have strangled her. Marveling at my unnatural disposition, I wondered what the poets who spewed ardently about parental affection could have meant. The crying, wetting, misshapen, grotesque bundle of newborn flesh did not inspire me with anything but loathing. I resented her untimely intrusion. Already her birth could be kept secret no more. The neighbors had heard her cries and came officiously to assist and give advice to my half-dead wife, while I had to scamper away to my perch under the roof, erasing all traces of my latest descent.

Miraculously Yoomi survived the days of fever, near starvation, and constant suction by the little vampire. She was back on her feet to feed all three of us, now carrying the baby on her back. We had sold the stereo and records, the clock and radio, the guitar and accordion, even the harmonica and cymbal. The time had come to part with our wedding gifts, her half-karat diamond ring and my Omega watch, which we had sworn never to sell. I again proposed to give myself up. Surely

9

the communists must have use for an English professor.
Maybe I could be their translator, intelligence decoder, or what
not, but again Yoomi prevented me.

It was early September and the food from our wedding
mementos had lasted only a week. Yoomi hired herself out as a
kitchen maid at a neighbor's, Char somebody, who was some
kind of a big wheel with the new regime. We had been smell-
ing his barbecuing beef all through the summer. The place
seemed a Mecca for the Communist cadres to congregate and
celebrate, their drunken, raucous singing lasting through the
night. These communists didn't seem to know choral singing
at all and everybody always sang in unison. The repertoire
was limited to the Red Flag, the Glorious Leader Ilsung Kim,
and other Party and Army songs which they never seemed to
tire of, which were too sacrosanct to allow accompaniment by
any musical instrument other than their own vocal cords.
Occasionally they tried some traditional folk songs. At this
point some rank amateur banged down on our Baldwin grand,
off key.

One of the first things every citizen had to do was report to
the authorities special luxuries such as the piano. Yoomi volunteered and contributed it to the cause to forestall its inevitable
discovery by the search parties, which might keep looking to
find more. Perhaps such cooperation might mollify their
suspicion and antagonism toward our house, if not quite win
their favor. The piano was moved to Char's. Yoomi's father
had bought it on her graduation from college with top honors
in her piano class. She had brought it with her when she married me. We had planned a recital sometime in September at
the Municipal Hall with the Seoul Philharmonic. Of course
none of the Communists had kept up with the musical scene of
the south and nobody knew her. To them she was just another
miserable housewife, a reactionary's deserted wife, with an
infant child to feed. But when they seemed to murder the good
music and ruin the piano, I felt an urge to show to Char and
comrades what a good musician like Yoomi could do with it.
Even their musical travesty stopped altogether and the piano
was never heard again. We learned later that the grand had
been moved to some public hall for the Liberation Day
ceremony on August 15, but the place was bombed and a piano
was the farthest thing from anybody's mind.

Her pay was the burnt layer of rice scraped off the bottom
of the pot and occasionally the leftover goodies from their
tables. At that time, when a peck of rice was worth more than
a piano, we had to consider this a generous remuneration. But
the strain of work so soon after childbirth ruined her health

despite the improved diet. She hemorrhaged continuously. Her shining eyes receded deeper and deeper into their bony sockets, and her skin grew sallow. Sweat stood on her forehead and dizzy spells forced her to steady herself by holding on to the wall or furniture. I told her to stop working; we could skimp, and the burnt rice, which we ate by soaking in water, would see us through a week. By then surely the Americans would be back. Witness the almost round-the-clock air raids by the American Air Force, completely paralyzing all daytime mobility of the People's Army.

But Yoomi wouldn't listen. She had to do it for her baby, who indeed prospered. Her cheeks filled out nicely, and her earlier formlessness gave way to a proportioned articulation of features. When she smiled and crooned in her contentment after a lengthy feeding at her mother's breast, there was even a hint of the innocence and beauty of the Raphaelite Christ child. While she was the epitome of health, her mother withered. I resented the little selfish creature and resisted my growing fondness for her.

September was drawing to a close, yet Seoul was still solidly in the hands of the Communists. The air raids seemed a mere surface irritation to the dug-in, deeply-entrenched ground forces. After what seemed to be a thorough devastation of anti-aircraft bunkers in a given area, the new formation of fighters and bombers the next day would be greeted with as vigorous salvos of flak as before from the same area. Time was said to be running out for the Communists. But it might run out for the Americans, too. After all, planes and bombs couldn't be inexhaustible. And time was definitely running out for us, our little microcosm of three, a nameless and lost speck in the vast macabre chessboard of indiscriminate death and destruction.

Whole streets were turning into honeycombs of pillboxes and bunkers. Naval bombardment had begun from American ships off Inchon, systematically erasing the city off the map. Fires broke out everywhere. A few houses down the block from ours got hit. What had been a sturdy concrete structure disintegrated, leaving a huge crater, while the ensuing fire spread and stopped just before our house. Yoomi and Mira had been moved out, and I was almost smoked out myself. We might absorb a direct hit ourselves at any minute. Wistfully I looked at the repapered walls of our main bedroom, how we had spent days looking for the right color and pattern, how upset we had been whenever a fly left a black spot and what meticulous care we had taken to remove the blemish without staining the rest of the paper.

11

Last-minute roundups of reactionaries were going on, which now included just about every civilian still left in the city who could not be positively identified as an activist in the new regime. As the first U.S. Marines crossed the Han, the detainees at various basements and temporary lockups, emaciated, bruised, mangled skeletons who had somehow survived the torture and interrogation without food, were led out and shot. Both banks of the Chonggay Drain were strewn with their bodies. Some were packed into abandoned air raid trenches and buried alive. Many were simply shot on the streets and left there to be trampled. Whole families, including the very young and old, were executed. The Communists became more vicious and wanton; if they were to die, they would leave no survivors to curse their memory and exult over their end. They killed anybody for no cause at all.

One night there came a loud knock at the gate. Our hearts were tight knots. Our legs wouldn't move. Mira started crying frantically, bringing us to our senses. Yoomi snatched her up and went to the door, at the same time motioning me to the attic. But there was no time for it. There seemed to be half a dozen of them and they were already through the gate, apparently having broken the latch. They were beaming their flashlights all over the house, especially toward the attic. One was going into the kitchen, another to the basement, a third to the back of the house. I had barely gotten into the outhouse latrine by the fence, when I realized one of them was coming toward it. In the three-by-five compartment I had no alternative but to jump into the tank, feet first, my hands pushing down the slippery sides. The thick mass on top closed over my head without a ripple. I was conscious of a flashlight overhead. The stamping feet on the creaky boards left and the door banged. I nevertheless stayed submerged as long as I could.

I heard Yoomi shriek. She thought they had found me in the attic when three of them vaulted into it through the access trap and turned over every piece of furniture stored there, poking into the corners with their bayonets. It was painful not to go out and reassure her of my safety. Mira went on screaming harder; probably Yoomi had dropped her. At one point I thought they were coming back to the latrine and was ready to duck again, but they didn't. About half an hour later, what seemed like an eternity, I issued out of the outhouse and ran to the inner courtyard. Hair disordered and face ashen, Yoomi was suckling Mira. She gave a start as if she had seen a ghost. She had passed out and regained consciousness only minutes before. She thought they had taken me away. Only then did we notice my odoriferous condition. We laughed like two lunatics. Thank God I had postponed installing the flush toilet. The cost of the new plumbing and septic tank system, there being no city sewage, had been prohibitive.

We had to leave the house. A shell had gouged a big hole on the street next to the stone fence, which had been blown off like dust. The roof had collapsed and we were squeezed between the sprung closet door frame and a fallen beam. A window slat dug into my calf, but Yoomi and Mira were unhurt. We had to get out fast. The dry wood had caught fire, and the smoke pierced and blinded our eyes. Shells were falling everywhere. The night sky was lit with a reddish glow that gave the illusion of soaking the whole city in blood. But the alleys were pitch dark, except for occasional flickerings through the openings.

Just as I turned a corner, with Yoomi and Mira close behind, rifle shots rang out. Instantly I drew back. Pressing close to the wall we retreated into the alley we had emerged from. A patrol of the People's Army passed. They paused briefly at the corner to peer into the darkness, but apparently more urgent business elsewhere didn't allow them to tarry. We came out of the alley, rounded the corner, and swiftly went along the other street. Dry plane leaves crackled at our feet, startling us. We kept walking fast, backtracking and detouring whenever a shell crashed near, a roadblock loomed ahead, or a patrol was audible. We were going in the general direction of the Han to the south, but the topography, jumbled beyond recognition by dugouts and shellings, was thoroughly confusing. To the south the sky was bright with flares, probably attesting to the American beachhead. Only the Americans would try to expel darkness, and we had agreed that our hope lay in getting through the Communist battle zone to the brighter sky.

Sudden tommy gun bursts were followed by the noise of people shouting and running.

"Stop or we'll shoot," a voice yelled. The tommy guns burped. Instinctively we had crouched flat to the ground. Shots whizzed past. Cannonade continued with their booms and crashes. A highrise down the block tottered and broke up. Whole walls and floors flew overhead and dumped all around us. We got out of the alley and suddenly came to the broad Namsan Avenue, pale with the shimmer of flares and fires and explosions. The avenue was full of enfilade. We had to get away from this highway of flying metal.

"Let's find a trench, an air raid shelter," I said.

"They say they're filled up with bodies," Yoomi said.

My spine crawled. I shuddered at the thought of what must

have happened to the man who had been fleeing in our direction a minute before. A half circle of grey was fanning slowly in the eastern sky, eroding the redness of artificial illumination. The chilly morning breeze buffeted our noses with whiffs of rancid smoke, the overpowering compound of burning gunpowder, wood, paint, earth, concrete, and human flesh. There was a flare right above our heads, disclosing our shapes. For the first time we looked at each other's face in the eerie light and were shocked at our skeletal haggardness, as if all the meat had evaporated. But we were not allowed the luxury of mutual scrutiny for long. A few feet from us lay a headless man's body, drenched in blood, still warm, kicking. The brains had spilt out of the bashed head a few feet away. Dark patches of blood stippled the whitewashed wall. Yoomi trembled and hid her face in my chest.

"Let's get into a trench before we get it ourselves," I said, pulling her behind me into an alley. There was a tearing explosion. The place we had just stood disappeared in a cloud of fiery smoke. More mortar shells rained upon the same spot. We could see fire spitting out of a machine gun emplacement a little distance away. Near South Gate we found and jumped into an unoccupied dugout, about four feet by ten feet. The floor was covered with a sheet of water. The walls were slimy. The smell of mildew, feces, and decay staggered us. Fresh pine trunks, their green-needled branches sticking up here and there, supported the ceiling of earth packed in straw bags. Where the bagging was torn, earth cascaded into the puddle of water on the floor with each ground-shaking explosion. Yoomi uncovered the flap of cloth she had put across Mira's face. She slept on soundly, quite unconcerned. One shell fell almost on top of the trench. The ceiling and walls shook, ready to cave in. The dust was suffocating. Instinctively Yoomi hid Mira's face against her bosom. The infant's nostrils fluttered, her eyelids quivered, her clenched hands waved uncertainly. Then she went back to sleep, her facial muscles relaxing, even hinting a smile. I was gripped with compunction. The little innocent life seemed the dearest thing in the world. I recalled how beastly my attitude had been toward this sublime being, free from taint and impurity. Her faint, still-lingering smile seemed the climax of all life, as if all previous generations had existed only to culminate in this perfection. So many lives had been plowed back into the soil to sprout this exquisite flower.

A hot puff of air, as if somebody had suddenly opened a heated oven, filled the trench, sizzling the wet floor. Flames darted into the trench from the opening. We gasped for breath. Our bodies were like burning brands. We doubled up and burrowed our heads into the ground, but the floor was aflame, too. Outside were rushing feet and loud voices.

"Napalms, napalms," shouted somebody running past our trench.

"Retreat to Position Two," another voice shouted, as the trotting feet scattered. Shortly afterward, there were other voices.

"Stop!" somebody yelled. Tommy guns clattered away, followed by screams. Cool air came into our trench and we could breathe. Mira let out a piercing cry. Her face was flushed like a ball of fire. Yoomi tried to comfort her but Mira kicked and thrashed, crying louder and louder. We heard footsteps approaching us. Yoomi bared her breast and tried to pacify Mira, but it did not work. The child dodged her head left or right, thrusting her hands mightily against her mother, and her face contorted with the effort, her cry growing louder. We didn't know what to do. Discovery by the Communist soldiers would be certain death. Anyone other than themselves on this battle line would be enemy agents or undesirables summarily to be executed. At that moment, just as the detachment of troops was almost above our trench, more napalms fell around our trench, and the footsteps ceased. Hot flames hissed past the entrance, and some leaped in, almost licking us. I pulled Yoomi to the other end of the trench, our feet sinking in the mud. Mira expressed her disapproval of the jolt by doubling the decibels of her cry.

"Help, good people. Help!" said a voice at the mouth of the trench. Our hair stood up and our breath stopped. A young man of about twenty was crawling into the trench. He dragged one leg, his torn flesh showing through gaping trousers. His entire face was sleek with blood.

"I heard you, good people," he said. "I knew you could not be bad. People with crying children can't be bad. Give me anything to tie up my wound with."

Yoomi tore a strip from her skirt before I had a chance to protest and handed it to the wounded man. He hurriedly tied up his thigh, stopping the bleeding in the leg. He stretched out his hand for more strips of cloth and Yoomi was about to oblige, which would have left her practically bare. I stopped her. The young man noticed it. He tore off his torn trouser leg, split it along the seam, and wiped his face. There was an ominous gash in his upper left forehead from which blood kept oozing. He bound his head above his eye and just below the wound, which seemed to stem the bleeding somewhat.

"Can't you stop the baby's crying?" he said, looking at us with annoyance. "They'll hear us for sure, just as I heard you, and we will be done for. They shoot any civilian. It is their last vengeance."

"Do they really?" I said incredulously.

"You'll find out soon enough if you let the child carry on," he said, urgently, imperatively. He made a lunge toward Mira but stopped short when Yoomi gathered Mira closer to her and shrank from him.

"Don't you hear them coming this way? I'll be damned if I'll get shot in this stinking hole because of a crying baby," he said, crawling out of the trench. A few seconds later, amid the crashes of artillery and mortar, we heard the nervous chatter of tommy guns and a long scream, which could have been the young man's, but we weren't sure. There were more feet rushing back and forth, more explosions.

"He was right. We'll get caught if we stay here with her crying her head off like this. We've got to leave her and get out," I said.

"Leave her?"

"Yes. But we'll come back for her. They won't kill a baby."

Horrified, she backed away from me, holding Mira tightly.

"If you want to live so badly that you have to abandon your own child, then go away from us," Yoomi said in disgust.

"It's not a question of abandoning. It's a question of avoiding suicide. It's survival, survival of us, you and me."

"What about Mira?"

"A lump of flesh, hardly conscious of its own existence!"

"Why is she crying if she's not conscious?"

"That's precisely what I mean. If she was truly aware of her position, she wouldn't cry. We have perception, a fully-developed adult consciousness, but hers is not even human yet. It's not much different from that of bugs. Besides, we made her. We can make many more like her."

I heard another detachment of troops approaching, their voices growing louder. Mira seemed to time her crying for a crescendo. In immediate reaction I put my hand across her mouth.

"Get away from her," Yoomi shrieked shrilly above Mira's crying, at the same time bending down and biting my hand so hard that a bone crunched. I jumped back in pain. The detachment was unmistakably coming directly toward us.

"Get out! Get out! I don't know you. We have no need of you," Yoomi was shouting. I had no time to think. I bounded out of the trench. Tommy guns burped behind me. A giant had grabbed me by the thigh. I fell down. Something warm suffused my leg. There was a loud thunder that completely deafened me and knocked out my senses.

The next time I noticed anything, it was broad daylight. I was lying before the gaunt remains of a building. Down the street, on both sides, I saw crumbling pillboxes and barricades with machine guns and dead soldiers slung across the sandbags. Farther down the street, around the Taypyongdong Rotary, a motorcade of American amphibious tanks, armored cars, and trucks was approaching, followed by thousands of Koreans waving flags and shouting hooray to the saviors. Where had they all been? I thought they had all been murdered or starved and no soul had been left alive in Seoul. In between the shouts and the rumble of the engines I heard a baby's subdued, hoarse whimpering. For the first time I remembered what had happened. I stood up and tried to run, but the big hand pulled me down. My left leg was a useless stump. It was the very same leg from whose calf a splinter had been extracted earlier. The bullet, entering at a small neat hole, had departed on the other side after wrenching out a big chunk of steak, bone and all. The rest of my leg hung by mere skin. How foolish the Korean saying that one doesn't get hurt twice in the same place!

I crawled across the street to the heap of earth from under which the sobbing of the baby continued intermittently, inaudibly. I started digging away frantically with my hands. Soon the nails broke off and the fingers bled. The crowd arrived. An American Marine walked up. To his surprise, I explained in English that my wife and baby were underneath. He had several of his buddies come with shovels. First came to sight a People's Army soldier with a broken back. Then, under a log, in a cubic foot of space, Mira was safe, although her legs were trapped in earth. The jagged end of a beam had rammed through Yoomi's chest.

* * *

"All right, Mira," I say. "I'll get the money ready tomorrow, and you can make the plane reservations and other preparations. But please write to me when you get to Florence."

"Oh, Dad, you are an angel," she says, hugging me. "I'll remember this always and pay you back, all of it and more. I know what kind of a sacrifice this is to you."

Does she? Perhaps. Strangely, she doesn't ask this time the usual question of what wicked thing I have done to her mother. Well, no matter. It boils down to the same thing, me picking up the tab, sweating and toiling to fulfill her big decisions. I'll have to withdraw from my Christmas Club savings, which I have intended for my next sabbatical trip to

Possession Sickness

"Get away from there," shouted George Khan. "You have better things to do than gluing yourself to TV all evening."

"I've got to see this," said Aileen, his 13-year-old daughter. "I've never watched a Korean shaman ritual. Have you?"

George rushed from the kitchen where he was washing dishes. Soap suds popped and ran on his hands. What he saw on the TV screen made him wide-eyed. It was Channel Eleven, the PBS, broadcasting live from Kennedy Theater on the University of Hawaii campus. Five shamans, wearing the ritualistic red and blue striped coats, sat in a semicircle, beating drums of different sizes and chanting in unison.

"They are calling the spirits, the sun spirit, ocean spirit, mountain spirit, river spirit," Aileen said. "There are as many of them as you care to name."

The drumming grew louder and more rapid, then slowed to a grave adagio, to be superseded by another breathless bravura. Suddenly they stopped. Total silence. The chief shaman emerged from behind the curtain and stepped into the middle of the stage. She was stately in her bright costume. A huge golden crown sat securely on her head, as if it were an undetachable part of her. She danced in wildly gyrating circles and diagonals, then collapsed in a heap as if she had fainted. Slowly her crown stirred; her head lifted, showing the finely chiseled features of her oval face with a sharp, high nose and black eyes overhung by thin but firm eyebrows. Her lips moved. A husky, deep, dark alto issued, rumbling like a subterranean echo. Then it changed to a torrent of words, garrulous, cajoling, protesting, abusive.

"Look how she made that somersault!" exclaimed Aileen.

The shaman intoned and moved with the grace and self-assurance of a master in full control of her powers. Her dance

19

was electrifying. Her chant entranced the audience who sat bolted to their seats, open-mouthed. The chorus of assistant shamans punctuated her inspired music and choreography with throaty exclamations. The whole theater, the whole universe resonated, reverberated with her as the binding medium, the focus of all energy. The spirits were descending gregariously in answer to her call. It was a good luck ceremony and no troublesome human spirit, dead or living, was invited. Only the propitious nature spirits thronged, shouting, cavorting, prancing shamelessly, riotously, in joyous rivalry and camaraderie.

"Isn't that something?" said Aileen. "I feel like jumping up and dancing. I feel dizzy and weightless. As if borne on clouds."

She turned to look at her father, who stood transfixed. He shook himself, looked alarmed at his daughter, then forced himself with a will to walk to the TV and turn it off.

"Father!" Aileen screamed, bounded forward, and turned the TV back on. The screen blurred, sputtered with dots of light, then returned to normal. "What has come over you? Maybe one of the spirits has jumped off the screen and possessed you. It's educational TV, not even PG."

Aileen resumed her seat but kept shaking her head incredulously, as if she couldn't get over his insensitivity.

"Why are you so dead set against anything Korean?" she lashed out after a short remission. "Weren't you born and raised in Korea? Look at your name, Khan. Who would think it was Korean? What are you ashamed of or afraid of? I want to learn about Korea, learn to speak the language, learn about my ancestry. Nothing can change the fact that I have Korean blood in me. Tell me who my mother is. Father!"

Aileen shouted a few times more and made as if she would lunge at him but changed her mind and leaned back on her rocking chair, becoming totally absorbed in the TV screen. George took a stand by the kitchen doorpost and, in spite of himself, also stared at the screen, his face ashen.

* * *

He recalled the first time he'd met Moonhee Kang at a church picnic. He was a fine arts major and she was in music. Gifted with a beautiful soprano, she was the soloist in her nationally renowned church choir. But above all she had a fantastic body: narrow waist, large bosom, shapely hips, long legs. Her closefitting, knit dress titillated men. George was himself a tall, wiry, handsome man and knew that women liked him. But, determined as he was to be a world-famous

20

artist, he never did anything about it. There didn't seem to be time for frivolities. It was his roommate who had insisted on his going to the picnic, arguing that a man simply couldn't live on work alone. George had been working on a seascape for days, often without sleep.

One glance at Moonhee and he fell in love. Too shy to initiate anything, he went to the church, to all its services, and maneuvered to get involved, obliquely, in the youth and choir activities she was part of. Then, after a few weeks during which she seemed totally unaware of his existence, she came over to him and asked him to draw a portrait of her. She had heard about him and wanted to test him, she said. There was no preamble, no apology. She simply expected to be obeyed as a matter of course. George was the happiest of slaves. After making a brief sketch of her he worked all night and returned the finished work the next day. She seemed captivated and could not take her eyes off the painting for a long time. "I like it a lot," she said finally, looking up with deep, mystical eyes.

After an evening service they took a stroll in the Tiger Park. By an unspoken agreement they strayed into the bush and made love. They met almost every day after that. It was an idyllic period when everything seemed right. Then she became pregnant. Of course they had promised to marry and even considered themselves already married, but they ran into opposition from both families when the necessity of formalizing the relationship was known. Moonhee's folks, well-to-do, with doctors and lawyers in the family, threatened to sue and break George. In turn, George's people, landed gentry in Cholla Province, refused to take a slut in as their daughter-in-law. After harsh words, threats and counterthreats, the young people were allowed to marry, on the condition that Moonhee live in the country with her in-laws until George graduated. She had to quit school: her condition was already noticeable and her college had a rule about that.

* * *

The curtain had fallen across the stage and the scene changed. Don Williams, the PBS reporter whom George had always suspected of wearing a toupee, introduced the principal shaman, Moonhee Kang. She had been metamorphosed into a well-dressed woman of the world in the latest fashion of New York, where her troupe had stopped before coming to Honolulu. She was perfectly at ease during the TV interview, the movie camera recording her every move, the bright lights, the reporter seated across from her, and the interpreter, the slightly nervous Professor John Halsinger from the East Asian Languages Department, University of Hawaii, in the middle.

"What do you say about the popular conception of shamanism as superstition, as hocus pocus, witchcraft, elaborate mumbojumbo that exploits people's fear and ignorance?" asked Don Williams.

"Misconception, you mean," Moonhee retorted. "It is none other than vicious slander. As for elaborateness, compare what you've seen tonight with the trappings of, say, the Roman Catholic Church. I don't see why we are superstition, while they are religion. Because we have many gods? Christians claim they have one big God, though they are never really consistent. Sometimes they allege two, Father and Son, sometimes three, the Trinity, not to mention the Devil and his retinue always hovering in the wings to take all the blame. They boast of miracles, prophecies, cures. We do the same. I had hoped America was a nation tolerant of all religions, free from prejudice and persecution, but it is as bad as Korea."

She went on defending her cause militantly, demanding equal time with the competition. Then some thoughtless witticism of her inquisitor's touched off a tempestuous explosion. Words tumbled out from her without pause, the literal translation of which nonplussed the usually suave, imperturbable Don Williams, at least temporarily.

"I didn't mean to say I consider shamans...," he mumbled.

"Remember you are talking to a psychic," she interrupted. "I may not speak English but my language is universal. I know what you are thinking."

"Madame Kang," he said, holding up the page of the *Honolulu Advertiser* with her photograph in it. "You made the news the moment you arrived in town, by foretelling the fire at the nightclub Casablanca, on Kapiolani Boulevard, where you happened to be with your friends..."

"I go to bars all the time in Seoul," she said. "It's my only form of relaxation. I have a few drinks, dance with a number of men, and I feel completely refreshed. I own a music-hall-cum-bar myself."

"Yes, a very successful one I hear," he said. "In fact you are successful in everything you do. You are president of the Korean Shaman Association, which you have organized."

"It was necessary," she said. "We are going to fight for our religious freedom. We will demand land grants to establish our shrines and temples and our communes."

"You are in a sense the founder of Korean Shamanism as a formal, organized religion."

"It's been there all along, long before the foreigners,

22

Buddhism, Confucianism, Christianity. But we have been driven underground. Our shamans are unlettered, operate independently, cutting each other's throats, and don't know what it means to unionize and work together. They have allowed themselves to be abused, ostracized, put upon. I had to twist their arms to make them join the Association."

"Do you still have serious opposition from within your own ranks?"

"Of course. They are jealous of me. They malign me as innovative and unorthodox, as unfaithful to the real tradition."

"Are you?"

She looked at him askance.

"You've seen what you've seen. Make up your own mind."

"It's certainly satisfactory aesthetically, as an art form, but..."

"Of course you don't know. All I can say is that people have to make reservations months in advance to see me perform. These are Koreans who have had shamans all their lives and they ought to know."

"Going back to the Casablanca fire, how did you know? What premonitions did you have? It can't just come like that, out of the blue."

"Yes, it does," she nodded gravely. "I was at this bar not more than a minute when a group of people recognized us and asked us to perform a ritual right there and then. Nobody presumes to be so bold in my country. I have my assistants screen all calls and requests. These Korean immigrants have forgotten their manners after living only a few years in this country. Regardless, I felt good that night and wanted to oblige. Though I was not in costume, I stood up to chant and dance. Suddenly two spirits came to me. One was that of the bar owner's discarded lover, and the other that of her unborn child. They had both died when she jumped off the bridge over the River Han. They begged to be comforted by a proper recognition ceremony. I called the owner, Mr. Pay, from his back-room office. He laughed, then became angry and had us thrown out as crazy women by his bouncers."

"But isn't religion supposed to promote morality and charity, not vengeance?"

"I wasn't vengeful. It isn't me that brings on or averts disaster. It is the will of the spirits. I have nothing to do except to be their medium, like our interpreter, Professer Halsinger, here. True they can be appeased through me and to that extent I influence the course of events."

"That sounds like an awful lot of power in mortal hands,"

the reporter quipped with a smirk. "Tell us how you get to be a shaman, what training or apprenticeship you have to go through."

"None," she said. "You either have it or do not have it. The spirits choose you and you can do nothing about it. You get called. If you refuse, they hound you with personal calamities of all sorts. You get sick, for example. We call it possession sickness. The spirits are giving you notice, as it were. If you persist in refusing, they ultimately kill you."

* * *

George recalled how her symptoms had started. The first was numbness in the abdomen. She was taken to a hospital for extensive examination, including X-rays, but they could find nothing wrong. At the same time she said her sensation had returned to normal. She was sent home and immediately began complaining about the same problem. Her skeptical in-laws had needle points stuck in her belly. Convinced by her lack of response that her condition was authentic, they hurried her to the hospital, but she was discharged again as before. This baffling pattern of recovery and relapse repeated itself several times. Early one morning she was found sprawling and screaming in the courtyard. She said a genie taller than the house had grabbed and tossed her out of the room. Both her knees were dislocated. They took her to a hospital and had them set, but they went out of joint when she returned home. This was repeated several times.

Meanwhile George had been away from home again, this time for his military service. When he came home on leave, he found that Moonhee had not been able to pass stool for an entire week. She had not responded to enema and was bloated. Her clammy skin oozed and stank. He couldn't recognize the stylish coquette and seductress of only a year ago. But the worst part of it was her inability to recognize him or anybody else. She hallucinated constantly and muttered gibberish. They took her to different doctors and hospitals, but nothing proved permanently effective. By now the neighbors whispered that the spirits possessing her should be exorcised by the shamans. People usually called them in only as the last recourse, when they were desperate, unless they were downright superstitious. George's family was neither superstitious nor religious but decided to take the lesser of the evils. A local Christian pastor was asked to come and pray. He brought his complete entourage of elders and deacons with all their reputed powers of prayer and healing. In vain they prayed the entire night. They even repeated their visits, still with no result. Unable to do anything with her, George left for his frontline post when his time was up.

* * *

"So there is no formal training you undergo," pursued Don Williams. "You don't go to a theological seminary, for instance?"

"No. We dispense with such pretentious tomfoolery. We will always have our membership, competent membership, because the spirits must communicate and they need a medium."

"How can you tell you have received the call?"

"It's not intelligible to ordinary people. If you are a chosen shaman, you hear voices and see things. People might call you a psychopath and even commit you to an insane asylum."

* * *

One night, back at her parents' home (where she had been staying because her in-laws could not cope with the situation), she sneaked out, dressed only in her nightgown. Taking a shortcut through the alleys and thoroughfares, dodging the curfew patrols, she made her way to the railroad station. Going up to the official on night duty, she warned him that unless he performed a big exorcism rite immediately, a terrible accident would befall him and the station. He called the police and had her locked up as a crazy woman. That night a freight train collided with a passenger train right by the station master's window, resulting in several deaths, including that of the night duty official. At the jail she ranted all night, pounding on the walls and swearing foully. Saying she had an important message, she asked the jailer to have her shown to the chief. Unable to endure her screams they took her to the chief's office next morning. She leered, made a pass at him, and coaxed him to do as she told him. Unless an exorcism was carried out, she said, something dreadful would happen to the place. The police threw her out bodily. The crowd that had gathered to watch jeered, spat, and threw stones. She stumbled and fell unconscious, bleeding. Finally, an old school friend recognized her and notified her family. They took her home and nursed her. The next day the papers reported on their pages the explosion of ammunition stored in the basement of the police station. Word of Moonhee's prophecy spread, and everybody sought her for divinations.

Such notoriety hardly suited her family. Her parents had

her sent away to their villa in Inchon with servants to guard her. It was a pleasant spot with a view of the harbor and she seemed to recover. Her physical health returned and she scored positively every time psychiatric tests were given. But, as in her bouts with abdominal paralysis, her hallucinatory condition played hide and seek with the examining doctors. Then she managed to elude everyone and disappear for two days. They found her on the beach, mired in a mudflat, half-drowned and famished. But the moment she saw her pursuers, she started to run. After they caught her, they had to tether her to a post. When she was brought home, bound like a felon, her mother wept bitterly at the sight and untied her. Moonhee jumped off and dashed out before anybody could stop her, ranting that she needed shaman ordination.

The Inchon villa was now attracting too much attention, and the family realized that the relative anonymity of Seoul was better. But lines of people awaited her there too, asking for her services as a psychic and exorcist. At the same time the shamans sent their agents and let the family know that Moonhee should be properly initiated into shamanhood. She was one of them, marked and chosen by the spirits to be their medium, their priestess, they said. None of them had chosen to be a shaman, a pariah to be despised and avoided. The spirits had called them, inspired them, by unmistakable supernatural signs, just as they had called Moonhee.

In some sense a shaman was like a vestal virgin or a nun, but there was no equivalent prestige. Exactly the opposite. People might engage a shaman, fawning while they needed her, but as soon as her services were terminated, they turned around and spat at her. The shaman fulfilled a function in demand, but it was a profession even the poorest refused to go into, however financially rewarding it might be. The stigma branded and doomed not only its practitioner but also her relatives, for generations. A shaman's husband was unemployable. A shaman's children couldn't go to school, as they would be shunned by their peers and blamed for every mishap. It was unthinkable that a girl from a good family with means should become a shaman. Being a shaman was in some sense worse than being dead. Moonhee's family urged her to end her life.

She slipped out of the house to return there no more and was given shelter by a shaman, who sponsored her initiation. It was revealed during the ceremony that her chief possessing spirit was George's older brother, who had died many years before at the hands of the Communists during the Korean War. He was the first-born of the lineage and was expected to achieve great things. His unfulfilled spirit had found harborage in her. Of course she was hospitable to other spirits too, but George's brother was her chief resident.

As she assumed her shaman role formally, with a long waiting list of clients, her natal relatives and in-laws dissociated themselves completely from her. Upon his discharge from the army George was compelled to take Aileen and leave the country to be freed from any connection with Moonhee.

* * *

"How do you tell them apart, the genuine shamans from the imposters and the psychopaths?" Don Williams queried. "You must admit there are the latter sort around."

"By the power they evince. The real shaman has superior intelligence. She will pass all your psychiatric tests, for example. Her predictions will come true. The insane are hardly coherent, let alone possessed of prophetic powers. However, many genuine mediums are mistaken as crazy, especially at the initial stage, when they are struggling for recognition. You've got to have some patience with them. The beginning shaman, unused to the access of power and often frightened herself, gets carried away, becoming delirious and incoherent. It is like a blind man suddenly opening his eyes. You feel as if you are airborne on 747 jet engines. You soar to the stratosphere and beyond, and you can see everything, even the minutest detail of the universe. You don't miss even an ant crawling out of its hole. You are both telescopic and microscopic."

Suddenly, she turned directly to the camera and, forgetting the reporter and the interpreter, spoke: "I know where you are, you Kang bastard, son of a bitch. I know you are watching me. You thought you were far away from me and safe. You were so ashamed of me you hid across the ocean. But here I am. I am famous and you are nothing. You'll come groveling, just as your relatives have. They are on my dole, because they are paupers. You will come crawling and begging or you'll lose the most valuable thing you have..."

The reporter was puzzled and looked between Moonhee and the interpreter. The latter stared at Moonhee in consternation and turned to Don Williams helplessly. She had spoken out of line, departing from the agreed-upon text, and using strong Cholla vernacular unfamiliar to Professor Halsinger. Moonhee stopped abruptly, then smiled sweetly, bewitchingly, to both men, as if nothing had happened.

"Let's get on with the interview," she said.

* * *

27

George called the Royal Hawaiian Hotel and asked for Moonhee Kang.

"I am Jungshik Kang," he said.

"I was expecting your call," she said. "Is it about Aileen?"

"Yes. Come to the Kaiser Hospital Emergency room right away. You may do whatever you like with me, but spare her. She is innocent."

"What happened?"

"Her rocking chair fell over while she was watching you on TV and she was knocked unconscious. How can you be so cruel, to your own child?"

"I had nothing to do with it. You must have gone soft in your head. I don't have that kind of power even if I wanted it."

"I won't argue with you. It won't accomplish anything. Come to the hospital and bring her out of her coma."

"Coma? It was just a concussion that knocked her wind out for a moment. She must be okay now. Go and do not leave her side."

"You really don't care, do you? You don't want to see your own flesh and blood!"

"Don't ever pull that flesh and blood stuff on me again. Who was the one that separated us to begin with? My coming into her life at this late date will only complicate her life. She is better off not knowing about me."

"She would grow up knowing her mother, proud of her heritage."

"Proud of being a shaman's daughter?"

"Why not? America has given me perspective, something you don't get in a less free and open society. From your talk on TV I thought you had gotten over those old Korean hangups yourself. Aileen should meet you. If, as they say, the shaman tradition runs in the family..."

"Has she shown any symptoms of the sickness?" she asked, her voice taut.

"No," George said. "But she must have potential, a predisposition. Besides, they don't call it sickness here, but rather a gift, a special talent. Money and fame come with it."

"You've been hopelessly corrupted. You call America free and open, with no hangups, but it has the worst hangups. Money. Fame. At least Korea puts things in their proper places. There is still distinction between good money and bad money. What's the good of a little more money? Sure I travel, I stay at first-rate hotels. But I see plenty of other people at this hotel, plenty of other people on the airplane, on TV. No, I want my daughter to be known as somebody really worthy, like a musician, scientist, writer."

"She may not have those talents."

"Then let her be a plain housewife, loved and happy with a family. Let her be anything but a shaman or psychic."

"Don't you want to give your own child the power of talking to the spirits?"

"Stop it. There is no such thing as spirits. It's all in your head, reading a plan into coincidence. Forget the whole business. I don't know you. I'll disown Aileen, just as you have disowned me. We are strangers. Never forget that. Goodbye."

* * *

The memory of the recent Korean Airlines tragedy at Seoul Airport on this same Honolulu-Seoul flight was still too fresh in everybody's mind. None of the 375 aboard had survived. As the plane got closer to the ground, all the passengers sat, fastened to their seats, hardly breathing. But George was relaxed and confident. Poor Moonhee, psychic and yet so blind! The spirits had no other way of overcoming the intransigence of her maternal protectiveness, sincere but misguided, like the paternalism of dictators that cannot be broken except by coup d'etat.

"Did we have to come all the way here to Korea for rest and cure?" Aileen said.

"Yes," George said.

"What was wrong with Honolulu?"

"The change of scenery will do you good."

"We could have gone to other places, Mexico or South America. Or Australia, Tahiti, Bali. Europe. Even Africa."

"I thought you wanted to come to Korea. What was all that talk about wanting to learn Korean and discover your roots?"

"I could have learned from you, from other Koreans in Honolulu, from books and cassette tapes. If you'd given me half a chance. Besides, you didn't have to sell your business, as if we'd never return."

A blue Pony cab, smaller than any compact George had seen in Honolulu, pulled up in front of them and a uniformed driver stepped out.

"To the Shaman Association Headquarters," George told the cabby in Korean.

"So you can speak the lingo," Aileen observed derisively. "What hotel are we headed to?"

"The best," George said. "I won't take any chances."

The St. Peter of Seoul

It was the first Sunday after the swift takeover of Seoul by
the North Korean Communists in July 1950. Less than a tenth
of the congregation was present at the Central Church, but
even that turnout was a surprising testimony to the loyalty
and devotion the pastor enjoyed among his people. The service
was in defiance of the new government edict prohibiting all
assemblies of seditious nature, especially those in the name
of religion. Its ranks thinned, the choir nevertheless sang the
introit stoutly, but one could hear a tremor of apprehension in
each chorister's voice. Those in the pews were visibly restless
and many kept glancing backward uneasily to the main
entrance. At the pulpit Pastor Yoo's invocation went up, filling
the chancel and echoing in the high open-beam ceiling of the
auditorium, but falling like a dud on the stillness of the floor.

The front door flew open and several armed men burst in.
They tramped down the aisle, their boots resounding on the
waxed boards. The leader, a stocky, hardened-looking man in
his thirties, had a pistol, but the others carried burp guns or
long shoulder rifles with fixed bayonets. They bounded onto
the platform, ignoring the side steps, and went straight to the
pulpit. As the pastor was pronouncing his last words of
prayer, with eyes closed, apparently oblivious to the disturbance, the men seized him, pushed him down the steps, and
led him through the church. The leader remained on the platform, cleared his throat, and started haranguing the congregation.

"You are all in violation of the law," he said in a ringing
Pyongyang accent. "You could all be arrested and thrown in
jail, but we will let you go this time. Do not ever return here to
listen to the garbage these American errand boys and
lackeys dish out to hoodwink and rob you. The church is

31

closed and the building is forfeit. Our People's Army instructors will give you speeches of a different kind. Come then and hear them. Go on home for now."

Suja Yoo, the organist, went after her father, imploring the captors to tell her what the charge was against him and where they were taking him. They pushed her aside unceremoniously and took him to a three-quarter ton truck parked outside. He was put on the back of the truck and a few of them guarded him with lowered muzzles, although they couldn't have feared any resistance or violence from their meek and submissive prisoner. The worshippers slowly came filing out of the building. Some headed for the vehicle to say goodbye to their pastor, but the severe, threatening frown of the guards frightened them away. Undaunted, Mrs. Wonhyo Wang, a woman elder, came to the truck. The guards blocked her approach with their rifles.

"Take me and let him go," she said. "He is guiltless. God will never forgive you if you harm him, even a hair of his."

The guards listened amused and puzzled, their ferocity relaxed somewhat. Her white hair and venerable carriage restrained them from offering her any outright rudeness. Their leader came back clattering down the stone steps.

"Get rid of her," he said gruffly, opening the passenger side door.

"Sir," she said, going up to him. "Our pastor has given all his life to God's work, helping the poor and weak. What you are doing to him is sacrilege, for which the price is eternal damnation."

"Not by our books, lady," he sneered. "You speak with a Hamgyong accent. When did you come south and why?"

"We moved here many years ago right after I got married. You have no right to take him, the anointed of God."

"Don't bother us with your gibberish. Consider yourself lucky, a Hamgyong turncoat. I'll bet you're a reactionary, a landowner that escaped the justice of the people. Maybe we should take you in and investigate. Would you like that?"

"I'm not afraid. Do whatever you want with me. I'll gladly go with you, but leave our pastor alone. I'll go in his place. I'll be his surety."

After looking at her derisively, he got in and told his driver to start. The guards shoved Mrs. Wang off as they jumped on the truck. Suja ran after it down the hill, shouting for her father, her eyes flowing with tears. She stopped at a corner, panting. The truck had disappeared in a cloud of dust. She stood dejected and helpless. Reluctantly, with a heavy heart, she turned to retrace her steps. The director of the choir, Kido Chang, who had the knack of singing his bass part while conducting, stood there watching her. She hurriedly wiped her eyes, disconcerted at being caught off guard in that compromising posture. Having grown up despising tears and the usual weaknesses of her sex, she felt unmasked, even disrobed, and resented him. Haughtily, pretending not to notice him, she walked past.

"Why didn't he leave the capital?" Kido Chang asked, ambling up in long easy strides alongside her.

"He didn't want to. Warden Shin, the Congressman, sent around a jeep for us, but Father sent it back, saying he couldn't leave his flock. He wanted to be the good shepherd who lays down his life for his sheep."

"What sheep? Hardly any are left."

"Even if one or two should remain, he can't desert them like the hired man of John 10 who runs when he sees the wolf coming."

"*Quo vadis?* so spake Apostle Peter to Jesus, his alter ego, and went back to Rome."

She darted a fiery glance at him.

"Do you have to play the cynic at a time like this? As a matter of fact, he spoke of that very thing that morning, except in his case he had never left the city limits. God speaks to his chosen directly in different places at different times. In different ways. Seoul is the Rome of this century and my father is the Apostle."

Her anger always provoked an inexplicable smile in him and a desire to banter, although he knew it was playing with fire. "You must be glad they got him according to the script," he almost said, but checked himself in time. There was a desperation, a pathos in her outburst that touched him tenderly. For all her outwardly spirited independence he knew her to be bewildered, frightened, miserable, to be in need of comforting.

"You mistake me. Surely you don't think I have anything but the highest admiration for his courage and faith. He's probably the next best thing to the Messiah Himself. I'm just a little bitter about the way God uses his best instruments, the eccentric, unpredictable, almost vicious way in which the best of us get manhandled."

"What do you think they'll do to him?" she asked, alarmed.

He looked at her pallid face and reproached himself.

"Probably nothing," he said, feigning a nonchalant tone. "Release him after some routine questioning."

He felt depressed and guilty for his palpable dishonesty. He had seen the thugs of the Youth Alliance of his county in

North Korea lead away a group of ministers to club and stab them brutally to death and leave them exposed in a gulch.

No one was allowed to go near and give them a burial. Determined relatives had to steal the vulturized, decomposed bodies at great risk to themselves.

"Why didn't you leave town yourself?" she asked. "I heard they've started cracking down on people from the north."

She looked at him with concern, then quickly turned away, her eyes on the dark mysterious Triangle Mountain looming beyond the church spire. Her sharp profile, with the pointed nose, bespoke her quick, resourceful, occasionally devious and cunning mind and stamped an austere yet passionate personality that he had learned to love.

"The Internal Affairs people came to my lodging house. I begged the landlady to say I had not been home for days. They left, threatening to search the house next time. She was trembling with fear. They told her that harboring me or any reactionary was equally reactionary, punishable by death. I had to leave the house right away."

"Where have you been staying?"

"At friends' here and there. But I think I've about exhausted their hospitality without endangering them."

"Was it too late to cross the river?"

"I could have gotten away after they blew up the bridge. I could do so maybe even now, if I had a mind to. But I've chosen to stay."

His tall angular body stooped and his eyes gazed at the pebbles of the sidewalk. They walked silently for a while.

"I've heard my own *quo vadis,* you may say," he said jauntily like a little boy bragging.

"Is it someone from the north?" she said, fixing him with a steady scrutiny.

"Yes," he said moodily, straightening himself and pressing his lips.

"Is she beautiful?" she asked.

He was taken aback by the incongruity of the question and gave an incredulous glance at her.

"Not in a thousand years," he said, laughing, but his features quickly hardened. "You saw him today, the one who spoke to the congregation. His name is Pilsoo Song. I saw him earlier in town driving in a jeep. Cocky, as if he owned the world. I was taken completely by surprise. At first I thought he had seen me and was coming straight at me to run me down. At that moment a procession of American POWs, probably those caught at Osan, happened to come shuffling along. There were about thirty of them, in irons, a ragged, beat-up bunch if there ever was one. Their bare feet were blistered and bloody, clothes torn and dirty, faces unshaven and unwashed. Big bones sticking through the skin, their tallness, their long legs and arms, heightened the emaciation and made them more pitiable. It was like watching a herd of pedigreed race horses, wasted and ravaged by disease or some gross maltreatment, being driven to the slaughterhouse for glue and fertilizer. You know what they say about how expensively they live and are brought up.

"Song's jeep stopped. Strangely enough, one of the POWs, perhaps attracted by his decorated uniform or perhaps momentarily deranged, left the line and shambled up to Pilsoo. He shouted, 'Tobacco, tobacco,' and kept pressing his fingers to his parched, chapped lips. The guard hit the POW with the butt of his rifle to bring him in line. Pilsoo called to the guards and told him to let him be. The POW came smiling and stretched his manacled arms. Pilsoo took the cigarette from his mouth and took it near the American soldier's expectantly open mouth. Pilsoo turned the cigarette the wrong end around and stubbed it right in the man's gums. With a scream the POW fell back and Pilsoo giggled hysterically. The guards and the onlookers joined in the merriment. I followed the jeep. He works at the Political Security Bureau."

"He didn't recognize you?"

"I had my back turned to him. Also, the gown must have made me indistinguishable. It was a close call, though."

"What's this man to you?"

The horror of the memories temporarily rendered him speechless. Song's men had dragged his father to the People's Court for instant execution after a verdict by handclapping. While he, his mother, and his brothers and sisters were sleeping, they cordoned the house off and set fire. Only he had escaped alive.

"Let me put it this way. The earth is not big enough for both of us. Either he or I must die at the other's hand."

Suja stopped, gazing at him with Christian, almost maternal eyes.

"I know what you're going to say, Suja," he said, waving his hand. "If the church will not vindicate my vengeance, I have no option but to renounce my faith in it. Our God separates the sheep from the goats. He is just and wrathful as well as benign and loving. He ought to be. Otherwise He makes no sense."

"This may be the moment of our supreme trial. Perhaps God stretches us to the limit to see what our breaking point is."

He didn't answer and only looked yearningly at her pretty face and her slender neck rising above the pleated collar of her

35

neat Sunday dress. Conscious of his gaze, she raised her chin primly and peered out at the distant sky.

"Maybe God is giving me a hint, a rather strong one," he said. "He wants to goad me into action. Seeing that I am sluggish and don't do anything to right the wrongs, He sends this snake my way again and again so I may witness him doing more of the Devil's work. It cannot be a mere coincidence. I must put a stop to it."

* * *

It was dark and the street was deserted. Kido had been hiding all day in a vacant shop with its windows and boards smashed, battling persistent flies and mosquitoes which, with the night coming on, grew more audacious, attacking his eyes and ears. He had watched for Pilsoo in vain and wondered whether he had chosen the right spot, whether Pilsoo had not been transferred to a post outside Seoul. In that case he would not be able to locate him. Only the Communist authorities would know where he was, and to inquire after him would entail Kido's revealing himself to them. Already movement around town was getting risky as checkpoints were set up and plainclothesmen stopped passersby everywhere. One had to carry residence and travel permits issued by the district offices. Since all males fourteen and up were liable to be drafted and sent to the frontlines, only children, women, and old men who had nothing to fear from the authorities had the necessary papers.

The itch from the mosquito bites grew unbearable and the flies sucked with needle-sharp pointedness. As he was about to leave, he heard footsteps rounding the corner and quickly hid himself back in the shop. Two uniformed men came with a man between them, his hands tied behind his back, who kept saying he was a loyal Communist. He'd had to join the South Korean Alliance for Protection and Guidance after his capture and torture by the South Korean police, he said, but he had continued to work for the destruction of the Syngman Rhee regime, believing in the ultimate triumph of Communism.

"Everything will be cleared up when we get to the Bureau," said one of the uniformed men in the metallic, high-pitched accent Kido knew to be his mortal enemy's. A thrill of delight and hatred went down his spine. As they approached the entrance of the alley, Pilsoo ran his flashlight along the walls of the houses.

"I heard a noise," he said to his companion.

Kido stuck to the ground, wishing that the earth could swallow him up, and stopped breathing. His hair bristled as the beam of light, shattered by the broken boards and furniture, danced in the looted shop.

"Probably a rat," the other said.

Their footsteps began receding. Kido followed them at a safe distance, looking left and right to make sure of his flight in case of discovery and pursuit. Pilsoo and company entered their office, a former garment factory, a block away from Clear Stream, the sewage canal. It was a squat, one-storied wooden structure, unpainted and in disrepair, probably chosen deliberately for its nondescript appearance to delude hostile air reconnaissance. Despite its sprawling size it was still not big enough to accommodate the traffic of people for which it served as the hub, and one could easily guess it to be a cover for an elaborate honeycomb of underground tunnels and cellars many stories deep. Kido waited under the eaves of a building from which he could observe the guarded entrance where they had disappeared. A sentry with a burp gun was ensconced in a sandbag-walled enclosure and checked the papers of visitors. People went in and out all night long, but Pilsoo either didn't leave his office or had left it by another way.

There were several other exits to the building and Kido watched each of them in turn for three nights. Despite his vigilance he saw Pilsoo only once more, and that in the company of five or six others, taking the way from the bombed machine shop in the south side. Kido had to leave him alone.

Then, one night, in an uncertain moon, the ruins of buildings bombed during the day gleaming somber and ghastly, with the streets blacked out for fear of air raids, the quiet broken from time to time by night patrols, Kido saw Pilsoo, with pistol in holster, picking his way alone through the broken tiles and glass. On the banks of the canal were lined up quick food stalls, selling noodles, bean curd soup, and rice during the day. A small hand-held blackout flashlight guided his steps among the debris littering the way. Like a shadow Kido glided out of the gloom of the alley from which his quarry had emerged and noiselessly followed him.

Hunter and hunted, bound as if by some invisible chain, advanced through the marketplace along the canal until the embankment dipped to a wooden footbridge. Its spans downed in an air raid, a passage had been rigged by placing huge boulders, submerged almost to the top in the black muck. The canal bed was dry at many places for lack of rain and was choked with garbage and rubbish dumped freely from the banks. Thousands of bodies, the bodies of South Korean National Army soldiers, policemen, government officials, and other minor reactionaries, had rotted there for weeks. The Communists, fearing a mass epidemic, had them at last cleared away with forced labor, including women and children, from the different sections of the city. But the odor still hung stagnant in the air, nauseating and slimy, sticking under the skin.

Pilsoo crossed the canal, jumping from stone to stone, his flashlight spotting the way, and went up the steps. He then headed for the roofless warehouse with broken walls. Through this building lay a shortcut to his office, half a block up the road. Kido gave himself a full minute before venturing on the stones of the canal bed. But once committed, he sprang across with the speed of a stalking lion.

Pilsoo was about to come out of the warehouse at the other end when Kido jumped out from behind a crumbled partition, knocking him unconscious with a *taygwondo* kick to the head. After pulling him to a corner, Kido took his pistol and flashlight and searched his clothes. The billfold had his identification, a major assigned to the Bureau as intelligence officer. There was also a brown leather-jacketed pocketbook. He ran the light over its pages. From July 15 on there were entries of the name Wonsok Yoo. The appointments seemed to have taken place at odd hours, sometimes at 3 a.m. The name did not occur after August. There were other names, with dates and hours, but Kido didn't recognize them. He slapped Pilsoo's face a few times and rocked him. With a groan Pilsoo stirred and squinted at the flashlight. His lips quivered when he recognized Kido. His face froze with abject fear, as if he had seen an apparition.

"It's me, Kido Chang, in the flesh. Feel me. I am no ghost. I didn't die in the fire. I jumped to where the smoke was the thickest and fell into the well, where I stayed until you cleared out. Did you think I had died?"

Kido chuckled and became loquacious, as if he had met with a long-lost friend and wanted to bridge the absent years by filling in the days and hours.

"Tell me about my brother Kiwon. Is he still alive?"

"Yes, he is," Pilsoo said eagerly, speaking for the first time and sensing a chance of coming through this reversal after all.

"Where is he?"

"He works at the factory, as a welder," he said, gulping.

"Have you heard of a one-armed welder? You have broken his arm. How can he be a welder?"

"He recovered after a month and he is really all right."

Kido rubbed the barrel of the pistol against Pilsoo's mouth, bloodying it.

"Cut out the lies or I'll blow your brains out this second."

Pilsoo licked the blood from his lips, tears running from the corners of his eyes.

"I know I am at your mercy. Why should I lie? You can check it all out yourself."

A thought crossed Kido's mind.

"All right. I'll test your veracity. Do you know Pastor Yoo, Wonsok Yoo?"

Pilsoo looked at Kido closely for a while before answering.

"Yes, I've worked on him. The Party wanted him to cooperate, to recant and make a radio broadcast renouncing his religion and his allegiance to Syngman Rhee's puppet government. But he was obstinate. He's been transferred to another authority and is off my hands."

"Wasn't it yourself who arrested him, at his church?"

Pilsoo's small eyes expanded to their limit.

"Yes, that was the order from higher up. After his arrest I was busy with other things and had nothing to do with him for a while."

"Where is he now?"

"At Diplomats' Club along with other high security cases."

"I'll check it out. In the meantime tell me more about my family. What happened to Kiwon's wife?"

"She went back to singing after she got separated from Kiwon," Pilsoo said. Miryo, Kiwon's wife, a pretty girl who had sung in the chorus Kido had led at Pyongyang Theater, was seduced by Pilsoo's father, a well-known lecher. When Kiwon went to the Songs' to bring her back with him, he was attacked by Song's gang. His broken arm still in a cast, he was thrown into jail as a reactionary.

"Pilsoo," Kido spoke quietly, closing his eyes in thought. "I knew I would meet you again before I die, but now that I am face to face with you, I don't know what to do with you."

"Kido," Pilsoo said, his voice vibrant with emotion, "I owe your family a great debt. Your father sent me to school and made my father foreman. My family never intended any harm to yours and wanted to protect you. It was the Party that made us do the things we did. We had no choice. If we hadn't, others would have come and done worse. But I have always felt close to you. In fact, I consider Kiwon my own younger brother. I took him under my wing when nobody wanted him. He was an outcast when he went crazy..."

"So he lost his mind?" Kido growled ominously.

Pilsoo realized that he had spoken too much.

"It wasn't my fault. It all happened while he was in prison."

But it was too late. Pilsoo raised his hands in vain to ward off Kido's fist as it crushed his temple. Pilsoo's arms dropped listlessly and his head cocked grotesquely to the side as if twisted a full turn on the neck. Kido righted the head and shook him. He put his ear to the chest and listened for the heart beat. The man was dead. Early in his teens as a student of martial arts Kido was introduced to the many points of vulnerability on the human body. Their great number never ceased to amaze him. Every living human being had seemed a walking miracle of uncannily favorable chance. Of course he had never had occasion to put his knowledge to the test.

The crumpled body before him, bearing no resemblance to the well-built, sturdy, vigorous mass of energy it had been only minutes ago, reawakened with penetrating vividness his consciousness of the mystery and fragility of human life, evil or otherwise. It was depressing, disquieting. All the rancor and anger he had felt for Pilsoo Song, the living person, forsook him, evaporated without leaving even a memory. The stark realization of the incommunicability with the lump of dead meat before him, the complete exclusion of him from it, the absolute, total irreconcilability baffled and numbed him. He felt forlorn, like a lone star in the blackness of space. Anything seemed better than this chilling isolation. Uttering a low moan, Kido shook the corpse once more, begging it to return to life, to get on its feet and fight back. He thrust the pistol in its stiffening hand, wrapped the cold fingers around it, and told it to shoot, to curse and spit and kick, to do anything but be dead and be nothing, the unresponsive, unarguable, unappealable finality.

Slowly Kido bestirred himself. The body had to be disposed of. A noisy patrol of half a dozen drunken men was passing by outside the wall. At the entrance of the warehouse they stopped. One came in. Kido quickly picked up the pistol from the dead man's hand and hid himself behind the partition. The man stopped on the opposite side and started urinating. Two others joined him, exchanging coarse jokes. After their business they all left and rejoined their companions waiting outside. Kido stripped Pilsoo's corpse and wrapped the clothes into a bundle. Carrying the naked corpse to the edge of the canal, he rolled it down the sloping bank. It fell with a dull thud on a dry spot. Kido climbed down, planting each foot in the cracks of the moss rock wall. He picked up the corpse and took it to a puddle that seemed deep and miry. He stood the corpse on its head and rammed it into the canal bed until he couldn't drive it in any further. The mud and water finished swallowing the corpse when he let go of the feet. He went up the bank, picked up the bundle of clothes, and went by side streets and alleys to Pastor Yoo's manse on the church grounds.

* * *

Kido went to the Diplomats' Club, wearing Pilsoo's uniform which had been altered by Suja to fit him. The guard gave only a cursory glance at the ID. The picture had been replaced by Kido's. Mrs. Yoo was an artist and made some touch-up changes to make it look quite genuine. Kido's strong Pyongyang accent lent to his authenticity. He was shown to the officer on duty, a lieutenant born in Seoul and of recent appointment, who flipped over the pages of a big book in front of him and said Paster Yoo had been moved the day before to the West Gate Prison.

"If you wait a little longer, you'll meet our commandant here," he said. "You know him. You turned the prisoners over to him yourself."

"That's right," Kido said, his heart thumping. A quick glance at the lieutenant convinced him that he had seen through the masquerade. "Unfortunately, I have to get going right now."

The lieutenant was rising. Kido drew out his pistol, gagged him before he had a chance to yell, tied him up, and led him out of the building. The sentry at the gate looked on wide-eyed.

"This reactionary spy is under arrest," said Kido, blustering and fuming. "Tell the Colonel that I have taken the traitor for questioning at our headquarters."

Everything was topsy-turvy. The tide of the war had turned ever since the September 15 landing of MacArthur's Marines at Inchon, the harbor forty miles west of Seoul with its enormous tidal differences of 35 feet, and long, narrow, shallow channels through miles of inaccessible mud flats. Surprised deep in their own territory and with the main supply line cut off, the entire Communist front south of Seoul collapsed. The stragglers and remnants fled through the hills and fields, throwing away their arms and uniforms, and the poorly trained home guards, rushed to defend Seoul, milled around like a lost colony of bees, adding to the confusion. The streets were like anthills with sandbag barricades at every corner. Apparently, against all odds, the Red Army was getting ready for a street fight against the approaching U.S. Marines. Naval gunfire from U.S. ships anchored off the coast rocked the city blocks. Bombers and fighters played hide and seek with flak, popping like white balls of cotton in the cobalt blue sky.

Kido found an empty bunker and led his prisoner inside. There was no need to beat him. The lieutenant was ready to tell everything. The Reds were rounding up important prisoners from various detention areas to march them north as they withdrew from the capital. He begged for his life, pleading his innocence. He had been a seminarian, due to graduate that summer to the ministry. That was why he had been particularly kind and considerate to Pastor Yoo, who had been his idol ever since he heard him preach at the seminary. When the pastor fell ill in his jail, the lieutenant had taken him medicine to relieve his suffering, though that sort of thing was strictly forbidden. The Communist commission had been just an expedient to escape assignment to the frontlines as a draftee. In the meantime he had been looking for a chance to desert and surrender to the U.N. side, but no convenient opportunity had presented itself.

His story sounded credible enough and his entreaties genuine. Kido almost relented, but hearing a patrol of Red soldiers in the street he decided he couldn't take the chance. It was not just his own life at stake; any attempt at rescuing Pastor Yoo would be foiled if this man should talk. This possibility, however remote the probability, could not be tolerated. Nothing should stand in the way of accomplishing his all-important mission, the urgency of which overrode all other considerations. He no longer saw the seminarian or heard him, a hapless victim ensnared by circumstances, whose fine sensibilities and past good deeds went unrecorded and unheeded, but found before him an obstacle, an alarm system positioned in his path, a time bomb that needed to be dismantled and neutralized. One well-aimed blow and the former seminarian was lifeless.

Kido was puzzled by his utter lack of remorse at having done away with two lives. He had plainly murdered them, undone the delicate spring of the mechanism called life. As a little boy he'd had nightmares for days after shooting a sparrow dead with his slingshot, thinking over the seemingly infinite ramifications of his destructive deed, the young it was to feed, the social network it had upheld, the geometric progression of offspring from it. But now, after destroying two human lives, officers of the Red Army, with responsibilities and commitments, attachments and aspirations, each with the potential of founding a dynasty, he felt no horror, no moral repugnance, nothing but fatigue and apathy.

Not even thinking about the dead, he found himself rethreading the chain of events that had led to his successful escape from Diplomats' Club. He knew better than to attribute it to any daring or finesse on his part. A thousand things could have gone wrong to betray and slip him up. Only freakish chance, a generous dose of luck, contrived to bring it off. The reflection unnerved him, made him tremble at the closeness of his escape. Unbelievingly, he felt himself, ran his fingers through his hair, and let out a sigh of relief at the reality of his being alive. He swore nothing would induce him to attempt a rehearsal of such a foolhardy adventure. His eyes caught the dead man's body at the other end of the bunker. The open glazed eyes stared at nothing and glinted in the shimmer of light through the opening. Suddenly Kido remembered that he had killed him, that he was alive and the other was not. A million germs, extremely magnified, readying for their feast on his handiwork, filled his vision. He shuddered with revulsion at his insensitivity, the moral vacuum in him.

His gloomy thoughts came to an abrupt end at the explosion of a shell nearby, which shook the ground and walls and broke asunder the crossbeams and rafters of the bunker. Dirt and sand showered down blindingly. The lieutenant's body was buried out of sight. Kido frantically dug his way out, choking with the musty, rancid smell of dust and gunpowder. Except for a few minor cuts and bruises he was all right. Although he feared a sniper attack or other assault from friendly guerrillas or deserters, he nevertheless judged it wise to keep the People's Army uniform on as he made his way to Suja's house along the streets, swarming with mustard-colored Communist uniforms.

* * *

She had heard on the shortwave radio that MacArthur's Marines had captured Kimpo Airport and were at Yongdungpo south of the river. Having heard and seen many last-minute atrocities, she feared for her father's life.

"Would it be at all possible...?" she didn't complete the sentence, her eyes beholding him without their usual fire and brilliance. After a pause she observed, "You have been phenominally successful."

"By sheer chance," he said, guessing what she was driving at and anxious to divert her.

"If only I were a man," she said, not heeding him.

"Luck does not run in a streak," he said. "The West Gate Prison is like a fortress with machinegun and mortar emplacements at the watchtowers. It would be literally the Lions' Den."

"But aren't you my Daniel? God will protect you, cloak you

43

with an invisible shield, make the enemy powerless."

"I wish I had your faith."

"Do this last one big favor for me, for the love you have professed before. I'll know you to be my true love. I'll do anything for you. I'll be in your debt for ever and ever."

"Only if I live to collect," he muttered to himself. He knew he could not avoid it. For a moment angry resentment swept over him. He almost shouted a violent denunciation at her as a crafty manipulator who thought nothing of sending other people to their doom. But her trusting smile, her liquid eyes, smothered all his protest. His only choice was to work out a plan of execution. He mistrusted the masquerade with Pilsoo's uniform and rank. There were too many of the brass there to be impressed by the rank of major. Maybe Pilsoo was already missing and they were out looking for any impersonations of him. The continued use of the uniform might be a dead giveaway. On the other hand, without the uniform he couldn't take a single step in the streets, and Internal Affairs people checked and shot civilian pedestrians at whim. He even toyed with the thought of getting himself arrested so as to get thrown in prison. But then there was no guarantee he would be placed near enough to the pastor. He would not be able to carry any arms and would be totally at the mercy of the Red jailors, unable to move around and look for Pastor Yoo or be of any help after making contact.

For two days he stayed at an empty bombed-out house by the prison, trying to find a means of entry. Artillery shells began to fall on the prison, and low-flying Corsairs strafed its towers, brick walls and yards. There had been stationed at the prison a regiment in addition to the prison garrison, and U.N. gunfire seemed to be directed at them. But no really big fire power was turned on it yet, presumably because of the inmates. On the third morning the troops of the regiment, with tree leaves stuck on their helmets and shoulders, climbed the mountain behind the prison toward the fortifications overlooking the river. Obviously they were going to make a stand. From within the prison could be heard, coming through the breached walls, volleys of crackling small arms fire, followed by screams.

At about eleven o'clock that night, as gunfire and air raids intensified with phosphorescent flares lighting the night sky, Kido entered the prison at the main gate, fortified like a regular bunker with sandbags and turf. Only one guard had the presence of mind to salute him. The others were taking cover, watching the fireworks in the sky, or looking on at the massacre of prisoners going on in the main yard. Some prisoners ran towards them and got shot down by the guards as they reached the gate.

"Where are the Class A prisoners?" Kido asked, using the classification given by Pilsoo and the lieutenant.

"A lot of them are gathered at the infirmary, second floor, in the East Wing, Comrade Officer," he said pointing in the direction beyond a few buildings. "They are faking one sickness or another, but that serves our purpose. We can shoot them all in one place."

The guard, apparently a recruit from Seoul, talked garrulously as he examined Kido's forged ID.

"Thank you, Major, but I need your special duty orders to let you in."

"Don't be silly. The Bureau has started moving after trying for hours to get a message through to you. The phone's been dead of course but no messenger has returned. Hasn't Lieutenant Chon from the Bureau been here?"

The guard shook his head.

"Never mind. I have to round up former puppet Congressmen for a special purpose. I have no time to waste over a formality now."

He walked past the guard, cowering him with his peremptory tone and gait. When he got behind a building, he quickened his steps, fearing that he might be too late already. There were corpses, still bleeding and stirring, piled on top of each other in mounds all over the yard. In a corridor a crowd of prisoners were running this way and that under a hail of bullets. Most of the cells seemed emptied of their occupants. The infirmary on the second floor was still locked. The inmates were yelling and kicking at the door, but the guards and prison personnel were running about busily and paid no attention. Kido went up to the door and shot the locks open. About a hundred inmates jostled out, though many of them were too weak to run even the length of the hallway, and some flopped in the middle of the passage. Those who got to the head of the stairs were fired on. Screaming, they ran back into their old room and dug into their beds.

Kido found an empty bed and covered himself with a filthy blanket like the rest. The guards came in shouting and ordered them not to move, threatening to shoot on the spot. Nobody stirred. Absolute silence reigned for a full minute, before the inmates gradually pushed the blankets off their eyes and slowly raised their heads like turtles to find the guards gone after the fleeing prisoners. The shootings and screams went on unabated outside in the yards and alleys.

Kido whispered to the man next to him, who happened to

be Chisong Pai, a former prosecutor. His body was swollen with hepatitis and the flesh under his yellow skin had lost its resilience, taking minutes to fill out when poked with a finger. Kido told him who he was, explained his uniform and pistol, and asked for Paster Yoo's whereabouts.

"He is right over there," said Pai, pointing to a bed by the window. Kido jumped off his bed and went over quickly, overjoyed. Suja seemed to be right after all: an unerring hand had guided him straight to his objective. But his elation was shortlived. What he saw was only a pitiful shadow of the robust, ruddy-faced preacher who could stand at the pulpit preaching or praying sometimes for over twenty hours and be no worse for it the next day.

Despite the commotion Pastor Yoo had remained immobile in his bed. His sallow, stubbly bearded face stuck out from under the dirty coverlet. His hair hung loose in unkempt matted strands about his head. His closed eyes puckered slightly now and then as a ripple of pain crossed his face. He had been suffering from dysenteric diarrhea and infectious sores on his buttocks, probably from sitting too often on the rusty edge of the latrine can. There was only one can for the entire ward and the inmates, weak though they were, were detailed in turns to carry it out under guard and empty it at a tank on the ground floor.

"He kept running to it almost every minute although his inside was empty," explained Pai matter-of-factly. Yoo was no worse than the others. Many of them had tuberculosis which, progressing unchecked, had made visible, savage inroads. Others were gastric, cardiac, or surgical cases. Those in the infirmary had the privilege of lying down on a bed, which was a great blessing compared to the harsh routine of sitting up or standing for hours observing strict silence and being interrogated and beaten a few hours a day in the ordinary cellblocks. However, with no medicine and care, a few dropped out dead every day to be filled by equally hopeless cases.

"That's Suncho Ko's remains," said Pai, pointing at a bundle by Yoo's head. A mining tycoon owning over half of South Korea's gold interests, Ko had suffered from stomach cancer and was unable to swallow even a spoonful of water. Although not a regular member, he had donated generously to the church. Pastor Yoo, his own guts gouged and burning, attended to the suffering Ko, comforting him and praying for him. When finally Ko died in a paroxysm of pain, Yoo removed with his teeth a lock of Ko's hair and bits of his fingernails and toenails. He also tore off a piece of Ko's underwear, picking off the lice and eggs embedded in the fabric.

46

These mementos were wrapped in a piece of paper scratched off the wall for possible future delivery to the family. Pastor Yoo had looked after other inmates as diligently as his health would allow.

"Some of us have become converts, moved by his example of selfless service," Pai went on. A wry smile interrupted him before he resumed. "We have all been appreciative, except for one person."

He nudged his elbow toward a bed by the wall. Congressman Namshik Hwang, constantly fussing and complaining, strangely resisted all of Yoo's attempts to help him. With a heart condition, he panted miserably even with the least exertion, but when Yoo carried him a bowl of water to relieve his thirst, Hwang would flinch in horror, saying he didn't want to catch Yoo's dysentery germs. In fact he didn't want to use the same latrine can that Yoo had used and defecated, to the disgust of the others, on a sheet of paper and threw it into the can from a distance, sometimes missing the mark. Nobody could understand Hwang's strange humor; there were surely deadlier germs than dysentery in the ward. But Yoo did not mind this personal rejection and insult and patiently helped him whenever he could.

"He is exhausted now," Pai said. "This beastly weather!"

The day had been humid and stifling hot. Not a single breeze stirred. The heated, sweaty, sickly air hung like a lid, silently and irresistibly cooking the weakened, beaten, starved inmates. Sticky perspiration oozed like thick glue through their grime-filled pores, scalding their skin. They called weakly for water, the unclean liquid doled out niggardly in rusty pewters from an unclean bucket along with the daily ball of millet and soy beans, but no jailer paid any attention to their cries.

Kido shook Pastor Yoo gently, who opened his eyes as if waking from a dream and unable to focus. After some straining he recognized Kido.

"What are you doing here?" he said in a cracked, raspy voice, looking over his Red Army uniform in amazement.

"I am here to save you," Kido said self-consciously. "This uniform was my passport to get in here. They'll soon be coming here to take us out and shoot us in the yard. I saw them shooting others as I came in. We must avoid them. We must get organized."

"Let's get them with the pistol when they come in," suggested Yonwoo Lee, the *Central Daily* publisher.

"We'll mob them when they come in," said Tongsup Chay, the First Bank president, although his thin body had nothing but bones and he limped horribly from untreated abscesses in

his back and groin. Pastor Yoo, who had not eaten anything
for days, struggled up with the support of others and sat on
his bed. His body might be ruined but his mind was unim-
paired. His eyes shone bright and calm. They listened to him
as their unchallenged leader, as the guiding light of good sense
and authority.

"We are all weak," Yoo said in an unruffled voice. "Mr.
Chang here has the strength of two men and has a pistol to
boot, but still he won't be a match in a shootout with half
a dozen guards with burp guns. The best thing is to play sick
or dead and catch them off guard at the last minute."

They heard footsteps outside and scattered hurriedly to their
separate beds. Eight investigators and guards came in. Kido
was pushed into a hole they had made in the flooring, a dirty
cramped place between the joints crisscrossed with wiring and
plumbing, full of dust and cobwebs. It might have been
big enough for a smaller person, but Kido was stifled as he
doubled up. His back stuck out and the square piece of flooring
didn't fit level with the floor. A bed post was planted on top
and Kido groaned as the wood bit into his flesh. The
investigators hurriedly checked the list of names and charges,
row by row, asking each prisoner whether he could walk a few
miles outside the prison. They said the prisoners would be
moved to a new and better hospital north of the city, safe from
air raids and well stocked with food and medicine. This was
tempting to many who had not eaten properly for days, but
they had heard about the Inchon landings from Kido and by a
previously agreed-upon signal from Pastor Yoo they all said
they could barely walk out of the infirmary. The investigators
made their notes and moved on to the next room.

Gunfire roared louder as the day broke and air raid sirens
screeched on and on. There was a loud explosion in the yard.
The inmates all stood close to the bars on their toes and looked
down. A shell had hit and made a deep crater with shattered
bodies plowed under or scattered around it. Some of them were
uniformed People's Army soldiers. More shells fell on the
buildings. One hit the infirmary wall, killing two men lying on
the beds next to it. The bombardment must have convinced the
Red soldiers that the prison no longer enjoyed a sanctuary
status. They panicked and ran for protective shelters. Just
before they vacated a building, they shot the prisoners in it.
Burp guns rattled down the aisle in the cells and hideous cries
and screams went up. The murderers would be at the infirmary
any minute. Kido had the inmates make their beds look as if
they were still occupied, then line up along the wall by the
door. As many able-bodied men as possible stayed close to the

48

door with pieces of wood torn from the floor or beds and any other solid objects usable as weapons.

The door burst open. A guard came in firing his burp gun at the beds. Kimun Lee, a lawyer, dived for his feet. As the guard stumbled to the floor, two others went for his burp gun. Three other guards rushed in, also firing the burp guns wildly at the entrance and into the room. Several inmates were wounded, one of them dying instantly. Kido shot two of the guards dead and wounded the third one who flung his rifle and fled down the aisle calling for help. In the uproar and confusion going on all over the building and outside, nobody heard him. Somebody snatched up the burp gun and shot him as he was reaching the stairs. The guard on the floor was strangled. The inmates now had four burp guns and a pistol with plenty of cartridges. Flushed with their success some were eager to go out, take the prison garrison by force, and liberate the prisoners. But Pastor Yoo advised caution, pointing at the hundreds of guards outside. The dead soldiers were stripped and put on the beds. The stronger of the inmates put on the uniforms and stood at the door as sentinels. Somebody had to go out and remove the dead soldier from the stairway. Kido went. Just as he reached the body, several armed men came out of the nearby room and headed for the stairway. Kido propped up the dead man and waited for them to come near.

"One of you must have shot him by accident," he said accusingly.

"Who are you, Comrade Officer?" asked the leader, a lieutenant.

"I am from the Political Security Bureau to make sure that none of the Class A reactionaries got away. The Bureau has a pecial convoy waiting outside. Lead me to the infirmary and bring me up to date on their status."

Kido spoke imperiously in the Pyongyang accent, the shibboleth of power.

"A group was sent there to eliminate them," the lieutenant said.

"Eliminate them?"

"Those were the commandant's orders. Did you not check with him beforehand?"

"I couldn't get to the headquarters because of the shelling. Well, then, where are those who went to do the job?"

The lieutenant hesitated and looked at his soldiers.

"The one you are holding was one of them," replied a private.

"What's going on here?" Kido shouted ferociously. "You

mean this American imperialist shelling and bombing has so completely broken your morale and discipline that you shoot each other rather than the enemy?"

He whipped out his pistol and pushed it so hard against the lieutenant's stomach that he let out a moan of pain and doubled up.

"You are all under arrest. Tell them to lay down their arms and go down to the commandant's office for further investigation."

His height and his booming voice all combined to awe the crew. The brandished pistol and the fire of rage darting from his rolling eyes convinced them that he meant business. Besides, all would be cleared up once they went to the commandant's office. At an acquiescing nod from the lieutenant they laid down their burp guns.

"Raise your hands," Kido roared.

They obeyed and lined up in a file with the lieutenant at the head. Kido told them to aboutface and march toward the infirmary. The lieutenant was about to point out that the commandant's office lay in the opposite direction, but Kido jabbed him with the pistol in the nape of his neck as he followed, picking up the rifles. At the infirmary they were stripped, gagged, tied, and put under the blankets. Their uniforms were donned by other able-bodied inmates. Pastor Yoo's counsel still prevailed: they were not to stir from where they were. However, it was decided to send a couple of the uniformed men to go out and look for food, as many were on the verge of starvation. They needed the strength to hold out until the Marines arrived. Shells continued to pound and smash the prison and its surroundings. Even when one came, however, with its shrill whirr, the inmates felt that it couldn't hurt them. They knew the shells to be the necessary preliminary to their salvation.

Two were chosen who had been to the kitchen before and knew the way. Kido would have gone too but the inmates wanted him to remain with them to direct the operations in case there should be a confrontation. The two men were gone over an hour. Uneasiness and anxiety gripped them. Some expressed the fear that the foragers might have been captured, tortured, and made to confess, that the prison guards were now preparing for a massed attack on the infirmary. It was suggested that the prisoners should all move to another place, where the guards had already killed the inmates or marched them off. Pastor Yoo was still in favor of staying put, but he was in the minority.

They were about to rush out into the aisle when one of the men, Ingoo Suh, returned with a bag of rice on his shoulder.

His uniform was spattered with blood. It was the blood from the other man, Cholho Lee, who was hit by a flying shell fragment that tore off his shoulder. They had got to the kitchen safely enough and the kitchen hands were willing to give them anything, rice, dried fish, and pickled cabbage, especially when they were told to leave the prison and seek their own safety. On the way out and back a shell shattered a wall and Lee was hit. Suh tried to carry Lee, leaving the bag of food, but Lee died from unstoppable bleeding. There were squads of Red soldiers heading their direction. Suh ran and hid the food and himself in a shed until they went away.

"Forget about leaving," Suh said. "The bombing has flushed them all out. They are all over the place."

The famished prisoners sat down to the food and dropped any thoughts of breaking out for the time being. As the night deepened, the gunfire became more deadly and frequent. knocking plaster from the ceiling and violently shaking the walls. Shootings and butcherings of prisoners went on throughout the night in the yard and in the different cellblocks. But no search party came to check on the infirmary.

* * *

The next morning came with a bright sun in a cloudless autumn sky. A cool wind blew through the ward like a purifying breath. Swallows and larks, springing from nowhere, could be heard singing and cavorting merrily. Cuckoos sent up their melancholy responsary in the back hills. All other noise seemed to have hushed. Gunfire was heard at a distance, only accentuating the eerie silence that reigned over the entire prison compound. The occupants of the infirmary kept looking down at the yard, strewn with white or blue-clad bodies singly or in heaps. There was no sign of living Red soldiery. About noon challenges were heard to the accompaniment of automatic weapons firing. Khaki-clad Korean National Marines crouched behind sheltering objects and cautiously entered the yard. They quickly stormed into the buildings one by one, making sure there was no lurking sniper.

Kido took Pastor Yoo home in a jeep loaned by the Marine commanding officer. But as soon as he reached the safety of home, the pastor's body became a burning furnace and no amount of aspirin or cold massage seemed to have any effect. He became delirious and, on the second day, literally tonguetied. This eloquent man, who had moved thousands to tears or cheers, couldn't speak a word. His tongue would not move. All he could do in his fleeting moments of consciousness was to

51

snort, hiss or grunt. An army doctor was consulted, who diagnosed it as acute meningitis and prescribed antibiotics, but the disease showed no response. Then Pastor Yoo started hiccuping. His family raised his head and poured sweetened water into his mouth. Somebody had to turn his head to one side, another held his mouth open, and a third pulled his tongue out to let the liquid trickle in without choking him. But the hiccups continued as regularly as a sinister metronome set at 15 a minute. They racked his bony rib cage and convulsed into momentary tension the sluggish, insensate skin, the sunken abdomen, the bony legs and arms. An acupuncturist was brought in, an old woman with deep-lined bark-like skin, who pricked the patient seemingly at random. As the needle penetrated his knuckles, his hand jerked a little.

"Hm, he feels that," she said casually.

"Is he going to be all right?" Suja asked tearfully, holding the old lady's shoulder.

"Sure," she said, quickly gathering her instruments and leaving. Outside she told Kido as a person not related to the family that the patient wouldn't live through the day. He kept this to himself. The still hopeful family asked him to go to a doctor of their acquaintance, a Dr. Won, who lived in Yongsan clear across town. There was no public transportation. Most of the streets were impassable with downed telephone and electric wires, sandbagged barricades, shell craters, heaps of smoldering ashes, and uncleared bodies. The torn, mangled, diseased humanity stumbled or crawled amid this bizarre wasteland. To be whole as Kido was seemed a supreme privilege. Military vehicles moved through some barely cleared lanes. The first wave of enthusiasm and elation over liberation had passed, and the citizenry set about grimly poking at the aftermath of destruction and carnage.

Dr. Won's neighborhood, being near a school quartering a Red Army detachment, had been leveled to the ground. His house must have been a grand mansion with trees, a lawn, a fishpond, and an aviary, the doctor being an ornithologist as well as a neurosurgeon of national reputation. Nothing but charred heaps of rubble remained. The doctor's wife, in dirty rags, was digging among the pile of burnt timbers, broken bricks, and rooftiles to salvage food they had hidden in the basement. Three young children, their faces smudged with tears and soot, watched their mother and occasionally assisted her. The doctor had been killed on the last night before the UN troops entered the capital. They had hid behind a concrete parapet as street fighting raged outside. A rocket hit and blew up the wall, directly where the doctor had been sitting.

52

When Kido returned to the Yoos, Suja was sitting at the edge of the raised floor by the courtyard. Her face looked haggard. When she saw him, tears started to her eyes.

"Father is dead," she said in a hollow voice.

"When did it happen?"

"Shortly after you left. Strangely enough he was calling for you. He strained his lips and tongue and we could distinctly make out your name."

Pastor Yoo's funeral service was held at the site of the burned-down church. The roof and walls of the main sanctuary had crumbled, but the steeple with its bell had survived like some lanky, grotesque giraffe with its hindquarters cut off. The bell pealed as clearly and resonantly as ever. It was a miracle the manse had survived intact, undamaged, although the oak and chestnut trees surrounding it had all caught fire and burned to cinder, leaving ugly blackened limbs like monstrous horns. A surprising number of believers came to mourn his death. They wept bitterly. His imprisonment and death were to them a symbol of their own suffering and grief, and he was soon transformed by their imaginations into the Christ figure.

"It's dark! The light is gone," they wailed, holding on to the bier and following the procession to the cemetery on foot.

As the coffin was lowered into the grave and the first shovel of dirt sprinkled, fresh wailing started. Everybody's eyes ran with tears. The only exception was Susok, Suja's twelve-year-old idiot brother. Typhus during his infancy had permanently damaged his brain. He was laughing and enjoying the whole scene as if it were a play staged for his amusement. Suja pulled him to her side.

"That's our father," she said, choking with tears. "He so loved you."

For a moment the idiot's attention seemed caught. He regarded the half-covered coffin seriously. Then he gave a shrug and turned away, as if he saw nothing unusual in it.

After the burial Kido escorted the family to their house, where mourners waited to greet them with more weepings. Kido slipped out unnoticed and walked along Bell Street. The same melancholy scenery greeted him everywhere. The street surface had been partly cleared for vehicular traffic, mostly military, but the charred walls of buildings stood gaunt like skeletons of dinosaurs with heaps of rubble at their feet, totally beyond redemption or salvage. He was inconsolably saddened at the widespread desolation. Death and misery had triumphed, mocking all human endeavor or achievement. He looked at the ruins of Octagonal Pagoda at Central Park. The magnificent stone structure, each layer sculpted by generations of masons, was now good only for landfill. Why did he bother to eat, drink, or move around? All the whimpering, crawling humanity, especially he himself, seemed to be the butt of a hellish joke.

He flopped down with exhaustion by the roadside on a chipped piece of overturned marble that had served as a cornerstone for a building. Why had he taken all the trouble to rescue the pastor, risking his own life against such overwhelming odds, blazing a trail of deaths, undoubtedly deaths of some innocent people, those youngsters who had no choice in being where they were or doing what they did, only to have the pastor die so pointlessly? But as his mind turned to this particular topic, there emerged from the general pattern of irrationality a glimpse of cogent explanation. He would not ordinarily have done what he had done for anybody, not if it had been his own father's life at stake. He'd done it this time because Suja had cleverly maneuvered him into it. A tear or a sigh from her vanquished him, depriving him of independent will, turning him into a robot of obedience. No wonder it had come to nothing. There seemed to be an inevitability, a measure of divine justice here. He fully deserved to be thrashed for letting a woman run his life. He struck his knees with his hands and rose to his feet. Dusk had fallen. The night air was chilly and crept up on his skin under the thin, tattered summer shirt and pants, presaging worse things to come in the approaching winter.

* * *

He was surprised by the reception he got upon entering the door of the manse. It seemed they had all been waiting for him. The word had somehow gotten around that before his death the pastor had appointed him as successor. The small matter of ordination by the Presbytery was quickly brushed aside. The organization had dissolved and hadn't had a chance to reconvene. The gathered elders and deacons greeted him as Pastor with all due deferences and reverences. In vain did he protest his complete astonishment, his unreadiness, inadequacy. Could he question the wisdom of the illustrious, saintly shepherd who had entrusted him with the wand of office to lead the directionless flock to the green pastures? Was he so willful and selfish as to consider only his own preferences and dispositions, allege personal disqualification, and hold back when the moment called for instant, decisive action? Couldn't he see the thirsting sheep ready to be taken to the quenching waters of worship and salvation?

"The church shall rise again immortal like the phoenix from her ruins," said Elder Hyongday Kwon, the oldest patriarch on the Session, with deep, quaking emotion.

"As the first act of your ministry," interposed Elder Unhwa Shim, stroking his formidable beard, "you have to officiate your own wedding to Miss Yoo, first thing tomorrow morning, so you can move into the manse."

Apparently that had been part of the dying man's will, too, which the Session was determined to carry out to the letter as expeditiously as possible. They seemed particularly impressed by the practicality and appropriateness of this detail, which gave them a new cause to approve their departed leader's fore-sightedness. They would not have had the heart to turn out his widow and children, but on the other hand the new pastor and his family, whoever they might be, had to be lodged at the manse. This arrangement got two birds with one stone. So the point was settled once and for all, without any further consideration or delay.

Working past midnight, they brought up dozens of other problems and agenda facing the church, how to cart off the debris, where to get tenting canvas, wood and other materials, whether the church should be built at a different part of the grounds to allow more front yardage, what military and government agencies should be contacted for one reason or other, what families should be visited and aided. The participants addressed each motion to Kido as official moderator but, after that formality, they promptly turned to each other, without even waiting for his acknowledgment, to heatedly debate the pros and cons. Kido felt ridiculously out of place, as if he presided over a lunatic forum, where nothing he could say or do made any difference. He wanted to get away and find Suja to ask her what this all meant, to tell her to stop this madness at once, before it went too far. But she was nowhere to be seen. Besides, he was ruefully admitting to himself, even if he should find her, he didn't have it in him to tear himself away from the solemn, earnest entourage to tell her what he thought of her manipulations and her dupes, these witless sheep who, with their principles, preoccupations, wisdoms, visions, were nevertheless blind as bats, not seeing beyond each other's rumps to understand who was really behind it all. The course had been set unalterably, irreversibly. He had to resign himself to being carried down the madding current, to sink or swim, through rapids and shoals.

Early the next morning, before he'd had enough sleep, he was awakened. The reporters had arrived, already quite well informed with details of exploits he had not performed. A

conservative average had him kill off, singlehanded, a
hundred Red puppet officers and men. They needed him only
to pose for pictures, not to corroborate the stories previously
authenticated by countless eyewitness accounts. Nobody took
his protests seriously. They smiled indulgently or admired his
clerical modesty. A conspiracy was afoot to create a legend, a
modern myth. It was not in his power to stop this mass will.
He had to acquiesce and be gracious about lending his name to
the romance. To scoff or debunk would be downright churlishness, unpatriotic and unnatural.

* * *

The bell rang, heralding another Lord's day, clear and
forceful, through the wintry air. The church, bigger and
more splendid than before, rose majestically on the hill domi-
nating the skyline, asserting its immortality, its ever-renewing
vitality, scorning the power of destruction. The U.S. armed
forces had diverted a quantity of their construction materials,
now pouring in by shiploads at Inchon, to the church with its
celebrated pastor. Carpenters, masons, and other craftsmen,
eager for employment, had worked feverishly to prove
themselves worthy of the grain wages. The interior was
well appointed and furnished with rows of varnished pews,
tinted glass windows, a waxed parquet, and a new pipe organ.
The chancel wall behind the altar was covered solid with
walnut-colored pipes, surmounted at the center by a golden
cross. Not only the sanctuary had been rebuilt; other buildings
had gone up on the compound, including a large dormitory
for foundlings, a brain wave of Suja's, among others.
Hundreds of homeless orphans, crippled, burned, blinded, came
to be fed and clothed and treated, and truckloads of powdered
milk, flour, rice, blankets, clothing, medicine, and other pro-
visions came for their support from the Americans, smitten
with guilt about the war. The church was a center of many
community activities, with people coming and going busily.
Behind the orphanage kitchen, away from the usual kitchen,
was added a shed to serve as the garage, discreetly housing a
newly purchased truck, well serviced and provided with spare
parts and two drums of fuel, but nobody particularly noticed it
or attached any significance to it.
The Sunday morning worshippers arrived in great numbers, devout and hopeful, seemingly unperturbed by the news
of Red Chinese entry into the war with fifty divisions, routing
and annihilating the jubilant Korean National Army divisions
that had reached the Yalu first and encircling the Eighth U.S.

Army and the U.S. X Corps, including its vaunted First Marines. The UN forces were retreating on all fronts, burning and blowing up huge quanities of supplies they had amassed and couldn't take back with them. The evacuation of Seoul had been ordered. This time Syngman Rhee had learned the futility and folly of lying about the real state of war, causing so many of his trusting citizens to remain in their places and fall into the enemy's hands. Even if he should lie, nobody would believe him. Everybody had gotten a little wiser. They had their radio tuned in to the Japanese and American channels and didn't depend on his Office of Information-controlled KBS. But the members of St. Peter's—that was the name adopted, despite its non-Protestant ring, to commemorate the staunchness of the illustrious Pastor Yoo—had no hesitation in coming to church this morning. At least they knew they wouldn't be the last to leave. Their hearts lifted up with the pealing of the bell, and the solid, new-built church, with its good shepherd at its helm, seemed to shelter them from the worst the Red Chinese and the Soviets could muster against them.

The massive pipe organ heaved up a gentle hymn of praise, permeating every corner and enthralling every heart with its insistent soft sweetness. As it gradually crescendoed, louder than all the bugles of Jericho, one had the illusion of being borne off or, rather, blasted off, on a rocket ship straight to the gates of heaven. The worshippers, brimming with gratitude, love, confidence, were certain that they held a confirmed reservation on the Heaven-bound express. They had faith in the engineer, the white-clad organist with the angelic appearance, the daughter of Pastor Yoo, the St. Peter of Seoul, and the pregnant wife of the incumbent Pastor Chang. They had unbounded faith in their new shepherd, the intrepid, all-daring man of action, who would lead them through hell, always bringing up the rear. They saw him seated on his chair, tall and straight in prayer, waiting for the prelude to stop. He was the pillar to hold up the falling sky. The very sight of him reassured them and gave them the strength and equanimity to face the seesawing armed forces, friendly and hostile, overrunning and wasting their homeland.

Kido sat trying in vain to collect his thoughts for the day's sermon, culled and collaged from the numerous anthologies, East and West, in his predecessor's library. He couldn't shut from his mind the thousands of refugees, their valuables on their backs and heads, milling at the railroad yard of Seoul Station to catch a train, the sky-high prices vehicles of any sort fetched for temporary hire, the fever and haste with which the entire population packed up and trudged the snow across the barren countryside. All the cleanup, reordering, reconstructing they had done in the city counted for naught. They were possessed with one thought, to leave the doomed city before it was too late. They had seen and experienced enough of the Communist rule, and they didn't want more, which they were sure would be worse. Everybody seemed convinced they were on the Communist blacklist, marked for elimination.

Kido pondered what his chances would be if found in the hands of the Communists. Certainly he would not be able to impersonate Major Pilsoo Song again. The whole world had heard about it and the Communists, with their reputedly accurate intelligence machinery, must have, too. But how was he to leave Seoul and St. Peter's with its new buildings, its trusting congregation, its pipe organ, and its dedicated organist? Pastor Yoo hadn't. As his successor he was expected to carry on the tradition. Suja had expressed her thought on the matter pretty definitely six months earlier. How had he been brought to such a pass?

As the organ flourished to a resounding close and Suja nodded to him, signaling his cue, he turned his face sharply away from her and stomped to the pulpit to intone his call to worship. He might be a consummate hypocrite, singing the stirring devotional lyrics, the distillation of centuries of religious inspiration, while his heart rankled with resentment, calculation, treachery, but he was no fool. As for hypocrisy, even Jesus had had his moments of self-doubt, but he'd brazened it out. Besides, this aspect concerned his character, the part of him which he somehow felt couldn't be held against him. Wasn't he the product of conditioned reflexes?

But being a sucker and not knowing it reflected on his intelligence, which at once demeaned and degraded him to something less than human. He would rather be a cheat than a dummy. He knew what his scheming, darling wife was up to. He might not be able to stop her, he mused grimly, but he was not blind, not this time. Perhaps it was something in her that she couldn't help, like some autonomous impulse she had no control over. He believed in the sincerity of her love for him, but he knew that because of it she would not hesitate to send him into the Lions' Den. For the sake of an image, an idea, a reputation, something to be proud of for the baby stirring in her womb? She had done it to her father: he was by now convinced that it was she who had, with her fixed notions about the good shepherd and the Apostle, dissuaded her father from leaving Seoul when he still could. But where were the descendants of Simon Peter to carry on and display, emblazoned on their heraldry, the fame of their ancestral loyalty and courage? Besides, one was loyal or courageous if he believed in what he was doing, but he, Kido Chang, the charlatan, the agnostic, didn't. He shouldn't be the innocent Isaac to be led to the altar to be a sacrificial offering, for the second time, to fulfill an arbitrary covenant between God and Abraham. Why hadn't Abraham offered himself, instead of his trusting preteen son, and seen what it felt like to be licked by the leaping tongues of flame? God couldn't be so prankish and wanton.

People were cruel and thoughtless about others' comforts and lives, could inflict pain and sorrow without batting an eye, because they could't see or feel the I, the self, beyond their own, outside their cubic footage of flesh and bones bounded by the thick, insulatory skin. Godhead was omniscience, omnisentience. No, it was Abraham's own insomniac, constipatory hallucination. He'd no right to impose thus on his only son. The erasure of time was conclusive, irremediable. It didn't make a bit of difference to posterity whether he was or was not a Peter, whether he walked with his head up in front of a firing squad or ran, dodging the bullets, groveling if necessary. He might make it in the latter case. Yes, he would try to get away, even if it meant doing it all alone. It was time he told her once and for all that she had manipulated his life enough, that from now on he was making the decisions.

But would he be able to get away? Was it not too late? He could cross the river and walk to Pusan by himself, roadblock or no roadblock, but not with his pregnant wife, his arthritic mother-in-law, and his idiot brother-in-law. Could he really leave them? A sense of fatality overtook him. He saw himself as a bug clawing at the smooth, slippery, perpendicular wall of a pan, watched over by a giant entomologist. The bug circled and clawed, fell and rose again, tried diagonals, doublebacks, somersaults, backslidings. Was it really worth all the evasions? Maybe there was some value in the dignity with which one faced the firing squad. You could die laughing or crying. Neither made any difference. But the so-called dignified way made a better story. Yes, a story!

He did not notice the impatient response from the organ, coming in half a second too fast on the final syllable of his invocation. He had no idea that his organist wife had learned to drive the truck expertly and had pulled it apart and put it together several times on her way to becoming an ace mechanic. Nor did he know that she had been carefully and diligently packing to see the family through for several months on the road. She was impatient to leave the service and call the G2 of Capital Division about the proximity of the

Identity

The wood crackled in the potbellied stove as a token gesture of defiance to the snowstorm outside. What little heat it generated seemed to elude human contact. My frozen feet and back weren't much relieved by the sight of Corporal Yoon, 19, who had been kneeling on the floor since supper. Lieutenant Kim slouched in his chair with his feet on the stool by the stove. Sergeant Shin sat or paced about Yoon, cracking him with a swagger stick for the slightest sign of "disrespect," such as shifting his weight or wriggling his torso. A student draftee, I sat at a desk between Kim and Yoon, recording the proceedings of the interrogation.

"What did you tell them last night?" Kim asked for the umpteenth time.

"I haven't met anybody, sir," Yoon said.

"Tell the truth or you'll be shot at once."

"We had not slept for three days and nights. When our squad was ordered to the rear, we thought it was to make us sleep. We had to sleep."

"But you must know the penalty for desertion, because that's what you did, desert your post while on guard duty. By neglecting your watch you and your men could have exposed the command post to guerrilla attack."

An ammunition dump and a supply depot had been blown up just two nights before, and Yoon's combat company was among those pulled back hastily from the front to reinforce the defense of the command post, five miles to the rear. At the front a fierce battle had been raging after a major offensive mounted by several divisions of Red Chinese and North Koreans. Our commanding general, furious, had given orders to shoot the culprits instantly.

"Are you telling me you risked death just to sleep?"

"We were too tired to think or stand up. I pinched my men, kicked them, jabbed them in the ribs with my gun muzzle. They couldn't hear or feel. They were dropping to the snow, some hugging the icicled pine needles like blankets. They would've frozen to death. I found an empty barn on a bombed-out farm and put them there. They slept like corpses. Nothing could have roused them."

"But one of them woke up to piss. He looked for you and couldn't find you."

"I was outside standing watch. I didn't go to sleep for as long as I could. I was in charge and knew my responsibilities. I bit my lips and twisted my ears to drive off hallucinations. Then I was clutching the snow and burrowing my head into it, like a warm bed. I crawled on all fours back to the barn, dragging my rifle. Then I passed out."

"Liar!" Shin yelled, cracking Yoon's knuckles with the swagger stick. The muscles under Yoon's eyes twitched. Water filmed his eyes as he stared, unblinking, at the wall.

"Didn't you put the men out of the way so you could go about your business?" Shin asked.

"I had no other business," Yoon said.

Shin was pouncing again on Yoon with the stick. Yoon's body stiffened, expecting the blow. Kim jerked his head, restraining Shin.

"If you admit you're a Communist agent and give us the enemy's plans, their positions and strength, we'll go easy on you."

"I'm not a spy. I've never been one. I have no information to give."

"Your men have deposed that one of the prisoners you recently captured recognized you as a comrade-in-arms during the Taygoo Offensive and called you by name. He thought you would be at Mt. Chiri as a partisan and was surprised to see you in our uniform. It's all here."

Kim held the folder before Yoon.

"I don't deny it," said Yoon. "But not all Red soldiers are Red."

"Are you also saying that not all UN troops are anti-Red?"

Yoon's lips moved to reply but stopped. He must have sensed the ruse. Kim went up to Yoon and poised his foot to kick. Colonel Chong, chief intelligence officer of the division, stepped in, acknowledging our salutes. Taking the chair vacated by Kim, he asked if there was any progress, at the same time extending his hand in my direction. I put the sheets of notes together and handed them over. Chong turned the pages rapidly, stopping when he came to Yoon's enlistment in the People's Army.

"So you volunteered?"

"Only in a manner of speaking, sir."

* * *

All the upperclassmen had been ordered to assemble at the school auditorium. A People's Army officer gave them a speech and told them to volunteer. He asked them to raise their hands if anybody objected. Nobody dared raise his hand. After two weeks of training Yoon was sent, equipped with a rifle and grenades, to join the Taygoo Offensive. His division consisted mostly of volunteer draftees like himself. After losing nearly all their men they drew back, running for days and days through the mountains, scarcely stopping even for water. Finally they came to a halt in the Chiri Mountains, cut off from the main retreating army to the north by the US Marines landing at Inchon. The southern coastal cities were being recaptured one by one by the South Korean army, and the Communist contingents scattered in these areas were also cut off from the north. The Chiri area, with its unending tower of mountain ranges and inaccessible terrain, provided the ideal rallying point for the straggling military remnants and civilian collaborators who were being hunted down and summarily executed by the returning South Korean forces. The partisans, reorganized into divisions and regiments, went foraging on punitive expeditions into the surrounding country, the recently liberated villages and towns.

One day they raided a seemingly undefended village, which turned out to be an ambush. Nearly all of them were killed. Yoon, who was guarding the rear, ran into the fields, away from the battle. Hiding near a village, he stole some clothes at night and walked to the nearest town, where he managed to board a refugee train for Seoul. He wanted to see whether his parents, brothers, and sisters were still alive. It took him three days to reach Tayjon by the refugee train, as military trains constantly preempted the tracks. He was picked up in a general inspection of papers and, after a few days of bootcamp, sent to the front where his combat experience enabled him to outperform the new enlistees. Recently he had been awarded a medal and promoted to corporal for dislodging an entire Chinese company from a strategic hill with his nine-man reconnaissance squad.

* * *

"Why didn't you disclose your People Army's background?"

"I didn't want to look bad, sir," Yoon said.

His past would not have come to light had it not been for the coincidence of capturing a soldier from his previous People's Army unit. His squad members had not reported the reunion so long as it was nobody's business; they'd liked having the capable Yoon as their leader. But now things were different. They had to save their own necks, and he was their scapegoat.

"You've been hiding, legally speaking," said Chong. "You've been deceiving us. Your service record means nothing. You're a spy. The only way to save yourself from the firing squad is to make a clean breast of it by telling us all you know about the enemy's next move."

"If you take the prisoner I've captured seriously, how can it be that I am a Communist spy, sir? He would have pretended not to recognize me."

"Don't argue with me!" shouted Chong. "Not every soldier is told who is sent out as an agent. What information did you exchange with your contacts last night?"

"I didn't meet anybody. That is the whole truth, sir. All I did was to fall asleep because I couldn't help it."

Colonel Chong put down the papers and looked hard at Yoon, as if he would pierce his very soul. His face and posture became solemn, like a judge about to pronounce verdict.

"Are you a Communist or not?" he asked.

"I have never been a Communist. I don't know what Communism means, except it is something I was told to hate before 1950, then to love, then hate."

Chong rose and left the tent with Kim. Shin was now lord and master and would have prated on and on, delivering frequent blows to Yoon for another hour at least, but he was called away to a card game. Yoon sat passively immobile. He was my charge. I raised him and put him to bed, giving him extra blankets and reminding him of the utter folly and futility of anything desperate like making a run for it. Yoon turned to me, his eyes as calm as if nothing had happened.

"Would you have done it differently?" he asked. "Put yourself in my place. We are about the same age. Could I have done it any other way?"

I could not reply. I just told him, without thought or sincerity, that everything would turn out all right if he didn't do anything foolish, if he told the truth, the whole truth.

In the morning I drove the jeep. Kim sat in the front and Yoon, handcuffed behind his back, rode in the back seat. His case was too big for investigation at the division level and was being turned over to the Army headquarters at Taygoo. So Yoon got a temporary stay of execution, and Kim, who had pressed for this decision, was happy to get away from the front to escort the prisoner to Taygoo, his home town. Even after crossing several hills all we could see were military installations and the little settlements of camp followers surrounding them. The state of war at this time was too volatile to induce civilians to return in numbers to their home.

After spirited driving, often skidding on the snow-packed road despite the chains, we managed to reach Miyari Pass overlooking the northern suburb of Seoul. The sun was just setting. Kim told me to pull up at the hilltop, off the road. He wanted to stretch his legs and attend to other business. I got off, too, telling Yoon to do the same. Yoon got down but didn't want to leave the jeep side. We two escorts went off in separate directions, keeping an eye on him. I got back first and started the engine. Kim returned slowly, pushing his arms above his head, turning his neck, jumping up and down. Arriving at the jeep, he rested his hand on the windshield and jerked his chin to Yoon to get in first. Yoon obeyed, and as he got halfway in, leaning his shoulder on the back of the front seat, he kicked Kim in the face. Before I could do anything, Yoon's massive head came crushing down on my forehead, knocking me unconscious.

When I came to, my right eye was closed and my left eye was so sore I could scarcely open it. My nose twisted and my jacket soaked in blood, I could just barely see Yoon running down the hill. I got out of the jeep and felt my way around to Kim on the ground. He was not breathing. His pulse had stopped. The pistol on his hip was gone, and so was the ring of keys, one of which unlocked Yoon's handcuffs, but my M-1 rifle was in the back seat. I picked up the rifle and ran down the hill, stumbling, shouting at Yoon to stop, the dirty Red. Before I lost sight of him, I aimed, although he seemed already out of range. My whole body shook with rage. I kept pulling the trigger, and he kept running downhill, bounding like a deer, disappearing quickly into the darkening valley. I flung the rifle and ran downhill, determined to chase him and murder him with my bare hands. But after a few steps I tripped, slid, and fell over a thirty-foot cliff.

When I regained consciousness, I was in the army hospital in Seoul, all bandaged and stitched up, in a cast. The colonel from the division was there at my bedside, pressing his congratulations on my shoulder, the only bare spot on my body.

"Lieutenant Kim is dead, poor fellow," he said. "But the main thing is that you've shot the spy dead. We don't have too many facts on him yet, other than that cock and bull story of his, but we will find out soon enough. I know he's a big one. Imagine giving him a medal."

I was silent. Yoon could have finished me off but he hadn't. Had my perfunctory gestures of kindness to him the night before been calculated to insure his goodwill, so he would spare me in just such an emergency, and had I repaid him with death for his misplaced humanity? But my thoughts wandered to something more immediate. What if they couldn't find anything on him? What if all his relatives were dead and nobody knew about him? What if he were a plain nobody, a high school senior cheated out of his college education? Hadn't I myself escaped being volunteered into the People's Army by the sheerest of luck, by hiding and shifting? What if at this moment somebody should play a practical joke and recognize me as a partisan comrade-in-arms in the Chiri campaigns? Nobody saw me in Seoul during the three-month Communist occupation. My father was killed in a manner known only to his Communist captors. Mother died in Pusan at the refugee camp, her body swollen with jaundice to three times her normal size. My brother Choo, whose face closely resembled mine, had been killed much earlier in an air raid. But didn't I have my official records, my official papers? No, the family registers and other records had all burned to ashes during the conflagration of September 1950 as MacArthur's Marines "neutralized" the city. There was no way to tell my past, my identity. Any freak coincidence could disprove it all.

"My card, my ID," I raved, tugging at the cast held down by several hands.

66

The Boar

Private Shin clattered back from the outhouse in his unlaced shoes. He went past his bed by the door and continued on down the narrow aisle between the row of sleepers. It was only a few minutes after turn-in time, nine p.m., but some were already snoring. The darkness did not impede his rapid progress to the end of the tent, where Private Chang slept. Shin shook him by the foot.

"What's up?" Chang asked irritably.

"I saw Inho walking into the company CP."

"Has it been five days already?" Chang said, sitting up, pushing aside the sheet.

"It must be. Nobody just cuts out of the regimental stockade, not even the Corporal Inho Lim himself. He must have come the short way down the mountain trail right after his release."

"Why didn't he come here first? He could report in the morning."

They came out of the barracks to go and meet Inho. Blackout was enforced and watch was set at the outposts along the perimeter of the garrison, halfway up the hill across from the opposite hills held by the Communists. Hugging the buildings and tents, Chang and Shin skirted the marshaling yard and stopped at the foot of the steps leading to their company command post. The windows on both sides of the front door were discernible under the silhouetted arc of the quonset roof. Chang told Shin to wait there, while he went to the mess beyond the ordnance sheds, the rocket launchers, and the mortar mounts to get some food. The kitchen chief, Corporal Kwon, came from the same province as Chang and would accommodate him no matter how late the hour, Chang said. Looking for a suitable place to wait, Shin went into the

67

planted slope by the steps. The blooming clover, cosmos and lilies exuded a sweet fragrance which soon became offensive to him: it reminded him of the pomade on his commanding officer Lieutenant Nam's pressed hair. On Nam's direction his platoon had to plant and tend the flowers daily. Who needed flowers after a sixteen-hour patrol? Shin sat on a bunch of white lilies and kicked his heels into the grass. The crunch of the bulbs and stems breaking under his buttocks thrilled him. The door of the CP quonset swung open, floodlighting Inho, who walked down the steps with a heavy, measured footfall.

"Inho!" Shin whispered.

"Who is it?"

"Me, Wonso. Sit here and let's wait for Kidong. He went to get some food for you. Did you eat any supper?"

"No, but I'm not hungry. I won't eat anything."

Inho started walking toward the barracks — short and pudgy, with a round face, eyes close to the sides, the wide space in the middle unrelieved by his flat nose and small mouth. Wonso felt an impulse to hug him, as he would his own brother, but he didn't. He couldn't. There was something about Inho that at once invited and yet discouraged intimacy. He had an aura of power about him, a power that could focus and zero in with deadly accuracy. Perhaps his being an expert shot, in fact the best marksman in the latest Division championships, had something to do with this impression. One did not trifle with him and tended to stand at a distance from him in spite of his comical, almost idiotic outward appearance.

"Are you sick anywhere?" Wonso asked, following sheepishly.

"No, I'm perfectly all right. Don't make me talk. Can't you see I'm in no mood for talk?"

"But if you don't eat, you'll get sick pretty soon. We enlisted men can't afford to skip meals because we are mad."

"You are the worst nag in the whole Korean army. I tell you again I don't want food. I don't want anything. Just leave me alone."

At that moment Chang arrived, panting, with a ball of rice stuffed with kimchi and marinated anchovies. Two friends pressing food on him was too much and Inho gave in. Flanked on both sides, he sat down on a stone beside a supply building and took the food. As the ball of rice broke between his flashing teeth and emitted its pungent odor, the onlookers salivated and swallowed. It had been hours since their supper, skimpy at best and quite unequal to the daily physical exertion required of them. Generally sleep banished hunger until the next morning, but now awake and freshly stimulated, they felt agonized.

But the torture did not last long. Inho had dispatched the food before they could count to ten.

"That was the first supper I've had in five days," Inho said.

"Don't they give supper there any more?"

"They do, but that jerk Nam saw to it that I didn't get it. He timed my latrine detail to coincide with supper time. I emptied all the sewer tanks every day."

"Was that really necessary?" said Wonso indignantly.

"It's all in the past," said Kidong. "Don't let that get you down."

"That's easy for you to say," said Inho. He fumbled for a cigarette in his breast pocket but found only a folded sheet of paper. Wonso quickly produced a pack of Hwarangs and Kidong lit a match.

"What's that paper for?"

"Order for my leave signed a week ago."

"Good. You can go home now for your father's birthday."

"That's tomorrow. It takes at least two days to get to Changsong, the nearest town. Then it's another twenty miles on foot by the winding paths in the Chiri mountains. The party will be over. He must think I'm a heel to miss it, after writing him I'd be home for sure, after bragging I would present him with a boar from the hills as soon as I got there. That was the first time I ever wrote to anybody."

"You can still go," Wonso suggested. "Your father will understand. You can use some rest, get fattened up, get back what you've lost in the..."

Inho rose to his feet and tore up the leave paper, as his pals watched aghast.

"Aren't you supposed to return it?"

"He can't mess my life up more than he has already. Boy, won't he suffer for it!"

"You're not thinking of anything foolish, are you?" said Kidong, alarmed.

"I'm going to shoot him."

Kidong and Wonso looked at each other.

"They'll shoot you for sure, if you do that. The best thing is to forget it. If every soldier thrown in the clink starts shooting..."

"I am not every soldier."

"Besides, you were wrong to duck his blows."

"I don't let anybody beat me up, not even God Almighty. I hadn't done anything to deserve his working me over like that."

* * *

69

It drizzled noiselessly the whole afternoon and into the night. The starless, overcast sky made it impossible to see beyond a few feet. There was a special alert on: Division intelligence had reported that a major Chinese offensive would be launched against the salient guarded by the Third Company that night. Private Inho Lim struck a match and covered it with his hands to look at his watch. It was eleven o'clock. There were only a few sleepers in the tent who, like himself, had just been relieved from earlier shifts at the trenches and foxholes. Putting on his uniform, Inho tiptoed out of the barracks and walked across the yard to the company headquarters. He knew Lieutenant Nam was the duty officer that night and would not be disturbed as all hands would be busy at the outworks.

The yellow dirt of the yard gave way to crushed gravel at the edge near the steps. Inho catfooted over the gravel, then purposefully waded through the flower bed to the far side of the nearest mortar unit. It would be awkward to be challenged and to have to explain his prowling at that hour. Inho knocked softly at the quonset door. Confirming the answering voice inside, Inho opened the door and quickly shut it after him. Nam lifted his eyes from the papers on his desk to the intruder, his chin still resting on his upturned palms. The lieutenant was in his T-shirt; his jacket, pistol holster, and helmet hung on the wall. The unventilated room was unbearably hot. Inho stepped to the front of the desk, saluted, and identified himself, with exaggerated, superfluous military formality.

"Don't you know you have to wait to be admitted? What is it that you want?"

"I have a question to ask of the officer," said Inho, unruffled. "Is it the heat that has forced the officer to comport himself in a manner unbecoming an officer?"

"What are you driving at?" barked Nam.

"I recall being beaten by an officer for unbuttoning my jacket while returning from a night patrol. He stood me up in the yard so that the whole company could watch while he beat me with his fists. I spat out the blood filling my mouth and he punched me harder. I dodged, and for that he put me in the stockade and half starved me. I find him on duty now, half naked. Who is going to discipline him?"

Outraged, Nam glared. There was no mistaking the purpose of the visit. From the beginning Nam had hated this cocky little corporal, who was lionized by the officers and men for his good marksmanship. Breaches of discipline being commonplace with him, Inho typified the laxity that pervaded Third Company from top to bottom. The corporal had to be taught a lesson and made an example of. Nam had come from a military family. His father, a three-star general, had served as minister of defense at one time. He had volunteered for this frontline post because he believed in working his way up from the bottom, the hard way. He had expected the troops to look and act like soldiers, to move like clockwork. What he found at Third Company was the opposite of discipline. The compound was strewn with litter. The troops were flagrantly unkempt, their quarters unswept and disorderly.

Even more flagrant was the disposition and behavior of his company commanding officer, Captain Pang, who saw nothing wrong with this environment and was in fact quite at home in it. His uniform looked as if he had slept in it. Often his shirt tail stuck out from under his trouser belt. He talked to his men in T-shirt or with jacket front open, and the salute seemed to have gone out of fashion between him and his men. The incomprehensible thing was his enormous popularity with his men, who uncomplainingly worked extra long hours at the outguard foxholes, on mine-laying details and special patrols. Third Company struck the lieutenant as a band of derelicts enjoying an orgy rather than regular soldiers performing a military duty. It might get things done, but that wasn't enough. There was the right way to do things and the wrong way.

"Don't you forget your place?" shouted Nam, straightening himself. "You are a corporal in my command!"

"Does that authorize you to be mean and spiteful? As I look at it, you have lost your command. We must talk man to man."

"That can never be, even if I wanted it. I am an officer and you are an enlisted man. The army is a strict hierarchy, a chain of command. Everything I do is for the good of the army, for the good of the country. There is nothing personal in what I have done. It was my patriotic duty."

"Don't give me that duty jazz. I know a rat when I smell one."

"For that I will have to put you in the stockade again."

"You will do that no doubt. But it will have to be tomorrow. For now I have to face you man to man. If you are my commander, not a phony one-striper, teach me with fists, which I understand, not with words. Let's go somewhere quiet and settle this. I don't want to mess up this place. If you're not a coward, don't hide behind your desk."

"You're crazy. An officer doesn't fight his man. All you'll be doing is assaulting your superior officer. You'll get at least ten years for that."

"If it is assault. But perhaps it will be something else, like

71

murder. Better get off that chair and defend yourself."

Nam jumped off his chair and reached for his pistol, but Inho was a step ahead of him.

* * *

The sun shone brightly. Larks and thrushes soared and circled, singing rapturously. The expected night attack by the Chinese Communists had not materialized. The overnight rain had freshened the leaves and branches. It was a beautiful June morning that cast its bewitching charm on the mideastern Korean hills. Captain Pang, weary from his night's vigil, came to his CP from the last round of inspection at the outposts, his face unshaven, his shirt unbuttoned, the waist of his loosely-belted, dirt-spattered trousers almost slipping off his loins. Sitting at his desk, he threw down his helmet and his crumpled, half-dried jacket on the back of a chair. He moved mechanically, almost in a trance, and longed for bed and sleep. But he felt uneasy. There must have been an error in the timing of Division intelligence, but that meant the continuation of the alert, with its inevitable toll on nerve and muscle made worse by the uncertainty and postponement.

"Where's Lieutenant Nam?" asked Pang, sinking heavily behind his desk.

"I didn't see him when I came a few minutes ago from my bunker," replied Lieutenant Cha. "I'd sure like him to explain the mess around here."

He swept a semicircle with his hand to include the broken chair in Nam's corner, the framed pictures hanging askew, the toppled clothes rack, the tumbled rubbish can, the spilt ink stand.

"Is everything okay at your sector?" asked Pang, without seeming to notice any change in the office.

"Yes. No enemy movement. Anyway, the visibility was near zero until morning. I wonder why they didn't take advantage of the weather?"

Captain Pang fell silent. He was preoccupied with the position of his defensive works sketched on a chart and pondered how he should readjust regimental artillery support to reinforce the forward outposts at the base of the hill, dangerously exposed to any massive attack. After straightening things up a little, Lieutenant Cha asked Pang to go with him to the mess for breakfast, but Pang told him to go on ahead. He needed to study more and could use the solitude.

The front door burst open and Lieutenant Nam lumbered in.

"Lieutenant Ilsong Nam of Second Platoon reporting, sir,"

72

Nam said, saluting smartly. Pang glanced up. Nam's face was bruised and puffed, his eyes almost closed. His pants were torn and his T-shirt was bloody. He had Corporal Lim in tow, dressed neat as a pin, in contrast to Nam's disarray. Stepping closer to the captain, Nam put a stack of paper on the desk.

"This is my report of what has happened, with all the details and circumstances," Nam said.

"Can't you tell me what's in it?" said Pang, turning his glance back to the chart he had been studying.

"Last night I was assaulted by an enlisted man."

"What did you say?" Pang said, looking fixedly at his lieutenant. "I don't understand a thing of what you are saying."

"I will repeat. While I was on duty here last night, an enlisted man came in and beat me up."

Pang stared uncomprehendingly at the officer.

"All right," he said at last. "Was the assailant a Chinese Communist or a North Korean? Surely it must have been an enemy infiltrator."

"No, sir. The culprit is none other than this ruffian standing behind me. I believe you are acquainted with him already."

"I make it my business to get to know all my men well. But I don't hear you right. You cannot mean that he beat you."

The captain looked at the two men alternately. Lieutenant Nam's high connections, which he had tried to ignore in his attempt to treat Nam like any other junior officer in his command, had been brought repeatedly to his attention. Regardless, the aristocratic lieutenant had a knack for getting on his nerves. He seemed bent on disrupting the existing order of things. In less than a week after his assignment, Nam put his platoon to plowing and sowing flower seeds around the compound. The war front was stagnant and stabilizing, with the truce talks slowly winding down to some sort of conclusion, but still there were constant skirmishes and engagements at squad or battalion level. Outposts and garrisons were constantly changing hands, and there was no point in investing so much horticultural energy in such uncertain real estate. Moreover, Nam woke up his platoon at an early hour and taught them to sing military songs in harmony. Wherever he appeared, the men jumped like startled chickens. He drilled his men through saluting and other basic motions, and punished them for not trimming their nails or polishing belt buckles and buttons.

Pang didn't care for any of this trumpery, whose military value was nil and which would best be left at boot camp, but he had not interfered. It was the young officer's first command, and he was flexing his muscles. So long as there was no radical obstruction of his military mission, he was prepared to overlook it. After all, what harm was there in a flower garden in front of the office? But perhaps his indulgence had been misplaced in this particular case. This mannequin of an officer was not a youthful romantic with forgivable, even admirable idealisms, but an overblown bag of conceit that definitely posed a threat to the mission of Third Company.

"Frankly," said Pang, "I don't believe a word of what you have just said. I believe you are under some great stress, perhaps overworked. You are not your usual self..."

Pang looked Nam over. As if that had been the cue he had been waiting for, Nam stepped closer, triumphantly.

"Look at my face. Look at my clothes. This is the evidence. Last night I was beaten up by this thug. He punched and kicked me for nearly an hour until I was knocked senseless. Then he had the effrontery to go to sleep in his barracks as if he had done nothing. I regained my consciousness and wrote this report. Then I went to his barracks to drag him out of his bed at gun point."

Captain Pang looked at Corporal Lim, whom he knew to be no ordinary country bumpkin. He knew Inho to be an unschooled, untutored mustang, fiercely independent, egotistic, cunning, unscrupulous, even dangerous, but serviceable even to the point of self-sacrifice if handled the right way, if his strong ego were recognized and flattered.

"What is your side of the story? Did you really beat up this officer?"

"No, sir," said Inho, his face frozen at attention, not betraying the least emotion.

Before Pang could react, Lieutenant Nam shrieked like a crazed animal, turned on Inho, clutched at his throat and shook him.

"You lying bastard! Heaven knows. Your conscience knows."

"The army is a strict hierarchy, a chain of command, sir. How can an enlisted man dare hit his officer, sir?"

"Are you going to stand there and say that you didn't come here last night at eleven o'clock and assault me right here at the company CP?"

"You are mistaken, sir. You are hallucinating. I was in my bed, soundly asleep. I had returned from my outguard duty and was exhausted."

"Stop it," said Captain Pang, as Nam was about to maul Inho. Pang told Inho to step up closer.

"Do you have any grudge against this officer?"

"No, sir."

"Swear you don't."

"I do, sir."

"Right. Return to your duty."

Inho left the officers. Nam's face turned all colors and looked to be on the point of blowing up.

"Go wash up and change. Those are no wounds of honor, I assure you. Meanwhile I'll tear up this report and forget everything I've heard. Remember you are an officer of the army. No officer is such a fool as to admit that he has allowed his own man to beat him. Don't ever repeat such a shameful story."

"You do not understand. I was the victim of violence. No man is proof to an accident of violence, and there is no shame in acknowledging it. The shame lies in not doing anything about it. We must refer him to a general court martial. We must call the military police right away."

Nam went on quoting article by article the Code of Conduct for the Armed Services.

"How long did it take you to write the report?"

"The whole night. I have consulted all the pertinent law books I have a watertight case against him. It is mutiny, punishable by death."

"You're free to do anything you want," Pang said as calmly as possible, suppressing the desire to punch him in the nose but doubting whether even a sledge hammer would make an impression on him. "You can call the provost marshal and hand your report to him. But how are you going to prove your charge? It's your word against his, and even if the court takes your word for it, all you'll have succeeded in doing is to show that you are a spineless coward. You'll be the laughing stock of the whole regiment. You had hands and feet, didn't you? Why didn't you use them? You're taller and bigger than that corporal. Nobody tied you up. An officer is not an executive working behind a desk with his brains only. He must expect to go out and kill the enemy, sometimes with fixed bayonet, hand to hand. I promise you one thing if you go ahead and prove your case. I'll never have you as an officer in my command. I doubt anybody else will either."

Lieutenant Nam's lips quivered and his eyes filled with tears as he struggled with the dawning knowledge. He withdrew the report and began tearing it up, biting his lips. Captain Pang looked the other way out the window and telephoned First Sergeant Kim of Operations.

"I am the Captain. Send out a one-man patrol, Corporal Lim, to the base of the hill. Yes, beyond Outpost Eleven. Cancel his leave. Right away. Let him stay there to set up a deadfall and capture a prisoner. No, don't relieve him. He can return only if he succeeds. Even if it takes a week."

Shortly before lunch the same day there was a big hulla-baloo in the yard. Nearly all the men and officers of Third Company formed a shifting, yelling circle.

"Hold him!"

"Don't let him get away!"

"Watch the tusks!"

Captain Pang emerged from the office and stood on the steps to determine the cause. The crowd parted and Inho stood forward and saluted.

"Corporal Lim reporting with his prisoner, sir!"

This was accompanied by a long shrill squeal from a boar now subdued, tied, and held down by Lim's smiling assistants. Captain Pang surveyed the assembly and looked at Inho and his prize. He frowned severely.

"Turn him over to intelligence for interrogation!" he thun-dered.

Inho stood dumbfounded, even cowering. A puzzled silence overtook the congregation. Corporal Kwon of the kitchen stepped up.

"Intelligence is ready to take over, sir," he said.

The captain nodded, aboutfaced, and marched solemnly back into the CP, unmoved by the clapping and cheering of his men. The lunch was delayed slightly, but nobody minded. Everybody enjoyed the ensuing feast, except Lieutenant Nam who refused to leave his quarters, where he sat composing a long letter home to explain his request for transfer.

Steady Hands

"Heard of Club Saigon just opened on Piikoi?" asked Carl Sommers. "It's crawling with little Viet chicks. Cute, too."

"I must head home," Stephen Gong said.

"What's the hurry?" Carl said.

"You know Marianne is waiting for me," Stephen said.

"So she is. Did I suggest or breathe anything treasonable? Duty and honor, that's me, Carl Sommers. All we'll do is stop in, have a look around, have a drink, and celebrate the occasion."

Carl, real estate broker and newly elected president of the Hawaii Vietnam Veterans Association, had dragged Stephen to their meeting and made him a full member, though Stephen had never been in the U.S. Army. Anybody who had been in the Vietnam jungle bearing arms against the Viet Cong was a patriot, an American veteran, Carl had argued, and others had concurred.

"There's a major operation coming up early tomorrow morning and I need steady hands."

It was brain surgery, requiring his utmost skill. More than the customary professional anxiety was involved. The patient was a fellow surgeon's son, John Nam, a senior at Punahou. John had jumped off the ledge at Pali Lookout. His girl friend, Mary Sung, was to follow suit, but she could not bring herself to do it. They had been protesting her parents' (both Koreans) discouragement of their courtship (John's mother was Japanese). The Sungs, with illustrious ancestors killed by the Japanese in Korea, could not accept John as their son-in-law. It was a messy business, very public, with police and press everywhere.

John had survived the fall, but the left front of his head, down to his eyebrow, was a crater that could hide a child's

hand. A plastic mold would have to be fitted in snug and tight
to mesh with the broken edge of the skull, so no ordinary
impact might dislodge it. Also the skin sewed back over it
should ensure normal hair growth and other physiological
functions.

"They look steady to me," Carl said after an affected scrutiny of his friend's hands. "I promised Marianne to return you
before eleven, didn't I? So it will be. Never break my word to
ladies. Delivery by eleven, safe and sound, hands and all."

The Benz screeched sharply at Beretania and Piikoi.
Stephen had not told anybody how literally he meant "steadi-
ness" about his hands. It was too frightening to own even to
himself. He would sooner strip in public or divulge the most
intimate secrets of his sex life than tell people, even his closest
friends, that his surgeon's hands could be shaky.

"It's not that..."

"Haven't got over your Vietnam yet, eh? It's all history
now. Look. If anybody has suffered, I have. Six years in their
stinking prison and all. But I've forgotten. You were there less
than a year. That's nothing."

Was it? Stephen wondered.

"Here we are," Carl said, parking. "Well, come on out. Have
just one drink and we'll shove off."

The colors in the neon tubes chased each other in a mad
swirl above the front door. The bouncer collected the cover
charge and let them in.

"Let's take the booth over there," Carl said, steering
Stephen on. "Get going, man. They won't bite you."

A round-eyed, long-armed Vietnamese passed by. Stephen
winced, shuddering at the likeness. No, it could not be that
demented Viet Cong who would have cut him to pieces. Many
light years ago, it seemed.

* * *

The artillery fire had stepped up sharply since dusk
all around Stephen's compound, the frontline first aid unit of
the Korean Tiger Division, though in the mixed-up battlefield
of Vietnam there was no clear front or rear. What was believed to be the rear could receive point-blank shelling without
notice and an alleged front could be inactive for days, sometimes weeks. Stephen, then Captain Sutay Gong, had been
assured by the Tigers, as the men of the Division liked to
call themselves, that the hospital was guarded "in depth".
Tanks were positioned along the fringe of the jungle complex,
then infantrymen in their trenches, then the artillery on the

high ground, overlooking all approaches to the hill mass. The mortars and howitzers boomed reassuringly from the heights, and the helicopters flew in regularly to evacuate the casualties to the field hospitals at Kayson or other big cities still held by the Allies. Though a little lively, the exchange of fire Stephen had been hearing that day was like the daily rain; it was nothing to be excited about. Then, probably close to midnight, everything became quiet. The belligerents seemed to have reached a gentlemanly accord to call it quits for the night and go to sleep. Stephen, exhausted by the day's work, turned over in his cot, trying to go back to sleep. The side of his tent was suddenly slashed and a screaming Viet Cong rushed in.

"Korean sonofabitch," he ground out the English syllables through his set teeth, his whole face writhing with hatred, as he lunged at Stephen with his bayonet. Stephen rolled aside and missed the steel by an inch. Leaving the bayonet stuck in the cot, the Viet Cong pulled out a knife and raised his hand to strike, his mouth curled in a sick smile of anticipation. Wedged between the cot and the canvas, Stephen could not do anything except stare, in disbelief, at the glint of the point aimed at his throat."

"Korean asshole, shitpot," the commando chanted as he lurched.

Stephen had closed his eyes.

"You Koreans have killed his family," the Viet Cong officer who had with others restrained the man explained to Stephen. "One of your men practiced *taygwondo* kicks on his kid brother."

Stephen spent the rest of the night in a trench packed with Korean prisoners. Anybody who spoke was punished mercilessly. The next morning they were marched out and joined by more prisoners, many of them Americans. One of them was Lieutenant Carl Sommers, U.S. First Cavalry. The daily squall started, pelting pebblelike drops. The prisoners were put in a long file and marched in a patternless meander through the jungle and rice paddies. Viet Cong check points seemed to pop up everywhere, from behind trees and rocks, from under brush and even under water. The guards left the Americans alone and even smiled at them but slapped, kicked or spat at the Koreans. The soldier next to Stephen, a Sergeant Kim, stopped to tie his shoes. The guard's rifle butt fell crashing down on the arch of his foot. Stephen had his turn, too. The guard walking alongside him suddenly wheeled about and booted him in the ribs, knocking the wind out of him. Think as he might, Steven could not figure out what could have brought that on. Unless it was the reputation of ferocity the Tigers had built for themselves in Vietnam. It was said to be a sort of safe-conduct to be a Korean in Vietnam. According to the legend, the Koreans, all blackbelts in *taygwondo,* giving no quarter, taking no quarter, were so feared by the Viet Cong that they gave the Koreans a wide berth and attacked only the softies, the Americans. The Korean soldier, with shattering recent memories of poverty and degradation, of civil war and of foreign troops trampling his homeland, suddenly found himself to be somebody feared, maybe respected, and walked with his head high in the Vietnamese cities and villages.

At the first Viet Cong village the Communists separated the Americans from the Koreans. Carl Sommers was taken away on a stretcher. A piece of shrapnel had lodged in his spine; he was delirious. When the Americans were out of sight, the Viet Cong guards took the Koreans to the village square and huddled them in a circle. An officer went on a makeshift podium and spoke in their musically whiny language to the assembled villagers. One of them, a ghostly old man with sunken cheeks and a sparse beard, leaped forward and attacked the prisoners with his tobacco pipe. One man fell prostrate to the ground, face bloodied. The officer spoke some more as the old man walked off, sated. A woman sprang upon the prisoners swinging a club. Two men fell to the ground. The Koreans milled around helplessly, packing closer to the center, watching the guns of the guards pointed at them. The officer spoke on and another assailant darted at the prisoners. Stephen, squeezed in the middle, waited for the blow that would snuff him out at any minute. The officer stopped in the middle of his peroration. A messenger had run up to him. They talked for a while.

"Korean surgeon, step out," the officer said. "Doctor, step out."

Stephen did not comprehend the Viet Cong's English, which sounded like the continuation of that murderous sing-song speech of his that would not stop until every one of them was dead. The guards came, pushed the other prisoners aside, and pulled Stephen out.

* * *

"Ya, this is just like Saigon," Carl said appreciatively, sur-veying the sleazy decor, the bead-curtained entries to the booths, and the young girls, in tight blouses and slit skirts, quick-stepping with laden trays.

"We are going to celebrate," Carl went on, ordering cham-pagne to the glee of the girls assigned to the table, already

80

pawing the two men.

"You said only one drink," Stephen protested, in vain.

"Cheers," Carl said, lifting his glass.

"Cheers," the girls echoed, lifting their glasses, their mouths crammed full of beef jerky and peanuts.

"Half the time in their stinking jail I didn't know whether to thank you or curse you for cutting out that shrapnel and saving my life. Now I have no doubts. Life has been good to me. You see here a successfully repatriated Viet vet."

At this point Carl was irretrievably distracted by the girl, seated in the corner between him and the wall, who was closing toward him and, with dexterity, reaching down under the table. The other girls chirped and shot furtive glances at Stephen as they gorged themselves. He had severely frowned at their familiarity and they did not dare to touch him. A woman in her thirties, gaunt and vaguely intimidating, came to the table. The girl sitting near the aisle next to Stephen rose hurriedly and left. The woman sat down.

"I am May Lee," she said.

"Hello," Stephen said.

"You are not happy? They bother you?"

"No, it's all right."

"You were not born here? Not American?"

"I am a citizen but was not born here."

"You Korean, no? You look like Korean, speak like Korean."

He almost shouted, "No, I am Japanese," anything to contradict her, silence her, put her in her place. He wouldn't be telling an outright lie either, though perhaps not the whole truth. His Japanese mother had died giving birth to him, but her legacy had followed him everywhere like a shadow as he grew up in Korea, a former Japanese colony. He recalled the many occasions when he had to dissemble about his Japanese maternity, which would have marked him worse than leprosy. His father might have boosted his own ego by marrying a girl of the ruling race, but he had certainly given a bum deal to his son, a half-breed that belonged nowhere. Now, in the U.S.A., especially Hawaii, the supposedly ideal melting pot of all races, Stephen still felt excluded from both sides of his blood. Perhaps that's why he had married Marianne Baker.

"Yes, I am Korean," Stephen said.

"I can tell. I have Korean friends in Saigon, Kayson, Dienphu. Many here in Honolulu too. Good friends."

May Lee fumbled in her purse and produced a photograph. Was he seeing things? It was Stephen's high school class picture. He had given it to Lap Sing. He had carried it around simply because it happened to be in his wallet. The yellowed paper showed some fifty boys in black buttoned-down uniforms and caps. None of them had meant anything to him. He couldn't have identified himself in it, had he not known his position in the rows. Lap Sing had wanted it and taken it, without asking or knowing which was him.

"A Korean friend gave my sister," May Lee said.

* * *

Though he treated the Viet Cong wounded, his captors made it clear to him that their basic relationship had not altered, that his life was spared for the time being entirely at their whim. Then, while he was operating at a field unit, U.S. helicopter gunships swooped down from behind the hill and devastated the valley. Stephen was wounded and lost consciousness. Hours later, his awakening eyes fell on a sickening scene of carnage. The ground was strewn with dismembered parts of human bodies. Trees were draped with bloody chunks of meat. If there had been survivors at all, they must have left him for dead. He tried to rise, but no part of his body obeyed his will. His hands and feet were numb. Fear gripped him. Perhaps he was already dead: his extremities were already rotting. Only the brain was left to witness the horror, then die. He recognized a sensation in his hands, a prickly itch as if they had gone to sleep and now the blood was recirculating. His hands shook in spite of himself like a pair of vibrators. Excruciating pain shot up from his right thigh. Cautiously he felt it with one quaking hand. A shell fragment had torn off a hunk of ham. His trouser leg was sticky with thick blood. Steadying his hands as much as possible, he shredded his sleeve, made a tourniquet, and staunched the flow.

The rain fell, torrential as usual, fogging vision. More worried and miserable about his shaky hands than about his serious leg wound, he started crawling, half crying. Like a painter without his vision or a musician without his hearing, Sutay Gong's career as a surgeon had come to an end. A Viet Cong patrol passed him about three paces away, the mud kicked off their sandals smearing his face as he lay flat on the ground in the bush. He stumbled into a small village in the jungle, the reed huts indistinguishable from the vegetation. Too sick to care where he was, he crept into the first hut and fainted. On the second night Lap Sing bound him to a litter and, picking up the poles at one end and letting the other end drag on the ground, took him away from the village. Her family had gone to inform the Viet Cong. She had to move him from place to place, weaving shelters from the leaves and vines and hunting for wild fruit and fish. His wound healed and he could walk again. But the shake in his hands remained.

In an unguarded moment he slept with Lap Sing, the yielding, primeval woman. Never had he known woman's flesh to be so sweet. Their Eden could have lasted forever. He could feast for hours on her large black eyes with dark circles like a lemur's and play on her satiny skin like an untiring musician on his instrument. One morning he found the shake in his hands had gone. As he gripped his fingers and felt the power in them, he missed the scalpel, the scissors, the stitching needle, the gowned assistants and nurses, the operating table under the floodlight where he was the absolute monarch. What started as a vague memory, an imperceptible stir, grew into an irresistible longing, an obsession. The pleasure of the senses palled. He had to get away, return to his element, his profession. Lap Sing sensed it too. Wordlessly, she led him back to the Allied Forces. On the last night she cried and he embraced and consoled her. Then, to his dismay, his hands started trembling again. He stared and stared at them, his mind a blank. Lap Sing stopped crying and patted and kissed him as if she were pacifying a fussy baby. He fell asleep. When the sun came up, it was time to go. He promised to come back for her and she nodded. He walked away from her, exulting in his steady hands; the previous night's relapse could not have been anything but a nightmare.

* * *

"Where is she now?" Stephen asked May Lee.

"In Malaysia, starving and sick, at a refugee camp for the boat people. She needs an American sponsor. She is pretty sure her Korean friend is in America."

"Why don't you sponsor her?"

"Vietnamese cannot. I was sponsored myself, so I cannot. American law. Besides, she is not my family any more. She has a baby."

"Whose baby?"

"Her Korean friend's."

Not quite knowing how he had been transported, Stephen found himself before the door of his penthouse with its lion-headed brass knocker. Quietly, he turned the key and tiptoed in. Marianne was already asleep. Changing into his pajamas, he slipped into the bed on the other side. She threw her arms about him and, after some mumbling, turned over and went back to sleep. A glow of happiness suffused him, as he watched her. All her nagging and domineering was gone and he saw the pretty oval face, radiating wholesomeness, that he had fallen in love with. He felt good and clean, as if he had taken a shower and scrubbed off all dirt and grime—Vietnam Association, Club Saigon, May Lee, Lap Sing . . .

He noticed that Marianne had set the alarm at six-thirty and, with a jolt of discovery, remembered the 8 a.m. surgery, in which he realized he was more personally involved than was professionally advisable; it was best to be detached from his patients, to regard them as intricate machines that needed fixing. Any emotional investment interfered with his judgment and performance. But was it being too emotional, Stephen wondered, to want the boy to regain his good looks and make a new start? He would advise him to expand his horizon and look farther afield. He could have his pick of the lot, black, white, yellow, brown, red . . . . He should above all stay clear of the Koreans and Japanese, the incorrigible adolescents of the Orient, locked in their eternal enmity. Stephen would bring the boy home and show off Marianne as a case in point. Yes, he would . . .

As he turned the light off, stretching his legs and closing his eyes with a sigh, he became aware of his hands knocking at his sides. Half distrusting his own senses, he lay in stupefied prostration, drained of energy and purpose. With superhuman effort, he slid off the bed and stumbled to the kitchen. He poured out a brandy and gulped. The intestinal explosion of heat subsided quickly, leaving his body cold and sweat-drenched, his hands quaking with sinister rhythm and insistence. He poured another glass, spilling half of it, and downed it to no effect. In the living room, he pressed with difficulty the sequence of digits on the press-button phone.

"Carl, I'm sorry to wake you."

"What's up?"

"Can your Association sponsor Vietnamese refugees?"

"For Pete's sake, what are you talking about?"

"I'm asking for a favor. I'll pay for the cost, whatever it takes. Can you sponsor a Vietnamese mother and child?"

There was silence.

"Who are they? Where are they?"

"Meet me for details at Club Saigon, now."

"Club Saigon? Steve, is everything all right?"

Stephen hung up and ran out the door.

Nostalgia

I eased myself behind the counter of my bar, the Harbor, sipping iced tea. It was about eight p.m. Jim Cannon, the bartender, wasn't due for another couple of hours. Until then I could handle the slack business myself. The air conditioning purred quietly, banishing the humidity outside. Embroidered tapestries, depicting Oriental myths, covered the walls. Lacquered Korean furniture, inlaid with mother of pearl, decorated spaces unoccupied by the booths. The Harbor might not be a swinging place grossing thousands of dollars a night, but so long as it paid for itself and gave me a minimal income, I wasn't too concerned.

It had been nearly ten years since I'd established my residence in Honolulu, but I still felt like the eternal peregrinator. I couldn't help feeling that nothing really mattered in this alien abode. Whether I was a howling success or not, there was nobody here to whom I cared to either brag or lie. However well I might get to know these people, Korean or not, I would be a mere statistic to them, just as they were to me. Only those bygone friends and acquaintances of my youth seemed to matter. I felt like a man on vacation away from home or, in my exalted moments, like a prince traveling incognito, ready to put up with inconvenience or contumely. I couldn't take anything too seriously. Nothing really touched me deeply enough to arouse me. Perhaps this was why they thought I was a good guy. I didn't drive a hard bargain. When I saw my counterpart in a contract tensed and trembling to gain at my expense, I smiled and gave way. It was all superbly comical.

With such a sense of detached amusement I was minding the bar that evening when who should walk in but Donam Hyon. It had been drizzling in that wishy-washy way typical of Honolulu in February and Donam was hugging a plastic

raincoat tightly around him. He flopped down at a stool at the
end of the bar by the door. Minutes passed but he made no
move to look in my direction. He had thinned, and a sandy
bristle covered his lower face. It had been over ten years that I
hadn't seen him, and I would not have recognized him had it
not been for his eyes slanting upward at the corners and his
sharp nose that chilled whoever he glared at. There was none
of his ferocity, dash, hauteur.

"Donam," I said, grasping his hand with great emotion.

He seemed taken aback. There was the smell of whisky on his
breath.

"Don't you remember me, Wonchol Song from Moon Rock
Village, Pyongyang County?"

"Wonchol Song." he repeated mechanically. His eyes
widened a little with a ray of recognition. He said, "What on
earth are you doing here?"

"I'm asking you the same question," I said.

After that he came to the Harbor almost every day and we
went out to drink. It seemed cheap and mercenary to entertain
him at my own place. After his retirement from the Korean
army as a Lieutenant General several years before, he had
been unemployed or rather refused to besmirch himself in the
rotten Korean system. He preferred to receive his pocket money
from his then wife, who owned a dry goods store. She was his
sixth or seventh—he couldn't be sure—not counting the first
one he'd married in North Korea. He was attractive to women
and had no trouble in attaching himself to them, but the
women he lived with could not put up with his temper and all
left him after less than a year. The one he now lived with and
who had brought him over to America had had the longest
tenure. She had lived with him for four years and their marriage seemed solid. Janice, whose maiden name was Chang,
operated a successful beauty parlor on Kapiolani Boulevard.
After her American husband was reported missing and
presumed dead in Vietnam, she went to Korea and met
Donam. She was marrying a general, cashiered or not, and
that was good enough for her.

It did my ego good to be sought after by Donam, even
though I had to pick up the tabs. Childhood fixations, such as
an inferiority complex, are the hardest to get rid of. We were
born on different sides of the tracks and I grew up envying
him and his family. They owned the very land we tilled and
lived on. Now I felt equal, perhaps even superior, to him, a
wreck of a man who lived on a woman's earnings, on remi-
niscences of his brilliant past, which was perhaps never quite
so brilliant when he lived it.

In 1944 he married the richest and prettiest girl in the county, and that was the year I got the draft notice from the Japanese Imperial High Command. I fled to Manchuria where our family had relatives, immigrant farmers eking out a bare existence. Then I became a bit bold and went to Japan by freighter. I wanted to see the world. Of course I got picked up in no time and sent to a South Pacific island. After about a month, seeing hardly any action, the war in the Pacific was over. I was a prisoner of war and shipped by the Americans to South Korea. The country was divided, the north under Russian rule and the south under the U.S. There was no traveling or postal exchange across the 38th Parallel. For at least a couple of years, however, people took chances and went back and forth, especially with the merchants who bribed the guards on both sides and smuggled goods and people. I had neither the money nor the temerity to attempt it and bided my time to go and see my relatives, thinking that the division was only temporary. I had really no compelling reason to go back. A third son had no place in the Korean household. My elder brothers took over the management of what little property there was. I had no wife or children.

Then one summer day in 1946, I believe, I saw Donam in Seoul leading a band of university students parading in front of the Capitol to oppose the Soviet-sponsored plan to make Korea U.N. trust territory. Their placards called for a free Korea without Communism. Donam, like the others, wore a headband with letters written in blood, and shouted the slogans, eyes popping and veins rising in his throat. The pro-American band he led was met by a pro-Soviet group coming from the other side of the Capitol. There was a frightful scuffle. They fought with rocks, sticks, and knives. A company of American-trained policemen arrived and charged into the melee, firing their carbines and swinging their clubs. The band of Communists scattered. Six lay dead, and thirty injured, several critically. The pro-Americans, who remained, were taken away in the waiting police vans. Proven innocent, Donam and his men were released after a few days. I went to see him at his lodgings in Mallidong.

He was full of patriotic fervor and cursed the evil times on which the country had fallen. The defeat of the Japanese was to usher in a new era of national glory for Korea, but she lay flat on her back, etherized, numb, cut up. He bemoaned the lack of leaders who could awaken a new national awareness and inspire and channel the energy of youths like him. He hated Communism as the ideology of bandits. He had his personal experience to prove it. The Communists had dispossessed his family of all their land. They would have been killed in the summary "people's court" trials, but they were just a step ahead. Engaging a south-bound merchant for a great sum of money, they left the county. The larger part of the way was by train. They had forged papers to show that they were going to visit relatives in Hwanghay Province. But the rest of the way, about thirty miles, had to be on foot through the mountains. By this time, contrary to their original understanding, the exodus had swelled to half a dozen families. It was a pitch dark night when they arrived at the border. Suddenly the whole earth seemed to light up. Search lights zeroed in and bullets fell around them. Dogs barked and the Red border patrols, obviously tipped off and waiting, closed in. The families scattered and crawled in the thick brush. Donam and his wife were separated from the rest of the family. They ran as fast as they could in the general south-ward direction.

"So what happened to your parents and the rest?" I asked after a good minute of silence.

"They got them," he said. "They must have."

He stood up abruptly, knocking over the chair. His eyes were fixed on a spot in the wall, and he stood as if he weren't aware of my presence in the room.

"I killed her," he said, in a thick voice. "I choked her to death."

I was stunned and concluded that he was speaking metaphorically. I laughed and put my hand on his shoulder. He pushed me off and continued the narrative. They'd had to run as the patrols were right behind, but she wouldn't move. She was having one of her fits. This rich, pretty wife was an epileptic, which was not known to him until after they were married. Her family had the illness carefully controlled with expensive medicine, and the outside world hadn't known about it. Donam took over the medication program and looked after her well, so well in fact that even after she came to live with him, her illness remained a family secret. It must have been the days of exertion and stress that brought on her untimely seizure. As the armed men searched, poking around with their bayonets, she started frothing, gurgling, kicking. At first he put his hands over her face, but it was no use. He put the knapsack on her face and bore down on it. The soldiers' search lights missed them. When they turned away, he got off and removed the knapsack. She was dead.

He came to see me a few weeks later. He had on a military uniform with a First Lieutenant's insignia. Inexorable deter-mination possessed him. He was now going to wipe out all Communists from the fatherland, so we could go back to our

homes in the north and regain what was rightfully ours. He
then told me that my relatives were all right the last time he
left them. After all, I thought, they didn't have much to lose
and perhaps they were better off under the Communists. But I
didn't tell him that.

Donam distinguished himself in the anti-guerilla
campaigns and reached the rank of Major before the war of
June 1950. In the ensuing turmoil we lost touch. The Communist invasion was swift. In three days Seoul was in their
hands. On the morning of June 28th, the People's Army
marched into the city, displaying their huge Russian-made
tanks and guns. The Red flag was up in front of the Capitol,
and Stalin and Ilsung Kim's giant portraits draped the City
Hall. Millions lined the streets, puzzled and curious, mostly
caught in the crowd while returning to their homes after running away from the unpredictable shells that exploded all over
the city during the night. Nobody had thought of leaving the
city until the last minute, as President Rhee had kept reassuring them that there was no danger to the city, while he and his
government slunk away, dynamiting the Han Bridge behind
them.

That night, while the populace was still confused and the
Red Army came to a temporary halt in their push southward, I
decided to flee south. The banks of the Han were guarded
by the Red troops and no civilian could cross the river. I knew
a spot up the river. The north bank was a cliff with pines and
rocks, but the southern shore edged a level plain that stretched
for miles, planted with rice and barley. I had gone there several times for fishing and knew the terrain rather well. I
eluded the guards and swam across. It was still a few weeks
before the summer rains and the crossing was not too difficult
although the current carried me further downstream than I
had anticipated. Thus I managed to escape the hunger, the
conscription of all males from fourteen upwards, and the daily
air raids that plagued the three-month Communist occupation
of Seoul. I also missed the devastating finale, the fire baptism
of U.S. naval bombardment which razed the city of Seoul to
the ground just prior to MacArthur's Inchon landing.

In fact, I had a rather good time of it. I was a war-profiteer,
if you will. It was all a chain of events beyond my control.
When I reached Tayjon, the temporary capitol, the Communist
momentum resumed and the Rhee government and military
were moving south to Pusan. Through an acquaintance I got a
job as a temporary truck driver for an army supply unit. When
I arrived to report back at the unit after a delivery, the place
was deserted. I had the empty truck all to myself. There were

thousands clamoring for transportation to the south, willing to pay any amount. They gladly parted with their life's savings to drive to safety ahead of the thousands of refugees, weighted under their bundles, dragging themselves along the dusty roads. When I got to Taygoo with a truckload of passengers, I was a rich man, with a truck nobody claimed. Eventually I owned several more trucks and had dozens of employees. I went into a few other ventures, import-export, construction, furniture, scrap iron, with varying successes. At one time I had visions of becoming a tycoon with the livelihood of thousands at my mercy, making and unmaking regimes. But quickly I realized my limitations. As things settled down during the post-war years, the ones with the ruthless tenacity to be really big took over.

I decided to buy the New Korea Theater, then up for sale. It looked like a steady income without much hassle. I was still worth several million dollars and was content. But nothing is secure in life, especially in Korea. In 1960 Rhee went under, following the student uprising. That didn't affect me, but in 1961 General Park pulled off his military coup and things changed. The new regime had to get their funds and promulgated the "Illegal Wealth" act. My accountant's nephew was in league with the coup leaders and they confiscated all my assets, including the theater and the house. In addition they were drawing up charges against me. Fortunately I had accounts receivable in America and by pulling some strings managed to emigrate.

As I said, it was about two months ago, in February this year, that Donam first showed up at the Harbor. He was a godsend to me. Here at long last was my link with the past, which was to make my existence meaningful. Our daily meetings never seemed to exhaust our material. After all, we had our ups and downs through two wars and four governments. His compulsory retirement from the Army took place under Park, who never trusted anybody other than those from his own province (and naturally got killed by them). The Park regime offered him some civilian jobs but Donam did not accept. He had only contempt for Park and his upstart minions. The scum had risen to the top, crowding out quality, he said. Curiously enough, neither of us had much to say about Hawaii. We might have been two tourists passing through, with no possible interest in the local affairs.

In the short period since our reunion I could see him visibly deteriorating. He drank to excess, although plainly he didn't hold his drinks too well. Then he began to alarm me with his odd stories. He was hallucinating. He said he saw at

the Ala Moana Center a young corporal he had sent out on a
scouting mission. He was a boy of seventeen and fearless,
always volunteering for dangerous missions. But one morning
he complained of a headache and begged to be excused.
Donam had already formed the plan of action and it was too
late to change. He was angry at the boy's malingering and
slapped him before sending him on. The corporal stepped on
a mine and died, his body mangled beyond recognition.
on a mine and died, his body mangled beyond recognition.

"I followed him from the store but lost him in the crowd at
a street crossing," Donam said.

"Don't be silly," I said. "You said there were eyewitnesses
to his death. They must have identified him somehow, by his
dogtag, for instance."

"But they could have made a mistake," he persisted.

I held my peace. Then, his drunken eyes boring into mine
in intense concentration, he said, "In case anything happens
to me, you take care of Janice, take over... kind of..."

"What nonsense is this?" I shouted. "Number one, nothing
is going to happen to you. Number two, Janice is quite capable
of taking care of herself. Number three..."

I was furious, genuinely indignant, as if he had proposed
something vile and obscene. As his sodden mind strayed elsewhere, the topic was dropped, but the thought recurred and
intrigued me. I had run into Janice on the way to pick Donam
up or drop him off and exchanged only the barest formalities.
But somehow I had convinced myself that she was the sort
of Oriental wife men dream of: understanding, forever yielding, obedient, self-effacing, and yet a rock of strength and
wisdom one could count on in time of need. She was Donam's
wife. Our relationship appeared in a new light, as if some profound destiny was evolving to join all three of us. I let my
fancy range.

Clearly the alcohol was weakening his brain. I tried to
divert him to other pleasures like movies, chess, sports, music,
even women. But nothing interested him, especially not
women. In fact they seemed to disgust him. When I took him
to the Blue Cloud, where willing "hostesses" clung like little
chimps, Donam gave such a frown that none dared to come
near. I had to avoid the subject of women altogether. He was
probably never unfaithful to his wife, a blessing few Korean
wives could boast, but I did not know whether that made him
a good husband necessarily.

Then there was a hiatus. He did not come to visit me for a
whole week. I could have called but frankly I needed the break.
I'd had quite enough of him and began to have second
thoughts about our friendship. Wasn't nostalgia or regressive

attachment, romanticized as homesickness, patriotism, love of one's kin and country, in fact a sort of Oedipal arrest? I attended to the postponed errands related to my livelihood at the Harbor with more seriousness and purposefulness.

The respite was not to last too long. He called and told me to meet him at a bar. I had other things to do and arrived a little late. He was waiting, having drained several glasses of whisky on the rocks which, however, seemed to have only sobered him up. I apologized for being late, but he cut me short.

"I saw a specter from the dead," he said.

"Another of the men you sent to their death?" I asked.

"No, it's that woman," he said, shivering.

I didn't know whether there were any other women involved in his life except his wives. Then I remembered his first wife, her tragic death, and the overwhelming effect it had on him as he recounted it. I was about to tell him that he had had no choice, that it had taken place a long time ago and he should forget it. But he spoke first.

"I didn't tell you about her all this time," he said. "That's why I wanted to see you specially tonight."

It was in November 1950, during the northward thrust of the U.N. forces under General MacArthur, he said. They had recaptured Seoul and were pushing on as fast as a marathoner could run, meeting practically no resistance. Donam, promoted to Colonel, was in command of a vanguard regiment on the western front. The Yalu River with Manchuria beyond was within a day's march. A bus arrived from Pyongyang, the recently liberated North Korean capital, with some thirty or forty entertainers. Donam distributed them among his junior officers, taking none for himself. But as he had just turned into his bed, his adjutant knocked at the door. He stood with a girl of about seventeen, and begged him to take her, since it was the wish of the entire staff. Otherwise they could not enjoy themselves.

There was only one bed in his tent, and he made her take it, meaning for himself to sleep on the floor. She did not refuse and quietly undressed. Then he noticed her exceptional beauty, the gentle rise of her bosom, the curving back, the tender waist, the soft dimple of her belly. He stepped toward her, removed the blanket, and pressed his body on her. Suddenly, the girl began to froth, gurgle, and kick, the whites of her eyes showing. Without thinking he picked up the pillow and was smothering her. The girl wriggled off the bed and begged him to forgive her. She had put on the epileptic act because she was too tired from the trip and didn't want to be bothered. A storm of rage seized him. He pulled his pistol and shot her under the belly. An ambulance came and took her away to the evacuation hospital, where he was told she died.

The incident was a trivial matter. People died like flies. Along the roads, in the fields and mountains, corpses, both civilian and military, lay scattered or piled in all stages of decay. Death was a commonplace to which everybody had developed an insensitivity. The death of a whore, especially recruited from the liberated population of North Korea, was the least significant thing. A soldier could shoot a North Korean because he didn't like the way he walked. All he had to say was that somebody had told him the wretch had a cousin in the Communist Party or in the Red Army. Donam's men, who removed the wounded girl from the tent, thought that she was a spy either trying to steal something from the Colonel or do him some bodily harm. No question was asked. When the bus came the next morning to round up the women to take back to Pyongyang, the conductor did not even miss her.

But Donam could not sleep the rest of the night. The following few days her face danced before his eyes, and he made bad tactical mistakes, killing half of his men. Fortunately, this coincided with the general debacle as the Red Chinese armies came rampaging in on the confusedly retreating U.N. troops, and Donam's errors weren't recorded.

"I saw her a week ago at the bank," he said. "I followed her to a restaurant nearby, Korean Barbecue. She was greeted there by the waiters as Madam. I stood outside and watched her through the window. She looks, she is, the Pyongyong girl I told you about."

"The one you shot in the stomach?"

"Yes."

"How can she be here? Corpses don't get visas."

"No, those at the field hospital could have made a mistake."

I protested in vain. He wanted me to go and confirm her identity. This was his only salvation. All these years he couldn't do anything; whenever he meant to do something, a voice accusing him of murder unnerved him. If she was alive, he would be a free man. He could start a new life. He would stop drinking, start a business, love his wife. But he had to be sure. I was the only friend he could trust with such a task. Besides he had figured out a simple foolproof strategy: I should go to her, saying that I was the doctor at the field hospital who had treated her gunshot wound.

Donam called every day to ask whether I had gone to find out. After putting it off as long as I could, I set out on the absurd errand. It was a charming little restaurant with about fifteen tables, all clean-swept and well-appointed. I could spot the Madam immediately from his description. She sat by the cash register at the entrance. I ordered a plate of steamed mandoo, meaning to go to her after it with the memorized script. But after I'd finished the dish, I lost courage. Finally, after ordering several superfluous glasses of beer, I went to the counter and stammered out my part.

Perhaps my hesitation and inexperience in play-acting made me sincere and credible. She was quite understanding and said that she'd been in Pusan during the war and no-where near Pyongyang, although that was her birthplace and the rest of her family was there. After apologizing as best I could, I left the restaurant feeling like a fool. But as I neared his house, I began to realize the consequences of this discovery to Donam. I came up with an expedient. I told him that I had seen her indeed and she was the right woman. She'd almost died but pulled through, thanks to modern antibiotics. For a long time her single obsession was to find Donam and pay him back in kind, but time had healed her hurt and she was now well settled and had forgotten all about it. But she never wanted to see Donam again. So in God's name he should stay away from her.

Donam listened, rapt, with a radiant smile on his face. I could not believe that he was so gullible. I was uneasy, shifty, and showed all the signs of an unpracticed liar, and any detached observer could have seen through me, but such was his need to believe that he did not even ask for any further corroborating details.

"She is alive," he exclaimed. "I never killed her. Things are going to be different with me. I know it. You'll see."

He embraced me with tears in his eyes. I didn't hear from him at all after that until a few days ago. Janice called me from the hospital. I was to come at once to the emergency ward. When I arrived, she told me that Donam had hung himself with the electric cord from the ceiling at the attic in the house. When she cut him down, he was still alive, but the doctor did not give him much chance. His windpipe had collapsed and his lungs had been damaged. But Donam wanted to see me. The doctor opened the door and ushered me to the dying man's bedside. His face was contorted and swollen. He breathed with difficulty. Janice whispered in his ear, and he struggled to focus his feverish eyes on me. He stretched out his hand for me to hold.

"Thanks," he gasped. "I had to ask her forgiveness. You see it had to be real to work."

He died a few hours afterwards, in delirium.

"I don't understand it, I don't," Janice said. "Everything was to have been different. He was going to work for a contractor in town. He even asked me out to dinner. Of course we had gone out sometimes, but it was always at my suggestion and insistence. He was loving and considerate and even wanted to have babies. Then today he returned, drunk and beside himself, his hair disheveled and his clothes torn. He shouted everybody out of the way and went upstairs. I heard a noise, went up on tiptoe, and found the chair knocked out from under him."

At his funeral Janice conducted herself with composure. The coffin was covered with flowers and there were a goodly number of mourners, mostly her friends. I was angry for some unaccountable reason and could have knocked over anybody that crossed me. "Epilepsy!" I muttered, biting my lips and suppressing my tears as I saw the coffin lowering into the pit and heard the hollow ring of the first shovelful of earth.

I took Janice back to her house. We were silent in the car. She sat, staring out the window, in her black mourning dress that seemed to wrap her like some precious, fragile thing. I will protect and honor you, I swore, restraining an overwhelming impulse to throw my arms around her and weep. The word "destiny" echoed in my ear.

A Fire

Allen Shin found the sign, Bargains Galore, written on a termite-eaten board in Chinese ink. The windows were caked with dirt, and the grey paint was peeling everywhere on the store front. Allen pushed the hanging curtain of beads aside and stepped in. The inside was a jungle of used goods, chairs, bookshelves, clothes, lamps, all kinds of odds and ends piled on top of each other. Narrow passageways meandered through the chaos, overhung by precariously-balanced chests of drawers, bed springs, plates, books.

"What are you looking for?" asked the old Chinese storekeeper, blinking his eyes over the spectacles that slid two-thirds down his nose.

"A bed," Allen said, discreetly turning from the old man's bad breath.

"Do you want a complete set, with the box spring and mattress, headboard, endtable, and dresser?"

"Yes, if you have something reasonable. Otherwise just a spring and mattress."

"I have a beauty for you in the back of the store. Has just come in. Not even unpacked yet. Come follow me."

The old man led the way briskly, then stopped.

"This is it," he said, turning around and making a proud sweeping gesture with his hand.

Allen was struck dumb. There was his entire household: dining set, TV, stereo, guitar, typewriter. Not a single item missing. So this was how Sunhee had disposed of it. The landlady had seemed mightily surprised when he'd turned up at the old apartment. Hadn't he met his wife at Los Angeles, where she said they were moving? No? As a special favor, the landlady had given back to Sunhee most of the security deposit, in cash, instead of waiting a month and sending a

97

check to their new address, as was the custom. The apartment had been taken. What a fool he must have appeared!

He could tell the storekeeper that these things were his, that they were stolen goods, in a sense. He had paid for every one of them with his own good money. He must have canceled checks somewhere to prove it. But prove what? That his wife had run out on him after selling all his valuables?

"Did you buy the whole lot?"

"Yes, it was a moving sale."

"Can I offer you whatever you paid for it and $100 more?"

"Make it $200 more for moving and other incidentals."

"More than what?"

"$1,800."

Allen knew the man was lying but didn't make an issue of it. He went nearer to the furniture. Here was the wreckage of his life, in a heap. It was like looking at his own carcass. Yet what he felt was more akin to amused curiosity than bitterness or anger. The old man followed him around, making encouraging comments. Allen's eyes fell on a picture frame, leaning against the leg of the writing desk, the backside toward him. On the plywood backing he could still read the date of the wedding picture.

"That's a rosewood frame," the old man said, lifting it up. "Look at the exquisite carving. Nobody makes this kind any more."

Allen knew well enough. He had special-ordered it from Taiwan through China Imports in Waikiki. It had cost him over two hundred dollars.

"All you have to do is take the picture out and put in your own," the old man babbled on, running his palm across the dust of the glass. It was still their picture all right, he in his tuxedo and she in her innocent white gown. The old man apparently didn't see the likeness between the groom in the picture and Allen before him.

"Wedding picture," he said, blowing the dust off the glass and frame.

Allen stomped out of the store. The bitch hadn't even the decency to take out the photograph. He strode down River Street and crossed Nimitz Highway to the waterfront. Coming to Pier 15, he sat down on a bollard. A luxury-liner with some foreign lettering, maybe Arabic, was docked at Pier 13. On the other side of the harbor a freshly painted Coast Guard frigate was moored at the Sand Island dock. A Matson ship was leaving harbor. A puff of steam left its chimney, and the whistle moaned deep yet shrill.

* * *

It was two summers ago. For the first time he had saved enough money to feel comfortable about taking a trip abroad. Rather than going to Europe or Mexico, he decided to go to Korea, the native land he had left at the age of four when he was adopted by Major Dunbar, the intelligence officer who had interrogated him. He'd been something of a wonder to the entire regiment. Barely able to walk, he had safely crossed the heavily-mined no-man's land.

"The lucky devil," the GI's said in amazement. "Not even a mouse could have made it alive."

The two-mile-wide belt of land had separated several divisions of North Korean and Red Chinese troops on the north from a matching force of South Koreans and Americans on the south. The Armistice was about to be signed and battles raged to seize last-minute advantages of terrain. The area Allen had traversed toddling barefoot was in the Iron Triangle, over which both sides dumped tons upon tons of ammunition to saturation bomb and flush out the enemy from entrenchments.

Allen's house was on fire. The smoke blinded and choked him. The darting flames singed his hair, eyelashes, and skin. The cotton in his quilt smoldered. He screamed for his mother and father. But the crackling of the fire and the thunder of shells and bombs hushed him. He ran to the door, but it was on fire. A falling brand knocked him to the floor. He crawled in the opposite direction. There was thick smoke and leaping flame everywhere. The barn, hayrick, wood pile, cowshed, everything burned. The houses next door were ablaze, too. He limped and crawled and found his way to the water-filled rice paddies. His burns smarted. He kept going over dikes, roads, streams, away from the burning village, the burning hell. He was now in the hills, but was scarcely conscious of the sharp stones and underbrush that bruised and cut him. The flash of gunfire and the thunder of explosions goaded him on all night, long after he had put hills and valleys between him and his village.

Major Dunbar was a bachelor who had risen from the ranks. He retired from the army after the Korean War and settled in Honolulu. But Vietnam called him again and he went, only to return soon after in an urn. Allen had not known how much he loved this man until then. He had long resented him for giving him the unsuitable name Dunbar. At school he had been the butt of ceaseless teasing, an Oriental with a Caucasian name. Now that the man was no longer alive, he recalled Dunbar's every mannerism, his intonation, his laughter. Dunbar had insisted on celebrating as Allen's birthday the day he had stumbled across the no-man's land into the U.S. army unit. This had always infuriated Allen, but now he was tearful thinking about it, hearing the old man's croaking voice, "Happy birthday to you...." He missed him terribly, his slouching posture, his shuffling gait, his untidy habit of throwing clothes all over the floor and furniture, his stink that no deodorant soap seemed to wash off. If only he could get him back as he was...It was years before he got over his loss. But never quite.

That's why he had decided to go to Korea. Perhaps his reintegration to his native land might help him forget everything, Dunbar, the U.S., the job, the acquaintances, all that clinging matter. He would find his original true being, uncluttered by spurious additions. He went to court and had his name changed to Shin, which he had picked at random from a list of a few dozen. He was sure Dunbar would understand. It had been like matrimony in a way and his loyalty should not extend beyond death. He was starting life all over again, with a new identity.

He went to Seoul, but the polluted, congested megalopolis with its nervous, fast-stepping population gave him no sense of homecoming. The real Korea, his native land, had to lie somewhere in the country. But what part of rural Korea? He had no idea where his village was. He remembered nothing distinctive about it. This was fine with him. The indubitable fact remained, his being Korean. Since he was not tied to any specific locality, he belonged to all of it, to any part of it. After inquiry at the Tourist Bureau he discovered that there were nearly twenty different Shin clans spread throughout the provinces. Again at random he chose a county in Kangwon Province near the Demilitarized Zone, just above the Iron Triangle of Korean War fame. The Shins lived in several villages all over the county. The village of his choice was called Cholpori. It was a half-farming, half-fishing community of a hundred families. The letter of introduction he had brought from the Bureau was addressed to the alderman of the village. Allen was a Shin, returned from America in search of his roots. The entire county buzzed with the rumor and conjecture ran wild. Several families came from outlying areas with claims of kinship, to be turned away reluctantly by too many conflicting circumstances. His exact genealogy unsettled, he was nevertheless soon accepted as one of them. The alderman insisted on Allen's taking his own beach cottage, rent free, for as long as he liked. The villagers brought him food and supplies and he had a hard time making them accept money in return.

100

The cottage was some distance from the village and was occupied only during the fishing season in late fall. For the rest of the year it was left vacant and stored fishing gear. It sat in the middle of a sand dune, wind-swept and shifting, dotted by clumps of stunted conifers and hardy weeds. Allen read, swam, strolled, and occasionally strayed close to the village with its thatched, close-built houses, reeking with sewage. He could not, dared not, go too close to the people, these kindly, smiling brethren with faces similar to his own, who nevertheless shared with him little else. Their constant nodding, bowing, smirking, giggling, all good-natured and friendly, annoyed him unbearably. But he enjoyed the sea and the strips of sand and gravel punctuating the craggy shoreline. He loved to go to the edge of a promontory not far from the cottage and peer into the clear water that revealed the deep bottom where the sea plants swayed like sensuous dancing maidens and the fish gamboled. He loved the masculine austerity of the bleak sand dunes. It seemed he had truly found his element.

Then Sunhee came. She took over the supply of necessities and discouraged visitors, especially the gamesome village girls. She was the alderman's niece or something, and went to college in Seoul. It was some time before summer vacation. She must have cut school to devote herself to the task of ministering to him. Her English was halting and ungrammatical, but she made herself intelligible by vigorously signing and drawing. She had black eyes, rather thick eyebrows, a lumpy nose, full lips, and a square jaw— a far cry from a flaming beauty. But she made up for her deficiencies by her vivacity, her eagerness to communicate, her determined cheerfulness that would not be dampened by refusal.

"I want to teach you Korean," she said. "It's a shame you don't know your own language."

It sounded familiar. He had heard it from Korean tourists passing through Honolulu, gravely shaking their heads at the American Koreans who couldn't speak a word of Korean, hinting at ingratitude, even treachery. Ingratitude for what? Famine and war?

"But I am on vacation," Allen protested. "I don't want to labor with a foreign language when I am supposed to have fun."

"You call this fun, being cooped up here all by yourself?"

"But I like it. You have no idea how much."

"You'll soon lose your mind if you keep this up.

101

I must help you, save you."

So Allen allowed her to do her best. The month was coming to an end, and it was time to leave. But Sunhee confronted him with the news that she was pregnant. When he offered to give her enough money for the abortion, she broke into tears. Did he think she was a machine he could turn on and off at will? She would kill herself first before she murdered her child. Did he have no humanity, no conscience, no fear of God? There was no other alternative but to marry her, duly witnessed by the Vice Consul at the American Embassy. He went to Honolulu first, at her strong urging. She would join him later, when her visa came through. There was a long waiting list, he was told. For eight months he sent $300 a month toward her support, not counting other gifts and allowances. Then, just before she left, she asked for $2,000 to settle her debts. He sent it, along with the air fare.

The person he met at the airport was not the big-bellied woman in her last month of pregnancy he had expected.

"I had a miscarriage," she said lightly.

"When?"

"Oh, a few months after you left."

"Why didn't you tell me?"

"I didn't want to worry you about it."

He glared at her.

"Were you ever pregnant?"

"Now, what is that supposed to mean?"

"Do you have the medical proof of your miscarriage?" he persisted. "Who was your doctor?"

"Do you doubt me, your own wife?" she shouted. "You have deceived me. You have never loved me. You have never trusted me. Is this love? Is this how husbands treat wives in America?"

Allen knew that he had been conned. All his plans had been shattered. There was not to be a new life. Knowing herself to be secure, now that she was on American soil, she openly scoffed at him. Did he think she would be tied down like a brood mare to start his dynasty, to make him the Adam of his race? She wanted to live, to savor in full the good life of America. She had to buy clothes at Carol and Mary, jewelry at the House of Adler, furniture at Jorgensen's. She had to eat out almost every night and only at the best restaurants. After two trips to the continental U.S. and several to the outer islands, they had quite exhausted Allen's patrimony. When this fact was brought to her attention, and she was asked to cut down on her expenses, she went into hysterics. When he returned home from work, he found the dinner unprepared. She wasn't his slave. He had to cook, wash clothes, and clean the house. In the middle of the night he was jolted out of his sleep by a violent tug at his hair.

"What are these deductions for?" she demanded, pointing at the pay statement.

Half asleep, rubbing his eyes, he studied the items. They were the medical insurance premium, union dues, social security payment, and installment payments to airline companies. She didn't believe it. She said it was a trick of his, borrowing money to stash away somewhere. No amount of reasoning helped. She was unalterable in her conviction. Night after night she woke him up to argue over the pay and the other women in his life, for whom he must be siphoning the money. Then she had a proposal. Since he was quite incapable of supporting her in her accustomed style, she was going to make her own money. She said she had met an old friend who worked at a bar, earning in one night as much as he made in a week. It so happened that there was an opening at the bar. He had to consent. Her hours were from evening till three or four in the morning. But she didn't come home after work. She said she slept at her friend's, since it was closer. She had to take care of shopping and other chores during the day. He was not home at the time anyway, so why should he care whether she was home or not?

His office sent him on a two-week training program to the head office in New York. He had a chance of being promoted to a managerial position, maybe even relocated to a better post. When he returned, there wasn't a penny left in their savings and checking accounts. He had to borrow from the credit union to pay the down payment on an unfurnished studio. After one night on the hard, uncarpeted floor, he knew he sorely needed a bed.

Walking slowly back to Bargains Galore, he paid the amount the storekeeper asked for the picture frame and went with it to his studio.

* * *

Allen jumped in his sleep, screaming. He was having a nightmare. He had been caught in a burning house, and half his body had burned. The pain was so real that he ran his hand over himself for reassurance. He was drenched in sweat. He opened a window. The nightlights of the city blinked drowsily. Muffled music ebbed and flowed from a nearby disco. A car screeched round the corner of the building. Late partying noise floated up from downstairs. He opened the refrigerator. There was no food. He took out a piece of ice from the freezer and put it in his mouth. Looking around the studio he noticed the picture frame, still wrapped in brown paper and resting against the wall. He picked it up and went to the oven. He opened the oven door and tried to slide the bundle in. It was too wide. But he didn't want to remove the wrapping. He took out the middle racks. Now he could squeeze it in sideways. Its length just fit the depth of the oven. The oven door clicked shut, and he turned the knob to broil. Then he went into the shower and fully opened both taps. As the water splashed his skin, he felt an exhilaration he had not known before. He sang at the top of his voice all the songs that came to his head. They kept coming one after another, astonishing even himself. He'd had no idea how extensive his repertoire was. He had come through fire and hell. He had beaten all odds. He was a lucky devil. Nothing could touch him.

* * *

The firemen had to axe the door down. The management had a good deal to explain and pay for. Several warnings of fire hazard had been issued against the building but had gone unheeded.

A Second Chance

For nearly an hour Professor Kichol Hwang had been closeted in his office with a student, patiently explaining why his paper merited only a C instead of an A or at least a B. A glance at his auditor's pimply face, smoldering in rage and disbelief, was enough to show him how far he was getting: Nowhere. He sighed. A sudden weariness came over him.

"Professor Hwang, long distance call from New York," Lorraine, the department secretary, shouted down the hall cheerfully, as if announcing some singular honor bestowed on the whole university. The interruption was a welcome relief, especially since the student got up and collected his things, apparently having given up the grade change as a lost cause. But from New York? Kichol guessed at once who it must be. If only he could get out of it...Could he tell Lorraine that he was busy and not available? He looked to his departing visitor and almost implored him to stay longer. But the student was brusquely walking out of his office without even turning for a goodbye. Kichol went gingerly to the phone. His hand shook as he picked up the receiver with the office staff looking on.

As he expected, it was Moonhee. Her voice had not changed. There was the same pure clarity, as if struck off a well-tuned piano, the same vivacity, earnestness, unbounded trustfulness, innocence, warmth and sweetness, reproach and accusation, as if years had not passed since their last parting.

"I'll be there by next flight," she said, "at Toledo or whatever the godforsaken place you are at is called. I had no trouble finding your home address after I located you at the university. Why don't you have a phone at home like other people? If you are so anti-social, you could put in an unlisted number. The advantages far outweigh the disadvantages. Suppose you want to call the store and find out if they are open. It was

105

by sheer chance that I found out where you are. An English
major in my class brought to me an article one day with your
name on it, 'The Rubric of Renaissance Sensibility,' or some
ghastly thing like that. I couldn't believe my eyes. If you
wanted to hide, you should have changed your name to an
Anglo-sounding one like Richard Taylor, or a Slavic one with
a -ski or a -vich, or even a Chinese one with all the nasality
you want. How about Chung Ching Cheng? Unless you have
some fetishism about names like some primitives or patriots.
You are a beast not to have answered my letters, all
twelve of them or was it thirteen? I've lost count. Perhaps you
never opened them. Weren't you even curious, after all these
years? I was ready to wring your neck. But I forgive you. To
talk to you is to forgive...."
　　She bubbled away. The music of her voice intoxicated
him and transported him across time and space to Seoul
before the war. He beheld her, a high-school senior
planning to study voice in college. It was her birthday
party, an evening of song and dance. Each guest seemed
equally at ease with soprano or alto, tenor or bass, and
even the most tawdry pop tunes turned into extravaganzas of
harmony. There was a band for the dance music, but the
principal accompaniment came from the guitarist, a
statuesque girl who sat erect with a forbidding dignity. She
was Wonjoo, Moonhee's brother Chanho's girl, a music college
sophomore majoring in composition. Chanho had talked a lot
about her and Kichol had once delivered a parcel to her
address for him, but this was the first time he'd met her.
　　Moonhee was radiant. She danced with several young men
and each time as she passed she tapped Kichol on the
shoulder and laughed, her eyes twinkling. There were three
American officers, military advisers at her father General
Ahn's Capital Division, and Kichol was engaged with them,
trying his best but feeling hopelessly inadequate in his
unidiomatic English. Their conversation never rose beyond a
series of unrelated questions and answers, the names of this
dish or that, this song or that, this piece of furniture or
that. But they praised his English. Often they were asked
to dance by the girls. Nothing could be more welcome and
they responded enthusiastically. The Americans were
conscious that these were high class girls to be treated
differently from the whores they kept. None of them dared
to approach any girl first and only waited to be asked. But
their break into society lasted only as long as the music.
The language barrier was insurmountable and after an
exchange of thank-yous and you're-welcomes, they had to

106

part, unable to exploit the body contact so established.

Kichol had to leave early because the nightly curfew was near. All the guests had chauffeurs waiting for them in vehicles with curfew passes. Chanho offered to have one of his father's drivers take Kichol home later, but Kichol refused. The cymbal was striking, the drum beating, the trumpet prolonging an extra high note. The music was coming to some mad crescendo and nobody missed him. Kichol walked down the flagged path, which followed the bank of a stream that tumbled into a lotus-covered pond just before the iron gate, where two soldiers stood guard. The silhouette of the two-storied, ivy-covered brick mansion loomed against the skyline of the Chongpa Valley. Kichol was almost at the gate, when he realized that someone was behind him. It was Moonhee, panting from the exercise. She pulled him off the path, away from the hearing of the guards. They walked up the slope of the surrounding grove. The ground was soft with pine needles. The air was redolent with the freshness of spring, with the heady perfume of azaleas and forsythia. She leaned against a convex pine trunk.

"Are you going away without asking my permission, the hostess?"

"I didn't want to interrupt. You were having fun."

"Fun! I was miserable, because you couldn't dance or sing with me. Besides you were looking only at Wonjoo."

"I met her for the first time...."

She changed the topic. "I'm eighteen now. What do you think of me?"

"You're gorgeous."

"Am I old enough?"

"Of course you are, grandmother!" Kichol raised his hand to pinch her dimpled cheek. He had known her since she was a toddler. Their families originated from the same county and they had grown up together. He had never looked on her as anything but a young girl, a younger sister, bent on teasing her brother and his friends. Suddenly she seized his hand with both her hands and showered it with kisses, then buried her face in his chest and started crying. Kichol stroked her hair, not quite knowing what to do. She lifted her face. Her moist eyes glistened. Her pretty pug nose touched his chin.

"Don't you know we are meant for each other?"

Kichol was even more puzzled.

"Hasn't your father told you? My father and your father agreed a long time ago, before we were even born, that we would be man and wife. Don't you know about this?"

"No. Nobody ever told me such a thing. I'm sure they didn't mean it. They were joking over a drink too many. You can't just marry because your parents want it. This is the modern age and arranged marriage is out of the question. What *we* want counts."

"But I want it. I've never doubted it. I thought you knew it all along and were waiting for the day we'd be old enough...."

She whimpered.

"Listen, Moonhee. I never said anything. You're the most wonderful girl. A hundred young men will jump at the chance of marrying you. But why are we talking about marriage? We're too young for that."

"No, we're not. In America they get married at fifteen or sixteen. One of the American officers, the one with the mustache, has a five-year-old grandson although he's not quite forty yet. Besides you're older than I."

"But I have no means of support. I'm sure your father has forgotten all about this pact, if it existed at all. He must want his son-in-law to be an established man or a promising young man, probably a brilliant military officer."

"I detest those upstart bumpkins with no breeding."

Kichol had had to run to beat the curfew, after promising to meet her the next day at a tea shop, ostensibly to help her with her English. He regularly showed up wherever she designated, taking care that their separate meetings did not interfere with his usual attendance at her house, almost every day during exam time, to help Chanho with his studies. Chanho was in premed, but nobody seemed less promising as a future doctor. On his own he would never have made it through the entrance examination, but the national university had a special provision for patriots' descendants. Like Kichol's father, General Ahn had fought against the Japanese in Manchuria and China. Of course Kichol didn't have to invoke the special provision.

After the pine grove incident with Moonhee he felt awkward and uneasy at the Ahn residence. He couldn't cross-examine her more about the particulars of their fantastic betrothal or how she had come to its knowledge. That would betray an unmanliness of some sort, diffidence, distrust. He had to act the part to her, strong, self-confident, and deserving. Nor could he dare ask Chanho or General Ahn. They might think he was joking or be indignant for aiming so high above his inferior position. He was keenly aware of the disparity in their present family fortunes.

"I'm teaching, too," the telephone went on breathlessly.

"Voice, of course, at a conservatory here in town. We have a weeklong recess for Thanksgiving. Don't you? So it's perfect. The flight number is American 861, arriving at Toledo...."

The local name brought Kichol back to his senses.

"Moonhee," he said. "You can't come here."

"Why?" Her voice seemed to snap.

"I won't be here," Kichol struggled for words, his throat tightening. "That is, we won't be here. The family won't be here."

"The family?" she almost screamed, like a stricken bird.

"Yes, *gajog*!" Thank God nobody in the English Department understood Korean. "Haven't you heard? I have two children, and a wife?"

She went silent. The noise of the line totally obliterated her. Kichol knew it was cruel. He could murder himself for it, but there was no other alternative. She was not to entertain any hope for their future, because there was none.

Her letters stopped. The weeks came and went. The finals were over and the grades had been turned in. Kichol thought of going somewhere, to Chicago, Los Angeles, Hawaii, maybe even Mexico or Europe, but decided to stay put. He was finishing an article on John Donne. It snowed heavily, blanketing the corn and wheat fields that stretched in all directions as far as the eye could see, the scattered farmhouses with their silos and granaries, the roads and highways.

It was December 24th. A loud party was in progress at the apartment next door. Kichol walked along Main Street. He had to get out and work off the black fumes choking his system. A couple, arm in arm and pressed so closely together that their legs threatened to get entangled momentarily, came toward him. He knew the man, Tom Wilson, manager of First National, where he did his banking. He nodded with a smile, but Wilson turned away, whispering to his wife, who giggled and snuggled yet closer to her husband. Was it so much, even on Christmas Eve, to acknowledge a greeting, let alone stop and say a friendly word, perhaps even introduce his wife? She must have seen him too but had kept looking straight over his head, over such an incongruity as a Korean on the main street of Bowling Green, Ohio.

Kichol resolved to transfer his account the next day, and furiously stomped halfway down the block, every footfall landing hard on the packed, frozen snow of the pavement. A near slip shook him up. After waiting for the light, he crossed the street more cautiously and retraced his steps

in the direction he had come. His wrath subsided a little
and he found himself seeking explanations.

Perhaps neither of them had really seen him. Didn't he
sometimes do that, walking down the hallway preoccupied
with his class material? One student said the other day that
she had waved to him but he stared right through her,
although he couldn't remember any of that. The couple
stopped before the decorated front of McInerny's, displaying
expensive gloves, lipsticks, furs. Wilson pointed at something
and the wife laughed. They both disappeared into the store. So
the man earns money and brings it home to his woman,
Kichol thought. They spend it, buying not only food but also
occasional luxuries, those little stopgaps to snatch a moment
of gaiety and excitement from the bleak background of
routine. So twitters the sparrow upon capturing an earthworm
for his female and brood after a summer-long diet of rotten
husks. Breeding goes on, the species continues.

* * *

But Kichol's cynicism soon gave way to an indefinable,
aching nostalgia. There was something vaguely familiar about
the way the woman had tossed her head, her ample hair
cascading, her marble neck gleaming. He recalled that walk
down the Inchon waterfront one summer night after leaving
his inn. He'd bought a bag of roasted peanuts at a carbide-
lighted cart, popped the pods, and put the nuts in her mouth.
Wonjoo, his friend Chanho's girl, laughed, tossing her head,
and Kichol was on top of the world. Life was meaningful,
awesomely beautiful. At her villa on the brow of a hill her
maid promptly opened the door. He could hear the maid's
moaning complaint and Wonjoo's wheedling. Her parents had
given the servant, a distant aunt, strict orders to look after
their daughter, but a servant was a servant after all and
Wonjoo knew how to deal with her.

The midnight curfew siren screeched when Kichol arrived
at the inn. He found the boat broker impatiently waiting to
take him by back alleys to the ferry, disguised as a fishing
boat, due to leave in an hour for a small village on the North
Korean coast. Kichol had forgotten all about the appointment,
or indeed the whole purpose of his being in Inchon. The guide
didn't give him time even to write a note for Wonjoo, who was
sure to come there the next morning to go hiking. Neither of
them had thought of Seoul or the loyalties they had left there.
The few days they had together seemed like the compression
of centuries. Every minute held new surprises. They had gone

110

to the neighboring forests. They had swum in the roaring tide surging up and down the craggy mudflats. They had wallowed in the fine, bleached sand. On his part, what had happened to him at the Counterintelligence Section of Seoul Metropolitan Police had effectually erased all debts. He owed nothing to anybody. The whole ugly business had exploded a week before, collapsing his universe.

He had returned late from a cinema and ice cream with Moonhee and was trying to catch up with some sleep, if that was possible at the bedlam of a house in the Chungnimdong slums near Seoul Railroad Station where he rented a room. Each of its seven other rooms was occupied by a family of at least five. A loud knock came at the front gate. Everybody was home, it being Sunday, but nobody made a move. Kichol ended up going. The caller identified himself as Detective Shim and knew his name, although he had never met him before. There were a few things to be cleared up and Kichol had to accompany him to the headquarters.

When they arrived at the police station, the detective asked Kichol if he had had any news of his father. Kichol answered no. Detective Shim threw a sheaf of newspaper clippings before Kichol, the headlines screaming his father's name. Pyongik Hwang was a member of the North Korean Politburo and was, among other things, in charge of coordinating subversive activities in South Korea. Kichol was dumbfounded. He could count on his fingers the number of days he had seen his father and barely remembered his face. Pyongik had spent all his youth fighting for his country's independence, and had been on the wanted list of the Japanese police as long as Kichol could remember. Except for an unsuccessful attempt to recruit his son for the Communist cause at their brief reunion after August, 1945, he had not been seen or heard from.

Politics, at least the sort found in Korea at the time, disgusted Kichol. Korea, the spoil of World War II, was divided and occupied by Russians and Americans, who set up their stooges to form 'independent' governments. There was heavy rhetoric on both sides, each claiming egalitarianism and accusing the other of exploitation and imperialism, although he could see no real difference between the two regimes. At American prodding the South had carried out a land reform, wiping out the landed gentry to which the Hwangs had belonged. Key industries, electricity, telephone, railroad, mining, all previously Japanese owned, reverted to the government. The North had also nationalized and collectivized, with the inevitable concentration of power in the hands of the privileged few. Each had their Russian or American military governors, called "advisers," pulling the strings. Each side bred its adherents and fanatics. Power was ever so attractive and always suborned the soul. Bloody street fights broke out everywhere between the opposing factions. Kichol withdrew within himself, refusing even to read newspapers.

In the meantime his mother, not even fifty yet, had died of an undiagnosed malady. Kichol was practically an orphan. His grandmother was still alive at eighty-two, but was half blind and paralyzed from her waist down. A village couple, distantly related, lived in the house, the husband farming what little land was left to the family and the wife cooking, doing housework, and nursing his grandmother. It seemed as if they owned the place and his grandmother was a charitable ward. He had to be content with the fact that his grandmother was still alive and managed to send him money. Besides he had an income of sorts, although nobody called it that. Chanho's family paid for his tuition and made him eat often at their table. He was asked to move in with them, which was sensible considering the amount of time he spent there, but he had declined. Having had servants and retainers in their better days, he felt it demeaning to live under the roof of his father's friend, although by a convenient distortion of values he saw nothing dishonorable in the other forms of subsidy without which he would surely have starved. What his grandmother sent barely paid for his lodging.

"Are you going to play innocent?" demanded Detective Shim, his voice rising dangerously. They had been joined by several others.

"But I am telling you the truth. My father and I are separate individuals, and I am not responsible for his actions."

"Shut up, you Red bastard!"

Before he knew it, Shim's fist had crashed into his face. His teeth were loose, and blood gushed from his mouth and nose. Kichol almost hit him back in rage, but checked himself and said, "I am a friend of General Ahn's family. They will vouch for me."

Next moment Kichol sprawled on the floor, hugging his stomach. In vain he tried to dodge the pelting of booted kicks. A blow to his head knocked him out.

"May I call my friends?" he said weakly, when he recovered.

Shim slapped him across the mouth. "You still know nothing about your daddy? We know all about you. We have checked with the General's family. So this is how you infiltrate

112

our high places."

A club stung his knuckles. At the mention of General Ahn's name Kichol's heart sank. He realized his defenseless position. They would probably shoot him as an enemy agent. There was no way to reach the outside, which had turned as hostile as his captors. There followed endless hours of asking the same things: What was his mission? When did he hear from his father? Who was his contact? As their methods grew even more violent and unbearable, Kichol wished he could invent something to satisfy them, anything to end it all, even if it meant death.

After two days of torture and interrogation, without sleep, they brought a basin of water and soap and new clothes. Kichol was told to wash up and change. They told him to leave because they were satisfied for now. He thought they were setting him up as an escapee, but he was in no position to refuse. He tried to get up but flopped back, his legs caving under him. They supported him to the door and the mystery of his release was explained. Moonhee was there with her father's sedan. She cursed the policemen, who cowered under the lashings of her tongue and helped him into the vehicle. She wanted to take him to her house but he begged her to drive him to his. Then he told her to go home and wait for him. He would be there after a short rest. Before she left, he asked her to lend him all the money she had. She seemed puzzled but complied. There was also the unpaid rent money for the month in his room.

He took a bus to Inchon and found an inn near the docks. There was a steady traffic of smugglers between South and North despite the coast patrol, and a passage could be secured for the right sum. Toward dusk, after a day of checking the docks for a reliable boatman, Kichol turned into the market street on his way to the inn when he saw Wonjoo standing in front of a fishmonger's stand. Her left hand on her waist, the hooked thumb biting into her belly and the thin, long fingers slanting downward, her right hand pointed at the fish she wanted. Her maid darted forward to haggle with the merchant. Straightening, Wonjoo turned around and, seeing him, stood still, tall, elegant, distant, yet inexplicably fragile and vulnerable.

"Hello!" Kichol said.

"Hi!" Wonjoo replied, meeting his eyes steadily.

Her finals were over and her parents had sent her to the port city where they owned the hill-top villa to improve her health. She had a touch of pulmonary tuberculosis, Kichol had heard from Chanho before. The maid was returning with the

113

fish wrapped in old newspaper.

"May I walk with you to your villa?" Kichol had said, hastily.

"Is it not out of your way?" she had said, her arctic composure giving way to a slowly spreading blush.

* * *

In North Korea Kichol found his father married to a young woman from whom he already had an infant son. Pyungik Hwang, the Communist functionary, showed no interest at all in what had been left behind in the South, including his son, and all his present work seemed to be of confidential nature. The father and son had nothing to talk about, and soon their company became oppressive to each other. Once he got placed on the editorial staff of a magazine with an adequate salary to support himself, Kichol found a lodging in the outskirts of Pyongyang overlooking the river. Seoul was eons away.

The work was easy, writing elementary composition from production figures supplied to him, judiciously interspersing the formulaic terminology at the right places, "heroic leader," "glorious revolutionary working masses," "overproduction," and other such jargon, which he didn't mind. Every language was entitled to its own punctuation, honorifics, idiosyncrasies. North Korea was developing a unique popular style, and however clumsy or heavy-handed, it was preferable to the vacuum or chaos of the southern literary scene. Returning home after a day's work and looking out the window at the boats rowing up and down the Taydong, he felt at peace and believed he was finally contributing to society.

The magazine sent him as a special correspondent to a settlement of immigrant Korean farmers in Manchuria. He was to report on their life and progress. It was the first opportunity he'd had of working independently. He could gather facts, weigh them, comment and evaluate on his own. As he interviewed the settlers who battled the elements with guts and bare hands, and recorded and narrated their struggle, he felt a tearful sympathy, agony, and pride. He became aware of the common bond between himself and them. He could have died for them, stayed there for the rest of his life working with them. Every cell in him tingled and reverberated with the story of the race—the vagabondage that originated from Central Eurasian steppes, trekking and meandering across the mountains and deserts of two continents, the persecutions, discriminations, genocides that hounded them everywhere they went and kept them on

114

the move, the narrow escapes, constant packings-up and marchings-on, panting runs, exhausted droppings on the road, children smothered in their cries, the uneasy settlement of the peninsula coveted by the hostile nations, Chinese, Russian, Mongolian, Japanese, Manchu, the thousands of years of invasions, national emergencies, midnight alarms, vigils, widows' keenings. The ten millenia of Korean history paraded past him like grim tableaux. The whole time he was there, he lived in a trance-like state of exaltation. He had forgotten all about the petty politics of the magazine or the intrigues and maneuverings of his social life at Pyongyang.

This deeply stirring, inspirational experience that had given him a new sense of identity and mission came to a rude awakening when he returned. A board of inquiry was waiting. The upper echelons had been mightily displeased with his dispatches. He should not have reported about the security force at the collective being outfitted with the uniforms and shoes left over from the Japanese army, nor on the utter lack of farming tools, food, and shelter. Against these crippling odds, the plucky Koreans were carving out a new destiny in a foreign land, building mud huts, smithies, granaries. It was the most moving epic of the century, the triumph of the spirit, the laurel of labor. But Kichol was told never to show the revolutionary workers at a disadvantage of any sort except after the fact, when the goal had been accomplished. So long as work was still in progress, the heroic workers had to be well-clothed, well-fed, well-equipped, producing 500 per cent beyond the target daily. He was severely reprimanded.To burn out the residues of capitalistic sentimentalism that jaundiced his perception a penance was decreed in the form of "voluntary" construction labor after work every day and all during the weekend.

One Sunday afternoon he had climbed a scaffolding to steady a beam. A rope slipped and he fell fifty feet, fortunately onto a pile of straw sacking. He was alive but both his legs had been wrenched out of joint and one arm had been broken. To while away the boredom at the hospital and also to do his reporter's job better, he had brought to his bedside books from the hospital library. He was fascinated by the Communist ideology, its motivation and history. But after two months of concentrated reading the inevitable saturation point arrived. Criticism eroded the initial enthusiasm. Was it the lingering capitalistic cancer? No, he knew he was capable of objectivity, if such was humanly possible. Why was there no other reading material in the state-owned libraries (and there were no others) than those of Marx, Lenin, and their

anonymous exegetical disciples? Surely, Tolstoy and Dosto-
evsky must rank somewhere along with them. So must
Shakespeare, Christ, Confucius. But there were none of these.
Whatever fiction was available had been authored by the
Korean People's Literature Committee and followed a predictable, inexorable pattern. Collective talent maintained a level
of technical competence, but there was no surprise, no ingen-
uity, no individual genius. Everywhere he looked he saw only
identical, eternally reiterative landscape. As his discharge
neared, he became depressed and restless. A moratorium had
been clamped upon his intellectual growth; he was not to go
beyond arithmetic to venture into the reaches of higher
mathematics.

A group of entertainers was making the rounds at the
hospital. They came into his ward, and the head nurse
introduced him as the heroic volunteer who'd got hurt while
working at their new People's Theater.

"We must express our gratitude in a special way," said
a high-cheeked broad-browed girl who looked like the leader.
Unaided by makeup, their faces yet glowed with a raw,
vibrant animation.

"Let's bring the largest bouquet to him," suggested
another girl.

They were all giggly and ticklish. Although physically
well-developed, their speech and manners suggested extremely
young girls. Having been involved in nothing but acting,
singing, and dancing since childhood, they lacked the sort of
sophistication customary among the conventionally educated
southern girls. But the sheer animalism they radiated was
refreshing, electrifying. Their short hairdo and puritan dress,
identically cut, could not suppress their vitality. Their
peaked breasts, energetic arms, strong legs burst through the
cloak of uniformity, demanding individual attention.

"Flowers won't be special enough," he said.

There was an explosion of knowing laughter. They doubled
up and rolled over. He grinned and breathed deep, his nostrils
dilating over this scene of devastating merriment. They
exchanged names. The leader's name was Soonja Ro. There
was a peculiar bounce to her steps; her whole body moved
in an impulsive, irresistible rhythm, imparting energy to her
ambience. He learned that she was a ballerina.

One November evening he was delayed at work, rewriting
an article to meet the absurd standards of the editor. He had
by now realized the futility of making any suggestions. Even
direct quotations from Marx and Lenin were suppressed as out
of context or misleading. The editor and his select staff

116

dictated the changes, and he had better accept them. He walked home in the chilling drizzle, getting wet and forgetting his date with Soonja, who was about to leave after waiting a full hour.

"You're shivering," she said with concern and unbuttoned his clothes. She undressed too and they turned off the light, although it was still early evening. Under the blanket, warmed by her body, strength returned to him. He clasped her so hard that her bones crackled and she moaned in pained delight.

"Don't leave my side even for a minute. I cannot live without you."

"Have you heard?" she said, pushing him gently to look at his face better.

"Heard what?"

"Our tour of Russia, China, Poland, and other Communist nations."

"No!" The blow seemed to take away his last hold on life.

"It will be a great opportunity. We will learn what other countries are doing and see all the great theaters, cities, villages. We'll have one or two things of our own to show them, too."

"When are you leaving?"

"About May."

"How long?"

"Only a few months."

He crawled out of bed and put on his clothes. Soonja followed the example.

"Don't be cross. It means a lot to me," she said, breaking the silence.

"Do you recall our talk about the measure of love, that the value of anything depends on what one is willing to give up for it?"

"Yes," she said, her face hardening imperceptibly.

He knew it was selfish, cowardly, futile, to ask it, but he had to. He wasn't strong enough to let her go, to leave her alone to make her own decisions.

"Can you refuse for my sake?"

"But we will be back together in no time at all."

"It is very important to me just now that you stay. At any other time it won't matter but it does now."

"I am indispensable to the troupe, though."

Encountering resistance, he became adamant and demanding. He shouted, begged, raged, and swore that he would never see her again if she went. She broke into inconsolable tears. He almost told her to go on the tour, but an unreasoning obstinacy prevented him. She wiped her eyes and

117

smiled through the film of tears.

"I won't go," she said, throwing herself at him and breaking into fresh wailing. He loved her above everything else, pledged his whole life to her, felt guilty and indebted, but purpose had returned to his life. He could live.

Their meetings became infrequent afterwards. She was tied up with her practices and various provincial tours, and he was sent on different errands, sometimes far-flung. When he returned from a one-week assignment to a coal mine in Rajin on the Russian border, she had left the country with the troupe. He lived like an automaton, allowing himself to be pushed around, willing or initiating nothing. He felt spent and old. He hardly noticed the marked change in the magazine's editorials, nor understood what the fever pitch of passion for national unification in the party congresses and statements foreboded. Troops were concentrating along the 38th Parallel and national mobilization was on. The air snapped with tension, with the imminence of war, but in his stupor he felt nothing, noticed nothing. It was just a month after her departure that the war came, in June 1950. Even when they finally put him in military uniform, armed him with a pistol, and made him a political officer, a combination of war correspondent and intelligence liaison, he still did not fully comprehend the significance. Only when he saw the first casualties did the reality and enormity of the war strike home.

They were on a course of self-destruction and there was no turning back. The tanks would trample Seoul, where he had his education. The artillery would pound to pieces the village of his birth. He would be literally shooting his classmates, boyhood friends, cousins and relatives, and they him. The only hope was that it would all be over quickly, with a minimum of bloodshed. At first, the hope seemed realistic. The medium T-34 tank of World War II vintage and obsolete in Russia, performed miracles, and the South Korean army was totally defenseless. Their small arms and mortars did not even dent the armor plate. The North Korean army was in Seoul in just three days and the vaunted Capital Division was good only at chauffeuring Rhee across the Han before the bridge was dynamited.

General Ahn, unable to survive the shame of abandoning his charge, shot himself, like a sea captain dying with his sinking ship. There was a touching simplicity to this mentality, but Kichol felt exasperated at its stupidity, its waste. Retreats were as inevitable in war as in games and sports. Hadn't he played soccer? But Kichol was quickly hardening against death in its myriad forms. Mauled, shattered, crushed, battered, burned, bloated bodies, military and civilian, decayed everywhere in the hot, humid monsoon. The army had its hands full and the populace was too excited, looting, collaborating, hiding, betraying, to organize burial parties. After a temporary check at the Han the People's Army pushed south at many points simultaneously, routing the South Korean army and meeting token resistance from the first American contingents, capturing their general. The Pusan perimeter was shrinking.

Kichol was left behind in Seoul to help organize a civilian government. It was a mess. The economy was a shambles, and no productive work of any sort could be done. Recruiting mostly street thugs, youth leagues were organized and given enormous powers, including summary execution, to press workers back to factories and shops. But almost immediately American planes reduced everything to rubble. The pocket of resistance in the Pusan perimeter had to be destroyed, the Rhee government driven into the sea, and that soon. But now the People's Army was encountering difficulties. A dozen divisions, equipped with new arms and supplies from America, opposed them. The American bazooka rendered the T-34 useless. The People's Army had to make a decisive effort before their superiority in numbers totally disappeared. Casualties had already been great from the delaying actions of the South, and most original divisions were less than half strength. Conscription was enforced at checkpoints and through house to house manhunts to fill the quotas of frontline recruits.

Kichol couldn't get information concerning Chanho and Moonhee and thought they had crossed the river in time with Rhee. Their house was the command post of a regiment. An agent reported that Wonjoo's villa in Inchon was occupied by a People's Army medical unit and her house in Seoul quartered general officers. Kichol's grandmother had died in January, peacefully, the servants told him. He heard the news unmoved. Life was here now and gone next. One could snuff it out with the flick of a finger. And she had lived long enough.

His father was in charge of army logistics and in a brief meeting at Seoul told him about the enormous obstacles in his task as the line of supply lengthened and got continually interdicted by American air power. It had to be maintained entirely by backpacking, using the pressed labor of the South, and that at night over the mountains. Father and son met like two business colleagues.

At one moment they were elated: the finger of history

pointed in the direction they were marching. They owed it to future generations to bequeath a unified, prosperous fatherland, to put new pride in their heritage. The next moment their spirits sank. The obstacles were numerous, unnerving, overwhelming. Air raids worsened, ever-increasing quotas for manpower from the frontlines could not be met, enemy agents abounded, starvation, epidemics, senseless, wanton death spread. The price was too high.

* * *

When Kichol returned from his ramble, the apartment manager Charles Friedson's front door stood ajar and Kichol heard the familiar voice. Moonhee was just stepping out, followed by Charles. She had arrived from Toledo Airport, carrying a handbag and a light suitcase. Her face, white from the cold, thawed at the sight of Kichol.

"Thanks, Charles, and good night," Kichol waved to the worthy fellow, who stood rooted in his doorway, watching with a vague smile. It was the first time anyone had ever called on his tenant. Charles closed the door after him. Moonhee was heading toward the stairway. Kichol grabbed her suitcase.

"Let's go to the hotel, " he said.

"Okay," she replied, smiling, looking at him amusedly.

It was the only hotel in town, at least the only one that went by that title. The others were all motels. The Ross Hotel was about half a mile away from his apartment. The owner, Walter Ross, seemed in high spirits. There was a live band and a lot of party-making going on in the dining hall. For the first time his place was full, but because Kichol was such a special friend of his, he was going to give up his own room to accommodate him, Ross said. Kichol had eaten at the hotel a few times and Ross had obligingly told him that he had flown the Flying Boxcars during the Korean War. He even had a wound to show for it and bared his arm. Those bastard Reds! He'd had to shoot everything that moved on the ground because even the most innocuous-looking civilian would turn around and blast with a burp gun. Kichol and Moonhee were shown to a table in a corner. Food was brought, juicy tender roast beef and baked potatoes. Neither of them could eat much.

"I bring greetings from the rest of the family," Moonhee said. "Chanho is a plastic surgeon, got a private practice in New York. They have two children, two real children, James and Jane, with their birth certificates and social security numbers, ha, ha. They are seven and five."

She stopped and scrutinized his face, a quizzical but benign laughter hovering around her eyes. Kichol picked up the glass of water and gulped.

"Of course they are Wonjoo's children," she said. "She sends her love."

* * *

Moonhee must know all about it, Kichol thought. He recalled coming to his office one morning in August 1950 after a sleepless, harried night. His quarters had been bombed during the night and he had narrowly escaped. Walking through the lines of people before the building, the families and relatives of those arrested, imprisoned, transported, or executed, he'd seen a few paces ahead of him a familiar shape. Her back was turned to him but there was no mistaking.

"Wonjoo!" he exclaimed, stepping in front of her.

Her darkened face lit up briefly with the shock of recognition, only to droop listlessly. There was none of the thoroughbred in her. He took her to his office and asked her why she was there. She was Chanho's wife and he had been caught with a short-wave transmitter and a camera containing a film of military installations. Her voice cracked and her lips were parched. Military justice in such cases was swift. Even possession of a radio had been forbidden and punishable by death. But Kichol wasn't thinking of what should be done with Chanho. As he looked at her eyes, sunken but not without luster, her rich folds of hair, her feet, her legs, her waist, the memories of their intimacy rushed back to him like a tidal wave. He had been celibate ever since Soonja had left him. There had been parties of celebration and to the conqueror women were available in any numbers, but Soonja had wounded him too deeply. He had renounced the flesh, in which he only smelled the scatological stench and saw the skeleton beneath. But his memories of Wonjoo had not tarnished.

"Can we pick up where we left off?" he said, despising himself for the banality and insensitivity of the proposition.

"You know it's impossible," Wonjoo said, her eyes averted. All his noble impulses deserted him. Frustrated animal desire took over. He clasped her waist and covered her mouth with his. She braced her arms against his chest and struggled. Suddenly her body relaxed and she asked him to hear her. She would do whatever he wanted with her if he would free Chanho. She should not have mentioned him. She was willing

121

to make any sacrifice for him, to use Kichol because he was nothing to her.

"Why should I do that? I could have him put out of the way and have you for myself. Lady, you are in no position to bargain."

She was crushed. He had destroyed her. He dragged her to the bottom of degradation and himself along with her, but he did not care. Life was worthless anyway. What was beauty, grace, refinement, virtue but a fleeting, cheating variation on the theme of rotting flesh? Wonjoo was inert and yielding, like a lump of mud. In the flux of conflicting emotions and images he recalled the body of a woman he'd seen near Hwachon with a stick driven up her vagina, half submerged in a swampy rice paddy and festooned with a ring of floating feces. He called the guard and had Wonjoo shown out. Chanho was brought to his office, his hands bound behind him. His lips were swollen, his eyes half closing, and his face, scarred with contusions and runny sores, puffy beyond recognition. They must have hamstrung his leg; he limped horribly.

"Have you anything to say in your defense?"

"I have nothing more to say. You can do anything you want," he said, opening with struggle the bloodshot eyes that burned with defiance and hatred. "There is one thing you can do, for old times' sake. Kill me right away."

Kichol liked his spunk. The Chanho he had known before was anything but heroic. By an unaccountable perversion, however, he was gripped simultaneously with a desire to humble and break his old friend.

"Wonjoo has been here," Kichol said with a leer.

"You leave your dirty hands off her," Chanho growled.

"If I am dirty, then so is she and so are you."

"You ingrate, snake, *doksa!*" A wad of spittle shot out of his mouth and landed on Kichol's eye, temporarily blinding him. Kichol punched Chanho's head. Chanho fell to the floor, face foremost. His nose started bleeding. He gasped for breath.

"Rat, snake, *doksa!*" he yelled with every breath. Kichol's booted foot bashed his stomach, his groin, his mouth. Kichol was determined to kill him and he almost succeeded. Chanho passed out. The doctor revived him. His wounds were dressed, and he was taken back to his cell. The next day Kichol received orders to join the 13th Division poised at the Naktong Bulge near Ohang. Before he left, he sent for Wonjoo and released Chanho with a safe conduct.

* * *

"We had no idea you would be here in the States," Moonhee said. "Chanho and Wonjoo thought you would be in North Korea, if you were still alive. At one point we wanted to do something about it. Chanho wrote to the UN truce commission and even went to the Red Cross office to see if they could learn your whereabouts, but came off with a fat zero. We found out there was no way to get any personal information from North Korea. The only other way was to send an agent there for the specific purpose of learning about you, and we hadn't convinced the CIA of the intelligence value of such a mission. However, we learned that your father had died, but even this bit of information had to be pried out of the CIA with much coaxing."

She stopped her narration and looked at Kichol intently.

"Did you know about his death?" she asked.

"No," he said, marveling at the placidity of his own response.

"You don't know how he died either?" she asked.

"No," he answered with some finality.

Moonhee did not pursue the subject.

"They were convinced you had died," she resumed. "They thought that had you lived, you must have made your mark already on the North Korean political scene and we would hear about you. You can't blame them for having a high esteem of your abilities, although it was a bit of a shock to see you in politics. Perhaps the war brought out your true talents."

She said it with a chuckle. Kichol glanced at her. There was no malice, no sarcasm. She wasn't capable of it.

"My true colors, rather," Kichol said with a shudder, avoiding her eyes.

"You know you're their benefactor and they'll never forget it. They'll do anything for you."

Kichol involuntarily looked at her once more, hard, to determine whether she was making fun of him. She stopped to meet his gaze head on. Those clear, lucent eyes of an incorruptible, eternal, primeval child! What an unbearable situation! Was it to be the joke of fate that his bestiality and treachery should be rewarded with gratitude and devotion, as if Kichol's mistreatment of his friend before the release had been a make-believe staged to take in his Communist comrades? It would have been kinder to be remembered as the villain and traitor that he really was, to have his ignominy shouted by the town crier, to be whipped and stoned than to be made out a benefactor.

"They came to the States soon after the armistice in 1953,

but I had come before that, in 1949, shortly after you disappeared."

She paused, her face clouding.

"I feel so guilty," she said, her eyes watering. "While so many of our people died and suffered, I was here studying comfortably with money sent from home. I feel like a vampire, a parasite that kills its host. I often feel I don't deserve to live. I have awful nightmares, those dying people holding out their hands, crying out to me, grabbing at me, as they fall to their death into the pit..."

She covered her face with her hands, suppressing a cry. She got out a handkerchief from her bag, dried herself, and smiled at him as brightly as the sun after a rain.

"So you see I'm still a crybaby. Tell me what you did after your last meeting with Chanho and Wonjoo."

"Why those details? They have no importance now."

"They do. I want to know everything that happened to you. It's to fill the gap for all the time I have been separated from you. I have never for a moment doubted that I would meet you again. I've never shared Chanho and Wonjoo's pessimism that you might be dead. You couldn't be dead, while I was alive. I knew it. I told you we were fated to be one."

"After all these years," Kichol remonstrated, "after your education in this country, after so much exposure to Western culture, do you still talk like a little girl from a 19th century Korean village?"

"I guess some things just don't change. The exact scenario was not worked out, of course, but I knew I would be back with you again. All that had intervened wouldn't matter. We would be brought together, the richer, stronger, better for our separate existences. I could understand everything you did and underwent, no matter what. So tell me what happened afterward."

Her curiosity, far from being contradictory to her avowed indifference to his past, appeared all too logical and necessary. Kichol had to comply. Far from being annoyed and resentful, he felt wanted and comforted. He had to tell and share.

"I was sent to the frontlines the next day after I saw them last, I think. I was sent to a task force to breach the Pusan Perimeter. But things were in a sorry state for the Communist forces. It was a hopeless gamble. Time was running out on them, while the UN forces were growing stronger every day. Two-thirds of the task force troops were made up of green conscripts from South Korea, those overnight soldiers who barely knew how to handle a shoulder rifle, who were pressed into the lines just as fillers without weapons. They had no inclination for the fight and watched out only for an opportunity to desert. But there were enough of the veteran NCO's, officers, and cadres around to force them into combat at gun point. August was ending and the Great Naktong Offensive was at hand. There were three other divisions massed around the Bulge at Ohang. Though the offensive was to be launched from all points of the Perimeter, the Bulge provided direct access to the Taegu and Pusan corridor and was to be the focus of attack. My function was liaison among the division headquarters in the area, hand delivering battle plans and intelligence through the brambles and rocks at night. There was no telephone or wireless communication, no vehicular transportation: the American Air Force had seen to that."

Kichol stopped. He remembered his meeting Soonja again at the battlefront. He'd been returning after a particularly wearying night towards daybreak to his underground bunker for a rest, when at the entrance he found her in a nurse's uniform. Her troupe had cut the tour short, and she had volunteered for a post to be near him. She had arrived early in August, but it took her that long to get to the front. Pyongyang and the whole countryside was under incessant aerial bombardment. Convoys, whether of personnel or materiel, could only trickle to the front. She said she hadn't liked the trip abroad at all and should never have left his side. She asked for his forgiveness. He just stroked her. Her entreaty was like a song composed by a poet of a different age, a different clime. The plaintive strain was touchingly beautiful and soothing, but the words had no relevance to the present or the past he could identify. They were together in each other's nakedness and the thunder of the bombs and shells, the confusion of dead and wounded, the mess of a thousand frustrated plans, the hurts and aches, screams and shouts, did not exist for them.

Kichol was conscious of Moonhee's expectant gaze on him. Her smile fluttered uncertainly for a while but never quit her face.

"The offensive was on, the one big supreme ultimate try. Our divisions crossed the river and closed in on the Bulge shortly before midnight, but the enemy had been alerted and waiting. Thousands of white phosphorescent flares burst overhead, lighting the night sky like broad daylight. Close formations of fighters and bombers, in concert with ground artillery, made mincemeat of us. Whole battalions got chewed up and disintegrated. The Naktong was dyed crimson with our blood. Bodies covered the surface like flotsam."

Soonja's medical unit, evacuating the wounded, disappeared in a direct rocket hit.

"My regiment, one of the spearheads crossing the river, was cut off and swiftly surrounded by the mechanized American infantry. Desperately we fought them at bay, until, all ammunition depleted, we surrendered. After a temporary accommodation near Pusan we were moved to Kojay Island. Thousands of POW's poured in every day. The counter-offensive had broken out of the Perimeter, pursuing People's Army remnants to complete MacArthur's 'hammer and anvil' strategy: the American marines had landed at Inchon in the north."

"The POW camp was pretty awful, wasn't it?" asked Moonhee.

"Quite. No international convention will materially change the lot of prisoners of war. Popular feeling demands that they not be treated better than the nation's criminals, let alone the poor of its citizenry, and war impoverishes everybody. The starving, suffering millions focus their hatred on these tangible causes of their misery and are outraged by any decent treatment. Our move to Kojay, away from public view, was therefore fortunate in that respect. A flimsy barbed wire fence surrounded the compound, dotted with overcrowded barnlike camps. Mine was the notorious Camp 76, which held as many as 5,000 at its peak. We slept huddled along the wall on a straw sack, our buttocks touching. Almost as many as came in went out, dead. Most of us had been already wounded, diseased, and starved at the time of capture. Only those really sick got any sort of medical attention. A rather novel method of screening was employed. The sick were carried out and lined up along the barbed wire. An American guard would come and strike the prostrate forms with an iron bar. Those that did not squirm under the blow qualified and were taken to the makeshift medical tent, to be given aspirin or alka seltzer, depending on whether the head or any part below the head hurt. Nine out of ten died in a few days. Those who failed the iron bar screening had to be taken back to the camp to wait their turn, until they got sicker.

"I became sick. I lost all appetite and could not touch the ball of rice, which was eagerly devoured by my neighbors. Understandably, they idolized me as a self-effacing philanthropist. What little I downed churned up a violent storm of excruciating pain in my stomach. I couldn't sleep at night and lost weight. Once, on a work detail carrying the drum of feces to be dumped at the beach, I passed out. But I came to soon enough and was spared the iron bar test. My inmates got me off the work details but I withered. Sweat stood on my brow and vertigo blanked me out for hours sometimes.

"At first the POW's were a broken lot, physically and morally. Everybody thought it was all over with Ilsung Kim, that Korea would be unified under South Korean rule with US backing and they would be released to become second-rate citizens in this new system. But in November word came through agents among the new POW's and the hawkers trading around the fences that the tide of war had turned with the entry of the Red Chinese, that if not unification under North Korean rule, then at least the old order of division into South and North would return. The Communist cadres had kept a low profile before but now got busy with organization and indoctrination work. Hakkoo Lee, a former brigadier, and his lieutenants appointed regimental and battalion commanders, turning the whole camp into a division. A standing politburo was formed to take care of policy matters. The organization thus started there was to spread to the other camps, separated from us by guarded fences, so that the whole compound might be organized into an army corps and stage a rearguard action behind the enemy lines.

"The Americans, with no previous experience in the handling of POW's on this scale, unwittingly aided this project. They decided to be model jailors, to show to the POW's the humanity and civilization of the Free World. The guards were instructed to treat us as guests and to accede to our every desire to make our stay pleasant. They provided us with sports equipment, for nothing was more wholesome than sports, building material and paint to repair and beautify our quarters, sheets in addition to blankets for better sanitation, books to improve our minds, paper and duplicating machines to vent our literary creativity. Pretty soon portraits of Josef Stalin and Ilsung Kim went up on the walls, huge slogans decked the camp sides, and leaflets and pamphlets circulated. The camp hummed with activity and bristled with spears and knives, now mass produced.

"The politburo asked me to attend a meeting. The organizational work had run into opposition at some of the other camps, dominated by rightist reactionaries, that is, conscripts from South Korea, who had petitioned the Americans to be separated from the Communists and sent to their homes in the South, not to the North. The ranks had to be tightened and at the same time strong representations made directly to General Dodd, the prison commandant, to leave us alone to take care of our own and to send us all to the North, without exception, according to the Geneva Conventions. Since we couldn't trust the interpreters provided by them, we had to write and speak in English ourselves. I was to do the job. Now my health became the concern of the whole camp: they fed me beef broth and fruit juice and even gave me medicines bearing American labels. With work to do and good health care, I became stronger.

"As a measure of internal consolidation the politburo made a list of unreliables in the camp from hearsay, took them aside one by one, and interrogated. A former high school history teacher who bluntly said he had to go and see his family in Seoul was clubbed to death. His body was hung by the ankles from the ceiling for all to see. Nobody trusted anyone, and strangled or stabbed bodies turned up daily. Since it was impractical to string up all the corpses, they were cut up and disposed of piecemeal, an arm here, a leg there, in the feces tanks. Apparently a similar consolidation program was going on at the other camps, according to their several dispositions, and our camp served as a collection point for the evictees from the rightist camps. Bearing bruises, cuts, and other marks of rough treatment, these dedicated Communists, in truth teenagers wanting to go home to their parents in the North, were accorded heroes' welcomes, although the camp was already spilling over."

"Didn't the Americans do anything about this?" Moonhee asked.

"No American guard could enter the camp, short of shooting our armed pickets. The humane principle aside, that would have been embarrassing as by now news reporters were swarming in from all over the world. Besides, a neutral nations observer team was poking its nose everywhere, as accusations of American brutality had been made at the truce talks.

"The politburo engineered a daring project, the kidnap of General Dodd. Overestimating his importance they thought that with him in our hands they would achieve the goal of getting guns, unifying the camps, and breaking out of Kojay. For the first time I felt obliged to raise objections. Such a break would serve no good purpose, even if successful, because the armistice talks were going on and, in the absence of explicit directives from Pyongyang, military action on our part might complicate things for the negotiators. I didn't tell them my real fear: the deliberate sacrifice of the American general and the following retaliation en masse, for the Americans had to be pushed far enough and had a knack for getting others to push them. I was told to shut up and mind my own business. Their attitude began to cool toward me and Brigadier Lee said my real sympathies were suspect.

"The kidnap plan went better than expected. Dodd came to see what was wrong with Brigadier Lee and his boys, got off the jeep at the gate, and walked, unattended, straight into the trap. We couldn't believe our own eyes. General Colson, Dodd's successor, got him released after pledging, among other things, noninterference in camp organizations and suspension of torture against POW's to turn them into anti-Communists. Intelligence reported that Colson's signed confession of crimes had greatly improved the bargaining position of the North at the truce table, and the whole camp had been memorialized for its glorious accomplishment.

"A new commandant came, General Boatner, who unlike the others before him showed no inclination to listen or talk and went ahead with the building of smaller, more manageable camps to relocate us. Since our strength lay in staying together, the politburo told every inmate to resist the attempt to the death. An elaborate plan was drawn up, which included the murder of all the prison command personnel, seizure of the weapons and ships, and landing at Pusan to commence the northward offensive. Of course there was no possibility of its realization. Boatner had reinforced his command with several Pershing tanks and scores of armored trucks. Higher, more secure watch towers, mounted with heavy machine guns, were manned with combat vigilance. Even if we should succeed in overcoming one or two armored trucks or watch towers, a remote possibility at best, instant retaliation would come from all points of the compass, pulverizing us.

"But as with all fantastic ventures, the far-fetched and impossible became commonplace and practicable by incantatory rote. Everyone rehearsed and knew by heart his part in the action, scheduled to coincide with the driving up of the armored truck to the camp. We were to comply and file out in orderly fashion, until lines of our men going past them a certain distance collapsed and seized the guards. The machine guns on the vehicles were then to swing around and knock off the closest watchtowers, while those still inside would issue from the cut-out sides of the camp and attack the different armored vehicles and watchtowers. The suddenness of several thousand men dispersing in all directions at once would confuse the gunners. Aided by the seized fire support, we would overcome the dazed guards. The planners, veterans of the Naktong Offensive, seemed to have forgotten the massacre of the Bulge and other places. And we had rifles and grenades then.

"I asked Lee about the latest intelligence reports on the exact moorings of the ships and their precise capacities to ferry all the 100,000 men on the island to Pusan. He rolled his eyes menacingly and bellowed at my obstructive questioning, but that didn't quite conceal his ever so slight wavering at the reminder of reality, the jolt at being caught off guard. Clearly he had no idea whether the plan would go even beyond the camp walls. His only purpose in getting the inmates worked up over the prospect of the Pusan offensive was to express his disapproval in the blood of hundreds of our lives, maybe thousands, the more the better, for some abstract propaganda advantage at the truce talks. Lee himself would not get hurt because he would be the last to leave the camp. The mess would surely win him the People's Medal, but the rest of us would be rotting in mass graves.

"I had to stop this deliberate murderer. I composed a letter to Boatner warning him of the danger and dropped it on an empty rice tub carted off by the guards. When I returned to my corner, Lee's henchmen jumped on me and brought me to the politburo. They demanded to know what I had written. I had better tell the truth because they had contacts at the other end. I said that I had asked Boatner to make an exception in our case, Camp 76. They did not buy it."

Kichol stopped. He knew that he could not go further. Did she want to hear from his own lips how one of his torturers had pulled out a razor and threatened to mutilate him if he didn't tell the truth? How Kichol had tried to turn it into a joke and stuck to his story? How when he'd regained consciousness, he'd found himself aboard a US hospital ship off Pusan? For the first time he felt annoyed and angry at having been pushed so far along. He felt tricked and betrayed. What right did she have to come poking after his trail of disaster? What grim pleasure, what sardonic humor was this? He almost stood up to strip and show her the stump of his manhood. Wasn't that what she was after? Better have a good look!

"What are you trying to accomplish? Didn't I tell you to stay away from me?"

"Must I spell it out? I want to be your wife."

Moonhee put out her hand to hold his. He flinched.

"You can't be thinking about the "arrangement" still. The

130

principals who entered into it are dead, if that is not obvious, and death ends all."

"Some things survive it, life insurance for instance, or civilization."

"I'm a changed man. You don't know what the war has done to me. I may resemble the former me, but the real me is something you would not recognize, something you would recoil from with horror. There is really no point in prolonging this. I must leave now. Whether you leave tomorrow or not is up to you. We have nothing in common. We are strangers. You don't know me."

"I know everything about you," she said, slowly, articulating every word.

"How can you? The very idea is absurd. Anyone who hasn't been there during the holocaust, who hasn't been through what I have, can't know. It has mangled and deformed us. You were lucky to stay away and study here, safe and whole."

"No Korean is whole, wherever he or she may be. Doesn't your John Donne say the bell tolls for thee? Believe me I have died a million deaths, been broken and maimed..."

She looked meaningfully at him.

"Do you mean...?"

She nodded. Their last telephone conversation had naturally shocked her, but recovering, she'd set about inquiring after him. The first thing she discovered was that he wasn't married at all. This led her to look into his past. Through the help of friends with Defense Department connections she was able to trace him to Camp 76 and the hospital ship.

"But, then, how on earth are you going to marry me?"

"Aren't you a simpleton?" she said, laughing. "You have studied your John Donne and nothing else, I guess. Read up on some basic manuals on human sex. Just as life doesn't stop for the loss of a finger or a toe, so sexuality does not stop for a little deprivation."

"You are obviously an expert."

"You'll be surprised to know I'm still a virgin, if that's what's on your mind. Not that it's important. I never had an opportunity. You were always there for me, and I had to follow a strictly regimented life to achieve even my present modest status in this country. There are just too many good musicians and singers around, and I have reconciled myself to my teaching career. My knowledge of sex is probably less than what elementary school children learn from their sex education programs. It's you who lack the basics. But it doesn't matter one way or the other. Our love never depended on sex, not sex in the usual way anyway. It has nevertheless sustained me all this time. It will sustain us forever."

He wanted to protest but could not. His skepticism, his self-reproach, his sense of inadequacy yielded to an irrational, insane hope. Perhaps her faith was strong enough for both of them. The fictional, the absurd and preposterous, became credible, even compelling, a potent religious truth.

"By the way, Chanho has been working for some time on sex transplant and restoration with good results and wishes to see you most particularly. Your case is sort of his life mission. Perhaps you should oblige him. You cannot deny him this chance to square his score with God, can you?"

She burst out laughing, amused by her own extravagance of expression. Her laughter was infectious. He could not help smiling. He laid his hand on her shoulder. The touch thrilled him. He felt an access of confidence, a sense of power, physical, palpable, real.

"We're both crazy," he said, "and you most of all."

She snuggled up to him and leaned on his shoulder, her face beaming, tears rolling down her cheeks. No jewel had ever shone more beautifully.

The band played deafeningly. The whole floor heaved and danced. Feet thumped, hips swirled, arms swung, bodies bumped and thudded. To enter the lobby after so much jockeying and jostling was like reaching a calm haven. Walter Ross sat complacently at the front desk. He was most understanding when they canceled the room reservation and winked them good night and Merry Christmas.

132

A Regeneration

When I met Arin for the first time in Seoul in 1946, I had
no idea she would become such an important part of my life.
She was with her brother-in-law, Osol Cho. They had come to
Inchon by boat from Shinujoo, North Korea, during a week of
stormy seas. Overland passage was already quite impossible,
as the Russians had built permanent border fences and
patrolled them with combat vigilance. Osol produced a letter of
introduction from his father, a close friend of my father's from
college days.

"The letter does not mention my sister-in-law," said Osol, a
tall, lanky, handsome man, urbane but laconic. "She joined me
at the last minute."

Arin, a strikingly beautiful woman with clear skin, jet black
hair, broad forehead, and high cheek bones, dropped her eyes
to the floor apologetically. Her bearing and movement had a
natural grace, nobility, and tenderness, left unmarked by the
trials of the voyage. A similar easy elegance surrounded Osol's
person and demeanor. They seemed perfectly matched and it
was incredible that they should be related otherwise than as
man and wife. In dumb amazement I beheld her as though she
had been borne up and thrown ashore by the waves like the
wonderful mermaid of legend. Would it be possible to hope?

"You are both welcome," said my father without reservation.
"My house is yours."

Seoul was then literally bursting with people and the
housing shortage was acute, although later events were to
make the situation still worse. People poured in from all parts
of the country in search of opportunities, but the main influx
came from the north, risking their lives to cross the 38th
Parallel by land and sea. North Korean dialects could be heard
everywhere: in the hastily put-up huts on the hillsides, in the

stalls at the market-places, in the streets where they turned out in great numbers as peddlers. Our house was one of the fringe benefits of my father's chair in economics. Finding the management burdensome, the university had sold it to him at a nominal price. It was quite spacious, especially since there were only three of us, my mother having passed away some years before.

The guests were each given a spare room. My sister Meehee became close to Arin in a short time. They exchanged many confidences. Arin told her of the brutality rampant in the North, confirming previous reports, and denounced her own husband, Osa Cho, Osol's elder half-brother, as a rank Communist. This offended Meehee's notion of wifely loyalty, but she got over it fast: Arin couldn't be guilty of anything base. In fact, my sister worshipped her new friend and came home from school directly, cutting out her calls elsewhere, to be with her as much as possible. They talked on and on, seemingly on the most trivial subjects. In about a month's time Arin and Osol found a house in Wonnamdong and moved out. Osol was interned at the university medical center and Arin bought a tea shop with a dozen or so tables. I had scruples about wooing her while she was a guest at my house and intended to visit her after they had moved out, but my work at the newspaper kept me busy. It was a chaotic, event-filled period in Korea's history. The nation was in turmoil. Hardly a day passed without an assassination, a riot, or the birth of a new political party. While the North was congealing into an iron regime, the South was breaking up into a thousand splinters to underwrite American-style free democracy.

I met Arin and Osol again in 1950, a month or so before the war. They had asked my family and some friends of theirs over to celebrate Osol's passing the national board. I was eager to see Arin again. The intervening years had only magnified her image for me. I arrived there promptly. For some reason nobody else could come from my family and there were only two other guests, both friends of theirs who had come from the North with them in the same boat. Arin tried to put a cheerful face on it, but I could sense her disappointment. She must have spent days preparing all the food. One of the men, Wonso Shim, had taught history at a North Korean high school and was now selling locks and keys at the South Gate Market. He discoursed on the relative merits and shortcomings of various imperial powers and concluded with the inevitability of Japan's downfall: she never learned to utilize the local resources of occupied territory.

"When they took the Philippines, Malaysia, and Burma,

they had to bring in their own prostitutes," Shim said.

"By your argument," retorted the other man, Masoo Pang, "the Russians would make model imperialists. They're expert at living off the land and traveling light. All through the main transport routes the Rusky semen has been liberally sowed in Korean uteruses..."

Arin rose abruptly and bade us goodnight, saying she had to go to her shop to lock up. Osol excused himself, saying he would have to see her off. Wine went around among the three of us remaining. None of us was ready-witted enough to come up with a suitable topic, and Osol seemed to be gone for a long time. Shim and Pang looked shamefaced, like children caught in forbidden pranks, and kept drinking briskly. The drink finally relaxed them.

"How could you be so tactless?" Shim rebuked Pang.

"It just slipped my tongue," Pang said defensively. "But you started it all. I was merely reducing your argument to absurdity. We were talking on an abstract level, weren't we? I had no idea..."

He stopped and looked at me. Shim looked at me too and smiled sheepishly, then turned to Pang.

"I think we can be open to him. He's like family to them and ought to know."

Ignoring some cautioning signals from Pang, Shim said, "Osol's brother Osa is a commisar for Pyongbook Province. He was able to rise fast in the Communist hierarchy because he sold his wife to his Russian boss. He made the Russian come to his house and ravish her before his very eyes, they say."

"She had no choice but to flee South," Pang chimed in. "Word has it that Osa remarried right after her defection with Osol became known. Therefore she's technically free now. But in public they still act like in-laws, although it's obvious they really love each other."

It could have been the drink, but I felt my head swim and my grip on reality weaken. The part about her rape by the Russian didn't bother me at all. What did bother me was the idea of there being something between Arin and Osol. One to one, on even terms, I could scarcely be a rival to Osol; he had, besides, all the advantages. The gate of heaven was closing and receding beyond the horizon. I reproached myself for being tardy. Perhaps it had been closed always, and I'd had no chance from the beginning.

"That swine Osa never really appreciated what a beautiful woman he had, a pearl to a pig."

"They should admit their love for each other and get married. There's not a single law or man to stand between them.

135

But they act as correct and formal as two solemn diplomats."

On June 26, just one day after the war's outbreak, I was dispatched to the North by the company jeep flying the press flag, but the Third, Fifth, and Sixth Divisions guarding the Kaesong-Munsan corridor to Seoul, as well as other units along the entire front, had collapsed and a full-scale retreat or disintegration was on. At Ujongboo our jeep was commandeered by bayonet-wielding elements of the broken army, and the photographer got separated from me while we made our way on foot to Seoul, jostling along in the stream of frightened people fleeing from the battle, piggybacking their children, carrying bundles, and driving reluctant domestic animals. The boom and thunder of artillery shells became louder, and the rattle of machineguns was unnerving. It was a slow procession, hampered by numerous roadblocks and off-limits areas.

I reached Seoul on the 28th, late at night. The entire blacked-out city was in an uproar. People milled around like bees in a shaken beehive. Retreating military vehicles drove through and often over the crazed population, shooting at those in the way. They headed for the bridge over the Han at Kwangnaru and at Yongsan, only to find both of them dynamited by Syngman Rhee, the fleeing father of the Republic. The crowds surged forward in one direction, then swayed back, pushing, shouting, trampling. I went to the newspaper but found its doors and windows smashed and its printing press and storage rooms locked. The telephone didn't work. Only the old custodian was there, collecting some of his and perhaps other things. He informed me that the publisher had closed the building the day before and no employee had come around since. I went to my house near the university but couldn't find my father or sister. After waiting a few hours, losing count of the artillery and mortar bomb explosions in the rainy night sky, I decided they must have found transportation and crossed the river in time. I left the house and went to Mapo, the ferry point.

The approach was already congested. From the embankment people pressed to the water's edge. The overloaded boats mostly carried soldiers who warded off civilians with their rifles. Those with inflated tubes or makeshift rafts went into the river fighting the swift current, swollen by early summer rains. Others got pushed in or jumped in out of desperation, only to shriek back to the shore or be whisked off and disappear in the foaming water. Mortar bombs, presumably intended to destroy the fleeing army remnants, landed all along the river bank, butchering the exposed, unarmed civilians who scrambled in all directions in the darkness. The blood-curdling swoosh and crash of shells continued unremittingly. The smell of fresh carnage filled the air, mixing with the stink from the older corpses, maggot-infested and covered with flies fattened like soaked beans.

Trusting to my swimming prowess I chose a narrow bend of the river and waded in. Before I took five steps I couldn't touch the ground and felt the current rudely toss me midstream. The fetid water was murky and thick like a soup of mud and putrid, noisome matter that floated subsurface to bump, surprise, tangle, and disgust me. The quarter-mile width was lengthened tenfold, twentyfold, as I aimed for the opposite shore. Every stroke seemed to carry me further away, to sweep into the broadening mouth of the river emptying into Kanghwa Bay of the Yellow Sea. I had to concentrate on reaching the shore, no matter where, so long as it was on the south side. The river fanned out into dangerous shoals and rapids, but at last I felt ground and crawled up a bank, exhausted. It was Sosa, about ten miles downstream. The day was breaking.

Three months afterwards, in late September, I was back in Seoul with the Fifth US Marines who had landed in Inchon under MacArthur's "pincer" strategy. I wore a leatherneck uniform, naturally without any insignia, and enjoyed the emotional welcome and adoration of the pathetic population with their starved, ghostly, skeleton bodies. I felt no compunction about arrogating the liberator's uniform. I had earned the right. In a significant way I had done my bit in making the Inchon landing possible. After I reached Pusan, where refugees slept and cooked in the railway station lobbies, I got a job as interpretor-translator for the Eighth US Army Intelligence through my former newspaper connections. There was no thought of starting the newspaper in the new capital. Few of the staff had got away, and there was no possibility of importing a printing press through the transportation channels already clogged with military personnel and materiel.

Promptly I was paired with a commando leader, Captain Newberg, formerly of the merchant marine, with some unsavory trading activities to his credit in the Huk-infested waters of the Philippines and the pirate-teeming coasts of the Indonesian islands before he got "invited" by the US Navy. With five other volunteers from the Korean Navy we were dropped on Yonghung, one of the numerous islands surrounding Inchon, and proceeded to take over the island, which wasn't much of a problem. There were only a couple of recently appointed local gendarmes. They said they had been forced into their position because their relatives were in the South Korean army. To expiate for their collaboration they were zealously cooperative. They supplied us with all the vital information regarding the visiting schedule of mainland inspectors and shipping and navigating conditions in the treacherous channels among the shallows, mudbanks, and rocks of the Inchon archipelago. Our work was already half done. There was no lack of local assistance, as all these islanders were friendly and had no particular cause to espouse Communism.

Night after night we went out to take soundings of the proposed approaches of the invading armada and spent the days in transposing the findings onto the charts and radioing them to the Seventh Fleet cruiser lying to sea some twenty miles away. The project was not without danger. We momentarily expected an invasion of power launches from the mainland. Someone was bound to tip us off. Our only chance lay in keeping a sharp lookout and radioing out for assistance, while we fought the invaders off with our automatic weapons, small arms, and grenades. Naturally we had chosen our garrison atop the highest point of Yonghung, one side of which was a sheer cliff facing the mainland. The danger of our discovery and mainland attack increased as our operations expanded to the neighboring islands. The worst times were when fog set in and cut off all visibility. Towards the end our mission included sneaking past Wolmi Island, the threshold of Inchon, and looking for mines.

We encountered no floating mines, but one night at low tide we found the familiar horned dome of an anchored mine, sticking above water near the main channel. This jolted the planners of the landing operation, and we were told to intensify the mine spotting work. Luckily, there were only a few of them in a string, which were neutralized immediately before the first landing party set out. The Communists, either thinking the area too unlikely for a huge amphibious operation or because they were logistically unable, left the channels more or less mine-free. The last few nights prior to D-Day were spent in going up to the seawalls girding the city and measuring their heights from the water level.

The streets of Seoul were littered with downed telephone and power lines. Charred, crumbling walls stood gauntly, still smoking among heaps of smoldering rubble. A woman in tatters poked among a pile of roof tiles and burnt timbers. The headless body of a Communist soldier sprawled across the curb. Two children sat crying by their dead mother. The younger one, scarcely a year old, kept shaking her shoulder, while the older one about three, looked wildly about with swollen eyes and mouth, stretching a hand to passersby. An emaciated man, sallow-bearded, with no arms or legs, lay on his back. Through incessant hiccups that racked his taut rib cage he kept muttering for a transfusion. A girl of about five, blind, her feet burned away, stumbled down the street, falling repeatedly. A section of the Chonggye sewage drain was choked with hundreds of speared and clubbed bodies. An uncovered trench at Chongno was packed with about a thousand civilians, former South Korean police, government officials, and businessmen with their hands bound behind their backs and bullet holes in their brains.

My house had suffered a hit, and the two wings of the U shape with the bedrooms, studies and living rooms had collapsed, leaving only the base of the U, the passageway with the kitchen and the bathroom, minus windows and doors, blown-off tiles, and parts of the walls. Meehee was there with Arin and Osol, Pang and Shim. They had all been hiding in a tunnel dug out at the edge of our property under the flower bed. Communists had put Arin in jail for being a reactionary. All North Koreans who had come south after 1945 were prime targets of Communist vengeance. She was released, however, when Osol went to his brother, Osa, who had come to Seoul as a political officer holding colonel's rank and was in charge of propaganda and security in the city. Her arrest itself was later found to have been engineered by Osa's new wife, who resented her existence.

Osa had wasted no time in tracking down Osol and Arin and announcing his awesome presence as conqueror. His intention had been to punish the pair for disgracing him, and he was surprised and disappointed to find them living in the same house observing impeccable correctitude. He had expected them to be man and wife with two or three children. He had no excuse for venting his malice. Besides, Osol was working at his old hospital tending the wounded of the People's Army that increased in number daily despite the boastful wallposters announcing continuous victories and the imminence of national liberation. On the day of her release Osol went to thank Osa for his good offices. Osa laughed, pointing out the irony of his brother thanking him for freeing his own wife, then fell ferociously on Osol, demanding a confession of his adultery with his sister-in-law. Osol maintained his innocence, while Osa beat him senseless.

One day Osol was returning home late after a drink with the Communist supervisors at the hospital. It was raining. He turned at the alley near his house, soaked to the skin. Arin was waiting with an umbrella. Osol took the umbrella from

her and held it above her as they walked to the house. She
made him wash up and change into dry clothes. In the darkness their hands met and they embraced for the first time. She
sobbed. She had come to the end of the tether. They had either
to be lovers or to part. Osa had come to the house that day and
almost raped her. She'd managed to escape, but the trauma
had shown her the ridiculousness of their present position, the
folly of the barren years of their self-denial and restraint. Tast-
ing the sweetness of fulfillment after such a long delay, they
were reckless and ecstatic. They dared the whole world to try
and separate them.

But the morning with its air raid sirens and workaday
routine awakened them to the danger they were courting.
Osa's redoubled jealousy and desire for vengeance would fall
on them and crush them for sure. Arin went to Meehee for protection. Osol was not allowed to leave the hospital as the work
volume multiplied. The medical staff ate and slept there.
Finding Arin gone, Osa came to Osol and asked where she
was. Osol feigned ignorance and offered to help look for her if
he could be let out for the purpose. On the way to their house
in Osa's jeep there was a raid of dive bombers. In the ensuing
confusion Osol got away and came to our house.

"We tried everything to get Father out," Meehee said. "Dr. Cho
went to his brother and begged for his release, but it didn't work."

My father was taken under custody when he went to the
university a few days after the Communist takeover.
Everybody was ordered to return to work on pain of being
branded a reactionary for noncompliance. They would have
come for him sooner or later. His place of detention was a cut
above other jails and concentration camps, as it held South
Korean notables, including members of the parliament whom
Rhee had never trusted and had not informed as to the real
state of the war or his intended move across the river. Their
Communist captors treated them decently at first. They hoped
to win their voluntary cooperation in the form of recantatory
statements and broadcasts or active participation in the party
and army administration. Failing in this, hospitality turned
into systematic torture, especially as the war went worse for
them. My father was finally confined in a damp, unventilated
basement with a dozen other broken men. With the US
Marines near at hand, the Communists marched them off with
their retreating forces. If anybody couldn't keep up and fell by
the roadside, the escorting lieutenant made short work of him
with a single rifle shot.

"I'm sorry I couldn't be of any help," Osol spoke, his face
the picture of self-reproach and misery. I darted a fierce glance

at the pair, Arin and Osol, whose adulterous relationship had consigned my father to his untimely death, somewhere, like a dog in a nameless ditch, while they stood in front of me, starved and sickened perhaps but alive.

I had to leave them for now as my jeep was waiting and I had already overstayed my allowed time. Our detachment moved with the advancing front. I couldn't incorporate my personal cause into the Eighth US Army intelligence work, but when feasible I made inquiries, interrogating prisoners and calling the returning police and civilian authorities about the fate of transportees. These efforts revealed nothing. When I next returned to Seoul I found Arin at our house. I cursed the sight of the woman. Why did she not go back to her own place to indulge her unholy passion for her brother-in-law?

"Dr. Cho is now held by the South Korean police for collaboration and will probably be shot unless you do something," Meehee said with great concern.

I made no reply.

"You've got to get him out," Meehee said, shaking my shoulder. "They've got the wrong man."

"They have?" I asked testily.

"Don't you understand he had to? Otherwise they would have made him shoulder a rifle and fight against the UN forces. No male adult escaped. Besides, without his working for them we wouldn't be alive today. We all depended on him."

I looked at Meehee in surprise. The food ran out in a week and she'd had to barter off everything, watches, jewelry, clothes, utensils, furniture, bedding, for food at ridiculously unfair rates in the open markets. Apparently all of Osol's rice rations from the hospital went directly to our house for the feeding of its occupants. After calling the right places I went to the East Gate Police Station where Osol had been under interrogation. The captain, signing the release paper, protested mildly, saying he had reports of Osol being an undercover agent with high North Korean connections. Osol thanked me as we left the jail. I resented his being so tall and handsome, although hollow-cheeked and haggard from his latest experience.

"I am surety for your good behavior," I said stiffly. "In return you are expected to enlist and go to the front right away."

He nodded. His legs moved heavily but he carried his head upright. I am still ashamed and bewildered by the intensity of the strange, irrational hatred I felt for him then. I sincerely wished that he would be struck down by the first stray bullet as he marched in a squad of infantry. But the recruiting officer was more intelligent. Osol was commissioned a medical officer and was dispatched to a battalion aid station with the 25th Korean Division.

Arin's tea shop and house had been demolished. After cleaning out the basement and covering it with sticks, boards, and rice-straw mat weighted down with stones and bricks, she managed to erect a shelter of sorts. On returning home one day at dusk from the South Gate marketplace where she peddled chewing gum, cigarettes, chocolate and other American-made goods, she found Osol waiting. Jumping into his arms and crying hysterically, she led him into their dugout bower. They had until 3 a.m. next morning; he had to catch his transportation to a new unit at four. She didn't want him to leave. A fellow peddler in the marketplace had told her how her husband's effects had been delivered to her: a sweat-begrimed handkerchief, a pack of cigarettes, a worn wallet in an envelope. She wouldn't have known them to be his, except for a faded photograph of her she had given him. Arin had been afraid that Osol would come to her only as effects in an envelope. Osol tried to tell her that being a medical officer in a relatively rearward area, his chances of being killed were now pretty remote, but she urged him to desert, to go into hiding for the rest of the war. Not being able to persuade him, she had to be content with giving him a photograph of them together and taking down his unit number and location. He suspected that she might try to visit him and told her never to attempt it. Civilians were off limits to the frontline areas, still full of uncleared mines and guerrilla activities.

After a few days, disregarding his command, Arin went to look for him in the front, walking most of the way and dodging checkpoints. She finally arrived at his hospital at night. The sentries couldn't believe their eyes on seeing a female civilian and were ready to shoot her as an enemy agent. They called the operating room.

Osol was amputating the fractured and gangrened leg of a private. They had run out of ether and the patient had to go through the operation unanesthetized. He fainted repeatedly but regained consciousness quickly to scream and writhe with pain. Osol was indignant at the irregularity and shortage of medical supplies. Without proper treatment the private would die a horrible racking death, like ninety percent of the amputees.

He came to the front gate. Borrowing some blankets from the guards he took Arin outside the compound to an abandoned bunker. They cleaned up the place, padded the floor with dry rushes and straws, then spread the blankets. The destruction and mutilation raging outside broke like impotent

142

surf against the fortification.

The Red Chinese entered the war that winter, and the UN forces, caught unprepared in their headlong rush to the Yalu, the Manchurian border, got encircled and routed on all fronts. Mutilated, mangled bodies piled in at the evacuation hospital. The operating table was like a butcher's chopping block. Most of the hastily amputated and treated patients, lacking transfusions or antibiotics, died soon of the shock or lingered on painfully as the unchecked infection spread through the rest of the body. Osol was to put together, patch up, make sense of the disgorgings of a giant meat grinder, deliberately and efficiently set to work by scientific brains, industrial powers, national budgets. They were the same Korean flesh, torn to bits, that he had cut into, gouged out, or sewed up in the summer. The only difference was that now the cold weather stopped the putrefaction, but the stink was replaced by frostbite. The casualties arriving at the hospital were still wearing summer uniforms with no underwear. When their feet were unshod, the toes were apt to break off, frozen fast to the soles. Even so, those who made it to the hospital were the lucky ones. Many were simply abandoned on the hills or by the wayside to freeze in the subzero temperatures. The retreating lines of men, themselves limping from hunger, wounds, and cold, passed by them, not heeding their feeble, piteous cries for help or their frozen extended arms. A dead jaw was hanging by skin to a mustachioed face. Gold gleamed on the teeth, a fine piece of dentistry with clever crownings and intricate bridgework. Osol reflected on the weeks of drilling, molding, fitting, and filing that must have gone into it, only to be shattered by a mortar fragment. He felt his own facial muscles go numb. He couldn't bite the frozen ball of rice that was brought to him for his meal. The grim irony immobilized him.

That night the commandant of the hospital, Colonel Lee, asked him and others on the staff to a restaurant in a nearby town. They drank and ate into the small hours. As the party was breaking up, the colonel took Osol to one side and handed him an envelope full of bank notes. Simultaneously he asked Osol to drop the inquiry he had instituted about the quota of medical supplies for the hospital. The whole truth dawned on Osol at once: the colonel had been thieving medicine and equipment, condemning poor boys to miserable deaths. He threw the envelope in his face and declared his intention to prosecute him.

The next morning he was arrested by MP's on charges of insubordination and disorderly conduct. The MP captain appeared later with a compromise: the charges would be dropped if Osol applied for transfer to a frontline aid station. Osol was indignant and wanted to pursue the matter to the death, but when a colleague of his, whom he had liked and taken into confidence before, came and told him that the commandant's actions had been for the good of a whole lot of other people as well, Osol realized the futility of his struggle. The corruption was too deep-rooted and widespread. He signed the transfer request but didn't have to go far as his hospital moved south while the frontline aid station came retreating to his area.

I was then in the northeastern front with the beleaguered US X Corps at Changjin Reservoir. The Marines were still slugging their way to traverse the sixty air miles through the narrow gorges, hairpin turns, treacherous defiles of the Tabak Range, its hills crawling with two Chinese field armies, to reach Hamhung Harbor for redeployment by the waiting ships. My intelligence detachment was airlifted to Ujongboo. I was working on some captured North Korean documents, when Captain Osborne told me to go over to a nearby American medical unit to quell some disturbance. A prostitute refused to be inoculated and was threatening to shoot herself and the medical orderly with the pistol she had snatched from him. The person in question, hair disheveled and half crazed, was Arin.

She had come to the area vaguely hoping to be near Osol's regiment and to buy her merchandise at more favorable rates directly from the GI whores. In a periodical roundup for inoculation, American MP's wielding clubs had come and packed her with others into a truck. When her turn came to go alone into a compartment with an American soldier, she had reacted violently. She wouldn't listen to explanations from the Korean interpreter or the girls who had all taken their shots and watched the scene with amusement. Fortunately, she still had enough sense to recognize me, and the Americans had to take my word that she needed no inoculation.

When we were alone, I asked her if Osol knew she was there. She said she had seen Osol not too long ago, just before his transfer to the Seventh Division, but he didn't know she was still at Ujongboo, which was as close as she could come to the front. I arranged transportation for her to Seoul so she could go to Meehee and stay with her, promising to come soon to take them both south. The order for the evacuation of the general populace had not been issued yet, but I knew it was coming. As events turned out, I couldn't keep my promise; my detachment had to fly to Taygoo on an urgent mission. There was no way to send them word. The situation had deteriorated rapidly as the main Eighth US Army command abandoned the third line of defense at Hayjoo. The next and perhaps last line of resistance was drawn at Pyongtak, thirty miles south of Seoul.

Meehee and Arin waited for my arrival until the last minute and almost didn't make it. Panic seized the city. Frightening rumors of Red Chinese brutalities and North Korean reprisals circulated. One's very being in South Korea, while the Communists had fled to the north, was incriminating enough. Hadn't they cheered the arriving UN forces as their liberators? Everybody was sure that they would be killed as reactionary collaborators. Besides, it was winter. They remembered the hunger of summer, despite the vegetables, acorns, wild berries and the crops of that season. It was easy to imagine what it would be like when the land became snow-covered and frozen.

The snow piled inches deep on Meehee and Arin's bundles, on their heads and shoulders. They had to run from one railway track to another. The marshaling yard was one milling, scampering, churning humanity. Dozens got run over while taking shortcuts under the trains. Still people kept crawling under them, under the very cars with bodies stretched from the wheels like fish on a hook. They waited and ran and waited and ran, unable to sleep. A train might leave any minute and they had to be ready, at the right spot.

After being pushed around in the scurrying crowd, without sleep for three days and nights, Arin began to see strange shapes dancing before her. The snowflakes turned into flower petals. The bleak scenery, the screech of trains, all turned into a harmonious sweet spring afternoon, a fragrant hillside with newgrown grass back at home in Shinujoo, soft and warm to the touch. All she wished to do was to luxuriate in it, to sleep forever.

Meehee woke her up. A train, consisting of coaches, coal cars, gondolas, and stakes, stood right before them. There was a desperate rush. They ran to the coaches, pulling each other along, but there was no getting near the doors. At the windows, smashed open, people pulled and clawed at each other to get in first. The gondolas, loaded with tanks, guns, and armored trucks, swelled up fast, like leavened dough. People fitted their bundles under and around the vehicles and barricaded themselves in the middle. There was a body under one gondola, dragged a few yards along the rail, the skull crushed under the massive wheel, the brains spilt out and frozen. People paid no attention, stepped right over it and climbed on.

Meehee and Arin tried to climb on to the roof of a coach, but the level center ridge was already filled with rows of people and bundles. Some put ropes around the ventilation holes and hung on to the convex slopes. The stake car Arin and Meehee finally managed to get near was already filled to the brim, at least ten feet high. People pitched their bundles and themselves in furiously. Still people were climbing on. They had scarcely settled one minute, squeezed between people and bundles, when a woman next to them screamed. Her child had been squashed to death under the bundles. But her wail was drowned by the whistle of the train, signaling departure. The crowd on the platform, which had kept growing, became frantic. More bundles flew in overhead and people clung to the edge, unable to climb in. Many got trodden underfoot and children got separated from their parents. Nobody heard their piercing cries in the general uproar.

The train moved out at a snail's pace, making innumerable stops on the way. It stood on sidetracks at small country stations, while the locomotive detached itself and went off to pull others. The refugees shivered sometimes for a whole day, exposed to the weather in the middle of a snow-swept plain. The sharp wind numbed their hands and feet and froze their breath. One night as the train turned a curve several fell off the slanting sides of a coach roof, but there was of course no stopping the train, moving after so long a delay, to pick up the unfortunates. It took six days to reach Tayjon, where the train seemed abandoned for good in the yard.

On the second night of standing still, in blinding snow and unremitting cold, Arin and Meehee decided to explore for another train. They found one nearby with a puffing locomotive hitched to it. There was no need to inquire about its destination: all vehicles headed south. Finding a boxcar full of oil drums, they went in, closed the door after them, and settled in a corner, ready to sleep in the protection of the four walls. Big striding steps came crunching the snow outside and stopped before the door. An American soldier slid it open, vaulted in, and came right up to the corner where the two women stood petrified with fear. He flashed a light in their faces and tried to hug them both. Arin whispered that she would bite the assailant's arm, so Meehee could run out the door and call for help. In the crisis Meehee could not think or argue. She grabbed at the chance of her own escape, bolted out of the GI's released grasp, jumped off the car, and ran blindly, tripping and falling in the slippery snow. She stopped panting before a warehouse. Only then did she remember that Arin was left behind alone to deal with the American. She tried to locate her old train, but instead she bumped back to the spot where the other train had been. The track was empty.

When I met Meehee in Taygoo, she was distraught with shame and guilt. She expected the worst had happened to Arin and blamed herself for it. She was determined to find Arin and make amends. Though she went to all likely places, railway stations, refugee settlements, at Taygoo, Pusan, and other cities, her search disclosed no clue to Arin's whereabouts.

A few months later Seoul was back in UN control and the citizenry began to trickle back in. Meehee went there to look for Arin at her old hangouts. Her makeshift basement had caved in and had not been visited or lived in. Meehee decided to look for Osol's medical unit, thinking that he might be able to tell where Arin was. Thanks to the special passes I had arranged, she was able to locate it but found that Osol, now a Captain, had been wounded in a mortar bomb fire and was in a convalescent hospital at Pohang.

The hospital was somebody's former villa by the sea. Its grassy lawn had pleasant walks among tall spruces and junipers and bordered the white sand of the beach. The breeze from the sea was refreshing. The beach, formerly full of idly sunning vacationers, romping children, and splashing swimmers, was now deserted. The hospital was quiet, although all the rooms were filled with occupants. In Osol's room a major with no arm had to be spoon-fed by the nurse. A captain had a broken spine and, paralyzed from the waist down, had to carry a rubber bag that had been installed in his chair beneath his rectum. Another patient had lost a lung and panted and sweated just to get off his bed. Still another had a hose stuck in a hole in his throat. Osol was confined to a wheel chair. He had lost both his legs. His head, bald with red shiny skin, had a few blotches of hair. His eyelids had been burned and shriveled and did not close the unseeing eyes, even when he slept. His lips had been burnt off, exposing the teeth and gums. No matter how hard he tried to close them, he only tugged at the tight, thick-healed skin. A bib caught the constantly dripping saliva.

"You cannot see Captain Osol Cho," said the clerk at the reception desk. "He doesn't want to see anybody."

"Please let me see him," Meehee pleaded. "I've come a long way just to see him."

"Sorry, ma'am," the clerk said. "We have to respect the patient's feelings. Even his wife hasn't been allowed to see him all this time."

"His wife?" she exclaimed.

It must be Arin, the object of her search. As far as she knew, Arin had had no chance to marry him, but what woman had a better claim to that title?

"Yes," said the clerk. "If you stick around a little longer, you'll see her because she comes here daily, at about this time in fact, though each time we tell her the same thing."

In a little while Arin stepped into the hallway and, not noticing Meehee's presence, advanced toward the receiving desk with grim determination, her eyes fixed on the clerk's face.

"Arin!" Meehee cried and threw herself in Arin's arms, weeping bitterly.

Why did it have to happen to her, the sweetest, the best, the most beautiful person? Meehee berated God. There was no good or bad, no meaning or purpose in life. One should cheat, lie, murder infants, betray parents. It was Arin that took the comforter's role. She thought herself lucky. Osol was alive and would never be taken away from her again. When he felt strong enough to leave the hospital, they would make a nice home somewhere. She would run a shop of some sort and he could turn to crafts. He should be good at it because he had unerring hands. In his numerous operations he had never made a mistake. His touch, sharpened by the loss of guiding sight, would be even keener and more artistic. Besides, he could look after their baby. She was pregnant, was quite well along and expected soon. Osol knew about it and would like to handle the child when it came. He would have to let her come and see him then, if not before.

Toward the time of her confinement Meehee went to Pohang to Arin's boarding house near the hospital. Osol had been apprised of it and asked to be told of the delivery right away. It was a difficult birth. The labor lasted two days, nearly killing both mother and child. It was a daughter with Negroid features which her Oriental side could not quite suppress. Arin had fallen into an exhausted sleep when the struggle was over. There was a phone call from the convalescent hospital. It was Osol. Meehee told him that it was a girl, seven and a half pounds. He thanked her, gave his love to the mother and child, and hung up. He sounded calm and contented.

Meehee shuddered at the prospect of informing him that he wasn't the father of the baby, whom both he and Arin had wanted so much. Perhaps they could bluff it out with him. Yes, why not? He was providentially blind. Don't tell him anything. Tell him the child looked like him. Every child looks

148

like an adult somewhere. They are all homo sapiens. No touch, however discerning, could possibly distinguish the color. Thank God the baby's hair was straight. As for the shape of the nose, the curl of the mouth, the ears and cheeks, touch was too detailed, too individuating, she thought, to perceive the generic type. The thought lightened her steps, but as she approached Arin's ward her heart grew heavy again to think of the crushing effect of the knowledge on the mother. Meehee contemplated switching the baby with another. There were plenty of unwanted infants everywhere. Maybe there were some born at that very hospital. She went to the director's office, but he was out.

For a long time Arin couldn't bring herself to look at the baby or feed her. She was deaf to Meehee's proposals and lay on her bed, speechless and unresponsive. The next morning Meehee was surprised to find her up already, stroking the child and feeding her. She even smiled at Meehee.

"I'll take the baby to him today and tell him everything," Arin said.

"But you can't leave the hospital," Meehee said, stalling for time to dissuade her from the fantastic idea. "The doctor won't allow it. You've lost quite a bit of blood and are in no condition to be traipsing around, holding a baby in your arms."

"She is light. I must go to him at once. He must be told."

"He's been told already."

"Everything?" Arin asked.

Meehee hesitated under her intense scrutiny.

"I am glad," Arin said smiling. "I want to be the one to tell him. I'll bring the baby with me so he can hold her himself. The baby has done nothing wrong. She is my passport now. The clerk will let me come and see him now. Nobody, nothing can stand in our way. Osol will understand and love the baby like his own. He's that kind of a guy."

When they arrived at the convalescent hospital, the reception clerk told them Osol had disappeared that morning. He was last seen going to bed the night before, but the orderly making the early morning rounds found him missing. They looked all over the hospital and in the neighborhood, but there was no trace of him or his wheelchair. The authorities were completely baffled. They had checked the sand, but there was no mark on it. He could have erased the tracks as he pushed himself along, so they searched the nearby waters but came up with nothing. They even suspected some kidnapping plot and were just about to contact the relatives. Arin collapsed. Meehee caught the baby just before she dropped off her mother's hands.

Arin knew that they would never be able to find him. She had vaguely feared something like this might happen. He had been postponing it until the baby's birth for her sake. Osol had talked about the despair and hopelessness of the seriously wounded, those crippled and impaired beyond repair, doomed to wretched dependence and degrading vegetation for the rest of their lives. The courageous among them sought release from it but were so clumsy at it that they got caught beforehand or did such a messy job that they only worsened their plight. If it were him, he would do a clean, perfect job of it. He would incinerate himself completely or weight himself down with lead to the bottom of the sea so no living soul could see his damaged body. He couldn't bear to be seen otherwise than in the prime of health, in his full physique. She had then laughed the whole idea off as absurd. Yet she had felt a shudder and had to hug him hard to be reassured by the warmth and firmness of his body.

For days Arin refused to eat or sleep. She stayed in her room, bunched up in a corner, in autistic stupor. She didn't seem to hear or see. I had her brought to Seoul and sought medical assistance, but none was available. When whole chunks of the human body, smashed and rotting, go untreated, it is almost criminal luxury and egotism to complain of mental disorders. The Eighth US Army had a psychiatric detachment but no amount of argument qualified her admission. They had their hands full with shell-shocked GI's. However, following the advice of one of the psychiatrists there, I proceeded to take steps to transport her to the United States. The Immigration and Naturalization Service hadn't forgotten my services and made things easy. Of course I had to marry her. The legal side of marrying someone incapable of knowing what she was doing posed no problem when I had cooperative officials on my side.

As I watched her improve in the war-free, benign climate of Hawaii, I grew to love her more than anything else in the world. I couldn't imagine a life without her. Why hadn't I come to this realization and done something about it sooner? Yet this one-sided infatuation tormented me with anxieties and doubts. How would she react to her changed status as my wife when she recovered her full faculties? She might despise me for having taken unfair advantage of her. I was prepared to give her a divorce at the slightest sign of her displeasure. The uncertain prospect made me dread her recovery as much as I wanted it.

The day finally came when the doctor, with deserving pride in his accomplishment, told me that she could go home. I thanked him and left his office with mixed feelings, proceeding to the waiting room. Her back was turned to me as she gazed out the window overlooking Kaneohe Bay. There was an air of composure and peace gracing her whole person. Her long hair hung loosely down her supple, curving back. Her face was a little pale, but her lips were rosy and her eyes shone with their usual sparkle. She smiled enchantingly. I went to her and held her hand gratefully. On the way home to our apartment we talked unhurriedly about the surf breaking along the shoreline, the cattle grazing in the meadows, the palms swaying in the wind. We stopped at the roadside to look better at the blazing sunset on the horizon.

She has never since mentioned Osol. Our daughter Anna has passed the junior orchestra audition for the Honolulu Symphony and performs violin solos with them. We have two other children, but there is no half-sister problem, inevitable in Korea where people are obsessed by genealogy. I am supremely a product of that culture. I recall my wonder at American families adopting biologically unrelated children and loving them like their own. Most amazing was the adoption of lepers' children, susceptible though not affected, most of them in their teens, who were nevertheless refused admission to public schools and were shunned and ostracized in Korea, their homeland. This touched me deeply. I would never be able to extend myself that far, however I might idealize and absorb the Christian love of fellowmen.

My acceptance and love of Anna has no such lofty motivation. She is simply Arin's daughter, the flesh and blood of the person dearest to me, and is therefore my own, too. I thank God that we live in Hawaii, the literal melting pot of the races. A girl with black features would be such a scandal that she would never lead a normal life in Korea and perhaps in some parts of America. The fact that neither Arin nor I am black attracts no particular attention here: nearly half of Anna's classmates have step-parents, often of different nationalities.

The very word, *kayboo*, 'step-father' in Korean, has the most unsettling connotations—emasculation, the image of a spineless good-for-nothing grafting on another man's leavings, the litter and dam. However strong my love for Arin might be, I don't think it would have survived the obloquy, the inevitable attrition over the years in a climate like Korea's where we would all be outcasts, pariahs. I am simply not that strong. In spite of my seeming independence, I am a highly social creature, who cannot live without the approval and good opinion of my fellowmen.

Now I am a step-father, with a vengeance, but I don't agonize over it, and I have to thank the high rate of divorce in this country. Who would have thought I would be the beneficiary of divorce American-style, which I used to abhor and denounce? I seem to accept and even applaud it, perhaps because my own marriage is solid and I can look upon the personal trauma and social disruption divorce entails with equanimity. To the more morally discerning, therefore, my thoughts on this matter may appear callous, egotistic sophistry. But no matter what the moralists or social reformers may say or do, divorce is not going to go away in a society like ours with mating guaranteed among its constitutional liberties. Shouldn't we join them, if we can't lick them, as the adage says? Maybe America owes divorce what little measure of freedom from blood and genes that it enjoys over other countries. Rather than weakening or eroding, as many fear, the easy accessibility of divorce strengthens and dignifies marriage and family.

What is the price of the low divorce rate, the so-called stability of the family-oriented Korean home but massive institutionalized adultery, especially on the part of the husband, who is considered unmasculine if he cannot boast a string of mistresses? Moreover, recent reports indicate that the liberated wife is quickly catching up with her husband in versatility and effrontery. Stability be damned! The American way of easy divorce is honest and straightforward. It's above board, a clean way of doing things. The partners involved choose to stay together. It voluntarizes and humanizes the relationship. There is no inexorable bondage of the genetically-bound biological litter. We have a community of discriminating beings reaching out for the suprabiological, the spirit, if you please. Perhaps psychoanalysts may attribute my eagerness to defend our family structure to some basic subconscious insecurity in me about the situation, but then they'll have to argue that Jesus was insecure at heart to have preached so much.

Exile

I wasn't too surprised when Deacon Shim asked me to a lunar New Year party at his house: somebody in the congregation was bound to make an occasion of it. This was the seventh party I'd had to attend in a month since the regular New Year's at the pastor's. Just bring yourself, they said. I didn't have to bring any food. At the door I presented my usual calling card, an envelope with a check enclosed, which the host accepted with a sigh of relief after the customary remonstrances and protests.

It all began last year, when Pastor Hwang came to the farm, smiling, speaking in a mellifluous Korean. I have no idea how he got my address. These pastors have a ferret's instinct for rooting out their targets. I didn't have a phone then, and I had assiduously avoided any association with my countrymen. Not only for the usual reason of self-hatred, which is said to be very strong among Koreans. And you can't blame them, either. Korea, with its succession of incompetent, cruel, egotistic rulers, had not been much of a mother to her children. Shame, revulsion, bitter disillusionment were the primary emotions she had inspired and ingrained. And so long as Syngman Rhee and his henchmen enjoyed the support of America, the country where fortune had cast me adrift, I had more particular reasons to hide.

With the pastor's visit, the quarter century of exile from my countrymen came to an end. My farm now crawled with Koreans, buying boxfuls of vegetables as if they had never seen them before. They came from Pearl Harbor, Hawaii Kai, even Waipahu, not considering the expenditure of gas and time that would more than offset the bargain. But then they are not known to be the most rational businessmen. I couldn't have cared less for their trade. Selling to wholesalers was much more efficient and ultimately more profitable. Sure I got more money per pound, and the cash income, a dollar here and another there, need not be reported, but I had to interrupt my work to accommodate them individually. Seldom did they come just for the produce; they took upon themselves the task of filling me with a lot of unsolicited information, the gossip of the Korean community.

I learned that there were about seven thousand Korean immigrants in Honolulu, most of whom had a female relative married to an American GI during the war, now divorced and operating a bar. Many lied about their income and lived in the disreputable government housing at Linapuni or Kalihi until after five years or so of saving they bought a house or a condominium, forever after to denounce the immorality of the American welfare system.

There were about fifteen churches of all denominations vying for aggrandizement. The pastors sought out newcomers or stole members from each other with favors; in turn, people took advantage and hopped from church to church, not overstaying the hospitality of any one place. There were also the professionals, University of Hawaii professors, medical doctors, dentists, engineers, lawyers, accountants, who would have nothing to do with their inferior compatriots but whom the pastors sought after with obsequious flattery. Although it was a well-known fact that these self-made men were tight-fisted and believed in getting ten dollars back for every one they laid on the collection plate, their membership enhanced the church's stature. They came to dinners and picnics strictly as guests. The tithes and special offerings came from the lowly bar girls, hotel cleaners, restaurant operators.

Pastor Hwang's interest in me was therefore more substantial than prestigious. My three-acre farm was probably as productive as twenty acres elsewhere; the subtropical weather allowed recropping throughout the year. I was in the fifty per cent or higher income tax bracket, despite all the business deductions my ingenious bookkeeper could devise. As the pastor was not slow to point out, my generous contributions to the church would be more than compensated by the tax credits they would earn. So I'd joined and in record time was made a ruling elder. With the honor came the dues. When they decided to purchase the pipe organ, all eyes turned to me. Whenever there was a wedding, a funeral, or a birthday—and their occurrence was frequent and unending—they invited me most cordially, expectantly. They felt no compunction about openly asking me for this subsidy or that, now that I wore the title. No royalty could have sold its dukedoms more dearly.

The main course was over, broiled short ribs of beef. Deacon Cho, the jeweler, observed that the motherland showed signs of unification. North Korea had agreed to meet with South Korea to work out the details of electing a pan-Korea congress. Unification would never be realized, rose the skeptic's voice of Deacon Koo, the realtor. We shouldn't trust the rhetoric of politicians. On the contrary, retorted Deacon Lee, the upholsterer. The division of Korea was a purely external imposition; the power vacuum after Japan's withdrawal had to be filled by America in the south and Russia in the north. But during the Korean War Russia was edged out as Red China moved in to fight the Americans. China and America were now friends. A neutral peninsula was to the advantage of everybody concerned, he argued. Deacon Shim, our host, suggested that the moment Korea was unified, we should all pack up and return.

"Would they feed us?" asked Deacon Pyo, the auto body man.

"What kind of life is this that we have here?" snapped Deacon Chong, who worked as custodian at a Waikiki hotel but never lost an opportunity to remind others of the prosperous textile business he had had in Pusan. "My inwards twist several times a day to see these Japanese and Filipinos bossing over us. Caucasians are okay, but these second-generation Orientals are unbearable. Just because they came a few years ahead of us..."

"They sure kick us around," said Hishik Ho, part-owner of a bar. "Remember the dirt they threw at us in *The Advertiser* about Korean bars? Those lies about us fleecing customers? They can get away with anything because we cannot strike back."

"We need political power," said Byongho Lee, who had a Korean music and dance studio in town. "There isn't a single Korean in the state or city government."

"But there are other opportunities," interrupted Pyo. "One can be a scientist, doctor, businessman."

"They are all secondary," opined Professor Suh. "To be politically thwarted, even if fulfilled in every other respect, is like emasculation. We are living in a political limbo."

"I don't know about that," Pyo persisted. "I would be a millionaire anytime, even if I never got anywhere near a government office."

"Cite me a single millionaire who has made it without politics," pursued Suh. "Can you operate a body shop without going to the regulatory agencies, for example?"

155

This clinched the point. Everybody remembered going through irksome paperwork for business registration and inspection, filing financial statements, exhibits, balance sheets, all in confounded English.

"It boils down to having more children," said John Shin, who operated a gift and jewelry cart at Duke's Lane. "It is a patriotic duty. But you know how difficult it is to have a child. Between preschool and babysitters, our three-year-old is a four-hundred-dollar-a-month liability. I don't think I'll have another one even if he should be the next president of the United States."

"But what kind of life are we giving our children?" asked Deacon Lee. "Back home as children we thought of becoming president, congressman, general. I ask my son what he wants to be and he replies fireman. What kind of ambition is that?"

"They work short hours, retire early, make good money," said Pyo.

"What's a dollar more or less? When Korea gets united, I'll go," Lee declared vehemently.

"Me, too," said Ho. "Without the language I am an awkward clown here."

Everybody had a grievance or two against the new country of their adoption and seemed impatient for repatriation. For endorsement of the general sentiment they turned to the pastor who had sat aloof during the conversation. Somebody urged him to recount his Korean War experience. The pastor demurred at first but gave in. However, as he began from 1944, the year of his father's death as a forced laborer on Guam, even those who had steered him into this course were dismayed. He was a draftee in the North Korean People's Army, fought the South Korean forces and their allies, and was captured by the Americans in October 1950, shortly after MacArthur's Inchon landing and the collapse of the North Korean army. After three years of detention he was finally released as an anti-Communist POW. When the narration reached his conversion to Christianity and his eventual ordination, several hasty amens and hallelujahs went up, depriving him of the opportunity to draw some moral lessons, as was his wont. People got up, refilled glasses and plates, broke into twos and threes. This, however, must have portended to the orderly mind of our Deacon Cho the advent of anarchy to be averted at all costs.

"Does it mean you won't be going back to the united fatherland?" he shouted, edging up to the pastor by the buffet table, craning his head, dodging or shoving the people in the way. The concourse around the food was so thick and defensive that the pastor couldn't have been in a safer sanctuary. Finding himself unheard and next to me, the jeweller seized my arm.

"Grandfather," he said. He never called me anything else. "We should hear your story. Don't you have relatives back home? Quiet, everybody!"

Luckily, the hubbub drowned his shouts and clappings. In the meantime I had escaped to the lanai. The chilly night air had driven everybody inside. Waikiki blazed in the distance like a country girl's first night on the town. Her highrises, bedecked in multicolored, twinkling lights, defied the looming darkness of the Pacific behind. Suddenly, I felt lonely and old. The hollow feeling that grabbed my stomach spread and touched my heart. It could be any day now. Already I had outlived in age my parents and grandparents. I had the feeling that mine would be a sudden, no lingering, demeaning death. Instinctively I stroked my arm under the short sleeve. The goose flesh was bumpy to the touch. Who would mourn me? Would there be any trace of me after, say, ten years? My estate, intestate, would revert to the state, and my little tombstone, if there was one, would disfigure and crumble. I wondered where Yongmee might be. Was she divorced for the second or third time and operating a bar like the rest? Or was she a respectable matron with sons and daughters, maybe even grandchildren?

* * *

I saw her last as a passenger in the front seat of an American military jeep in Seoul thirty years ago. My bus lurched dangerously to a stop, making the curve by South Gate, its usual overload of passengers falling and piling like dominoes. While squelched under the weight of those on top of me, I saw the jeep drive up along the side right under the window. She was wearing dark sunglasses. The American soldier bent over and put his arm around her. The people in the bus straightened up. Oblivious to their own discomfiture, they smiled, feeling superior to this Jezebel, the fallen and untouchable. There was no trade lowlier than being a GI whore. They giggled, exchanging coarse jokes, loud enough for my sister's benefit. Some affected magnanimity and said her kind was good for the country's economy: the export dollars were 100 per cent net earnings as her ware didn't cost anything.

"Not entirely," a judicious wag pointed out. "Look at

157

her get-up. That must have cost her a pretty penny."

"Her honey gives that too," the trade expert said.
"She must wear something, no matter what she is."

Yongmee sat erect and unflinching, staring fiercely into
the space ahead. I sweated, squirmed, and wished I could
disappear and erase the memory of it. It was painful. I saw
only the shame and ugliness of prostitution, never the beauty
or love. I blamed myself for everything, for not taking care
of her and Mother properly. As the heir and namebearer of the
family, it was my duty to shelter and feed the women. I had
to do something fast, however desperate or irregular. Mother
must have suspected all along what Yongmee was doing and
got sicker every day. Yongmee moved out and soon stopped
coming home altogether.

Then, a year or so later in the Pusan refugee swarms of
July 1950, I ran into her friend Hesook. She told me that
Yongmee was in America and had written her about my
whereabouts. My papers had been ready and I should go at
once to the American consulate. Hesook had been about to
advertise in the papers. Relieved that she had not done so yet,
I asked her whether anybody had come to her asking for me.
She said no. After some hesitation I went to the U.S.
Consulate, disguised as an old cripple. Surprisingly, things
went fast and I was on the plane bound for America. Till the
last minute, however, even after the Northwest Airlines
DC-4 had taxied out and speeded up for takeoff, I momentarily
expected it to be stopped and Kwak's men to board the plane
to get me. Only when we left Haneda, did I savor the reality
of my deliverance. Luxuriating in the velvet of the seat, I
slept as I had never slept before.

It was a new world that I woke to in Honolulu, where
the immigration procedure was completed. The ticket was for
New York where Yongmee was waiting, but I decided to
get off at Honolulu. Perhaps I was paranoid, but I felt I
couldn't risk it. The long arm of vengeance or justice, I
feared, knew no border. After trudging for days all over Oahu
I chanced to be at Pupukea Plateau, on the North Shore. At
an isolated papaya farm Mr. Kealoha, a big Hawaiian, six-
foot-three and nearly four hundred pounds, looked over my
papers to verify that I was no stowaway and took me in, more
willingly perhaps because I asked for no pay. I lived at the
servant cottage and was on call twenty-four hours a day.

When he went on a trip to the mainland later, I gave him
a letter to mail from Chicago or anywhere in the middle of
the North American continent. I told Yongmee not to look
for me and promised to explain everything when the time was

right. Although I kept her New York address, I have never written to her since. I should write her now. Perhaps they would forward the mail even if she has moved. Most of the Kwak gang have probably died during the war or forgotten about me in the intervening decades. Syngman Rhee died a long time ago, in Honolulu of all places, and his successors did not inherit his concerns. Nevertheless, nightmares and cold sweats were my frequent sleeping companions.

In fact I owed my saving of Mr. Kealoha's life to one of those nightmares. That night had been an especially bad one, and I couldn't go back to sleep. Getting out of bed, I noticed that Mr. Kealoha's pickup was not in the garage, nor were his fishing gear and boat trailer. He liked to go nightfishing and it was full tide. After looking around the property, I felt a strange desire to walk down the hill to the shore. The wind was high and sang shrilly. I fancied I heard something from the beach. The surf was throwing slammers into the cove, the salt spray fogging the air thick for miles around. The pickup was parked on the shoulder of the road at the edge of a haole koa grove. The boat had been unhitched but the custom-built eight-foot surfboard was left on the pickup. I never had any interest in fishing, although I'd had to come down to the beach many times to help my boss. It seemed a singularly boring, unrewarding occupation, but he loved it. He said it made things right between him and his maker. I peered into the darkness, into the pale line dividing water and sky. Then as the wind whistled and the spray of salt dampened my skin, I heard a voice, a feeble desponding groan, that wafted uncertainly on the dashing wind.

"Hang on, Mr. Kealoha," I shouted at the top of my voice, although I was down wind and there was no chance of his hearing me. "Shout louder so I can see where you are."

There was silence for a few minutes. I was frantic. Perhaps a wave had swamped and drowned him. Then on the next shift of the wind I heard him again, out beyond the cove. Taking the surfboard, I splashed into the cold water. The wayward sea thrashed me and the jagged reef cut me up. Once the surfboard took off out of sight and I dismally contemplated swimming out unaided, but luckily I recovered it, jammed between reefs, and maneuvered it over the inshore tumblers. He was clinging to a shelf of rock at the far edge of the cove. Every now and then a big incoming wave washed over his head and he hung on, unable to climb up or jump off into the water. It was uncanny how he had gotten washed up on the ledge after his boat had overturned some distance from the mouth of the cove.

Brought abreast of him by a wave, I pushed him off the rock. In vain I tried to steer him to the surfboard. This mountain of man, numbed with cold and fright, pinned me down and stood on top of me. I came up desperate for air, fighting off his strangling arms. In the next swell that washed over us, I kicked hard and dived with him in tow. Under water, his buoyancy made him lighter and more manageable. I propelled him toward the board, which twisted and bucked like a wild horse. Luckily, the big man's hands found the board and his arms went around it in an inexorable embrace. Using myself as a counterweight, I steadied its unruliness and nudged him to spread himself more evenly. From the rear I swam and pushed both man and craft until we were out of the swirling cove and headed for the open shore.

The huge but gentle and predictable undulations off the reef gave way to churning, boiling grinders that exploded into millions of fragments as we closed to the beach. We couldn't ride over them together. He was nearly done in from exposure and exhaustion. Though a fair swimmer, I couldn't have made my way in without the surfboard. Nobody could. But his condition didn't seem to allow any delay. I slid off and told him to move up the board and stretch himself, belly down, while I hung on behind and pushed it in. He told me to stop, divining my purpose. We should wait in the deep water until day came and people should come and look for us, he said, but even as he spoke, his big frame shook and convulsed with cold. I told him to hang on tight and shoved him off over the first rampart of the reef.

The board shot away like an arrow to disappear behind the ridges of surf, steel-grey against the dark furrows. I barely managed to fight off a breaker bent on smashing and impaling me on the thousand subsurface teeth. The sea heaved up as high as Pupukea Plateau, then slid off to a great depth, to the very bowels of the earth, it seemed, blocking from view everything but the towering wave tops, roaring and breaking into showers, rivulets, and cascades. Something slimy caught at my feet; my whole body shrank with a scream, which was, however, quickly smothered by the clamor of waves that seemed like monsters poised on frothy rows of seething hills to pound and pulverize me. It was unfair to have to drown like this in the middle of the Pacific. Hadn't I paid my dues, those years of dodging and hiding in Korea, then the twenty years of servitude to an adipose Hawaiian?

The waves rose and fell, the walls gliding skyward with

leviathan grace and celerity, the tremendous crests overhanging the yawning trough that widened into Kwangha Boulevard in Seoul. I stood in front of a tobacco and candy shop and pointed at a pack of American cigarettes under the glass counter. The wrinkled owner slid open the back and reached for it with a shaking hand, suspiciously eyeing me as I put down a thousand hwan note.

"It's time," said Inho, already off the sidewalk and crossing the street.

"Take your Lucky Strike, sir, and the change," the old man croaked behind me, but I was walking briskly after Inho, positioning myself so I couldn't be seen from the hotel entrance across. Samgyoo and Sokchin, who had watched from the corner and given the signal, walked leisurely up to the hotel. Just then the front door swung open and the politician Yongnam Cho swaggered out, flanked and followed by his bodyguards. I pulled out the pistol from my inside breast pocket and lifted it above Inho's shoulder. The bullet went home and my target reeled. I bolted and ran into the alley by the hotel. While Cho's entourage barely registered what had happened to their leader, my pals yelled, "Catch the assassin!" and from among the pedestrians and onlookers sprang forward several of our planted men, joining in the chorus, "Catch the assassin!" The programmed hysteria of their conflicting shouts and directions stalled the crowd just long enough.

"I see him there!" shouted Sokchin at the head of the crowd, pointing at a young man in the alley who, frightened at the onrush coming toward him, had started running. Sokchin and others caught up with him soon enough and beat him senseless.

I wandered into a *makkoli* shop and ordered a kettleful. An aching, tingling warmth spread through my body, as of a thousand bells going off at a signal from cell to cell. My head became clearer. The place was packed with early evening drinkers, yelling, arguing, laughing. At the next table sat two men discussing politics, the usual topic, lamenting the fate of a Korea liberated from the clutches of the Japanese dog only to be halved and torn by worse wolves. Why didn't they do something positive, instead of jawing about it like jackasses? I almost shouted. My fist came down on the table with a bang, which the waiter took as an order for more *makkoli*. Obligingly he brought another kettle and asked if I did not want side dishes. They had fresh abalone, cuttlefish, corvina, beef short ribs.

"No!" I thundered and he left me alone. While I sipped

my frothing bowl of *makkoli,* my left hand went up
unconsciously to feel the reassuring hardness of the iron
under the coat. I had faith in my friends, in Sanghoo Kwak,
our leader. We had no ambition and we didn't sell ourselves
to any clique. We wanted merely to clean up the political
mess, to weed out the charlatans, especially those
opportunists returning from America with CIA backing and
money. All the funds Kwak got us came from his own
patrimony, he assured us. His family had been one of the
richest landowners in Cholla Province. But why didn't we
go after the biggest stooge of them all, Syngman Rhee, the
Princeton graduate? His turn would come eventually, Kwak
said. The small fry had to be taken care of first.

He must know best, I told myself without conviction. We
would take care of each other, he had reassured us repeatedly.
Did he mean it? How did the oath of mutual protection square
with the harsh fate of Byongin Kang? He and I both had been
in our early twenties, and I had been drawn to his engaging,
life-loving nature. Then, a week after a brilliant job of
dispatching the Red demagogue Honsoo Kim, Byongin was
denounced as traitor, beaten mercilessly, and locked up
in the unventilated cellar of our headquarters at Yonjidong to
die a slow, painful death. When the others were away, I
climbed down the ladder to him, despite the injunction
against communication with the proscribed. The dim light
through the barred, dirt-caked window at ground level revealed
him lying on the damp floor. I went closer and he opened his
eyes dreamily. Then his body became taut and defensive.
Blood welled from his quivering lips. He tried to suck it in.
More flowed down his cheek to his matted hair.

"So it's you they've sent to finish me off?" he'd croaked.
"What are you waiting for? Go ahead."

His eyes strayed to my hands, half in fright, half in
longing for the release of death. I spread them out to show
their emptiness and sat down by him.

"Do you think I doublecrossed you, too?"

"Haven't you?"

"What's wrong with meeting old friends from home and
going to a rally to educate myself? I never told them about
us."

"But you should have told us about them."

"I didn't see any point in doing that. I only wanted to
know what I was doing, and they made me see things in a
different light. I don't think Kwak is on the level with
us. I am sure he is Syngman Rhee's man."

"Hush," I cautioned him as we heard steps upstairs.

"I don't care for myself. They've done a good job on me," he said, coughing up more blood. "But I care for you. They are using us. I talked to a man from Henam and he said he hadn't heard of the Kwak family. Where does he get all the money and the arms?"

Another cough interrupted him.

"But I never squealed on you guys because you are like me, all *dungshin*, chumps. I was going to quit after the last job and told Kwak so. This is how he wants to part with me."

Newspaper boys went past the *makkoli* shop, shouting extras. The waiter came back with several copies and passed them around.

"They are going to kill everybody," said a middle-aged man sitting at a table behind me. "Anybody with a name, any patriot with a record of fighting the Japanese, anybody who might offer the slightest competition or opposition."

"Aren't we lucky to be nobody!" another responded.

"To be dumb *jimsung,* you mean," said the first speaker. "Because that's what we are expected to be, to shut up and to have no mind of our own. Something must be terribly wrong with us, with the way we've been brought up, maybe with our genetic makeup. We simply cannot tolerate dissent and discussion. It's got to be total obedience, one-man show all the way, or else..."

I switched them off at this point and started reading the tabloid sheet. Everything had gone as expected. The suspect would not talk for a while, and the whole storm would blow over as in the other cases. There was another section with the photograph of the suspect's sister, a wispy thing with her hair covering half her face. She was weeping over her brother's unconscious body. She said he had left the house to get some money and buy medicine for their dying mother. They had been tending her and it was his first trip outdoors in days. Recent refugees from the north, they had no friends and her brother could not have been mixed up in politics or murder. She looked about twenty. Her sorrow, innocence, helplessness showed through the black and white of newsprint.

I arrived at the Yonjidong house about eight p.m. to be greeted by awkward silence.

"Why are you so late?" rang out Kwak's metallic voice.

I did not reply.

"Anyway congratulations on a job well done. Here!"

He proferred a bowl of *makkoli*. I drank it at a gulp.

"Hey, go easy on it. You must have had some already," said Kwak.

163

"It's so unfair," said Inho, pouring himself a bowl. "We have been waiting for you all this time, not touching a drop. And you know how thirsty I can get."

There was a long table laden with plates of sashimi, oysters, turnip kimchee, laver seasoned with sesame oil. Everybody ate and drank lustily. Sokchin sat at the other end away from me, occasionally darting a stealthy, watchful glance. I felt no appetite and kept drinking.

"I know what it feels like after the first job," said Kwak, smiling knowingly and putting an envelope and a key in my hand. "Go to Room 512 at the Bando. I have lined up the best for you. Relax. The job's done. She has a gorgeous body and the most delicate soft skin."

"Send her away," I said, returning the key. "I have to go somewhere else."

"Where?"

"Home."

"But there is nobody there."

How right he was! My poor mother, who had struggled all her life to raise my sister and me after the Japanese killed my father for underground activities, had died not too long before of malnutrition and untreated gastritis. Neither of us was at her side. Yongmee was away with her American somewhere. Having just joined the group and eager to prove myself, I had volunteered to tail Yongnam Cho in his barnstorming tour of the countryside. A sudden anger and hatred flared up inside me. Kwak stood my stare unflinchingly, with a sinister grin.

"I must go," I said, rising.

"Don't! You must learn to listen for your own good," shouted Kwak, grabbing my shoulder. I shoved him off so hard that he fell crashing on the table of food. Unconcerned, I took a step to the door.

"Stop, you dung-eating *kay*! You think you're a big hero because you plugged one lousy politician!"

There was a click behind me. My armhairs stood up like pins. The space before me went blank and the floor dropped off underneath. I walked mechanically, suspended in a void.

"Let him go. But you have to be back here tomorrow noon for the Manhee Song job. Twelve sharp or you are not one of us. Remember Byongin!"

The unlighted street was filled with shadowy pedestrians scurrying home before the approaching nightly curfew. I hailed a taxi and told the driver to go across the river to Liberation Village, the colony of tumbledown shacks spreading like mildew on the sides of South Mountain to house the thousands and thousands of refugees from the north, the

164

legacy of the country's liberation from Japan. He made a sharp U-turn and drove furiously. I got out of the taxi. Thanking me for my generous payment, the driver came out of his car and offered to guide me. He said he lived not too far off. It was my first visit to the area and the darkness made the search doubly difficult. I gave him the address, taken from the newspaper account. We came to an unlighted hut. The same girl in the picture stood in the door. I offered the driver some more money, but he refused and went down the winding footpath to his car.

"Are you from the police?"

"No."

"Are you from the newspapers? My brother is not guilty. Clear this up so he can be near my dying mother."

She started sobbing. The tears glistened in the glow of the kerosene lamp. Her mother lay, eyes closed, under a quilt.

"Did you call a doctor?"

"Brother was going to."

"Where does he work?"

"Nowhere. We came recently from North Korea, fleeing the Communists. They killed our father, and my brother would have been next. We owned a rice mill."

Her name was Wonha. Next morning I gave her money to fetch a doctor and buy food. As soon as her daughter left, the old lady opened her hollow eyes, fixing them on mine. Her cheekbones stretched and almost pierced her sallow skin. A mist formed in her eyes. Her hand lifted weakly but fell down. I grasped it, dry and light as paper. Her pulse was weak. There was a tug toward her mouth. I brought her hand to her lips. Raising her head half an inch, she pressed my hand to her parched lips. She tried to say something, but only inaudible wheezes issued forth. Then her hand dropped, pulseless. When Wonha came with the doctor, she had the afternoon extra reporting her brother's death.

We carried the pine box containing her mother's body to the cemetery at Wooidong. Wonha had been distant and expressionless all the time, as if she was a stranger who had nothing to do with the whole affair. I was about to lower the coffin when she clutched it and begged me to bury her also. Her weeping turned into violent coughing, which she tried in vain to smother, pressing her face to the wood. When the spasm was over she sagged, exhausted, on the box, her limp hands dangling over the sides. I lifted her to put her down on a mat nearby and saw a puddle of blood on the white pine. Her mouth and chin were also spattered with red.

Coming down the hill I told her to take care of herself. She shook her head. Her illness had advanced beyond cure, she said. I told her to go to a doctor, but she said all the doctors cheated. They gave shots of placebo instead of streptomycin, the new wonder drug for tuberculosis. I told her to buy the antibiotic herself. But there was no guarantee in that either, because drugstores sold bottles with the right American labels but something different inside. Pharmacies openly bought back empty penicilin and streptomycin bottles with undamaged labels. I would teach them a lesson, I swore. We stopped at the next drugstore. As Wonha stood by the door, I went up to the ruddy-faced pharmacist in a white gown. There were other customers in the store but I managed to draw him to a corner. I pulled out my pistol and poked under the hem of his gown.

"White and clean," I mused aloud, stroking the cloth with mock reverence. "I wonder how blood would look on it."

"What is it that you want?" he gasped, the color fleeing his face.

"I want streptomycin," I said, putting down the cash. "You wouldn't think of cheating a consumptive, would you?"

"Oh, no, never. I have the genuine stuff, just got from the Americans this morning."

Wonha suggested that we go to the doctor she had been going to off and on near Liberation Village. The nurse at the clinic told me to wait outside. Totally ignoring her I sat down by the doctor's desk, casually took out the gun, and, hunting for a cigarette, asked the nurse to show me how she dissolved the medicine in water. The doctor offered me his cigarettes and told the nurse to bring the ampule of distilled water. He would inject the medicine himself.

I tried to persuade Wonha not to go to the police for her brother's body, but she wouldn't listen. On our way from the cemetery, after burying the son next to the mother, I knew we were being followed. She was shaky and hardly in her right mind, but I had to send her home by herself in a taxi while I tried to shake the tail and track them down instead. They were Sokchin and another man I had not seen before, probably a new hire. Losing them near East Gate, I thought it best not to go to Wonha's house that evening. At daybreak the third day I came to her house by the most circuitous road I could imagine, but as I turned in the gate, I saw the top of Sokchin's hat beyond the fence. The other fellow was not with him. As he turned the corner, I struck him down with the handle of my gun. Quickly I dragged him into the house and was about to tie him up before we left, but he was already cold.

We went to Pusan, to Masan, to all the cities, never staying more than a few weeks, using different names, disguising ourselves as best we could. We managed to keep just a jump ahead of the police and my *dang* vigilantes. Only once did I come really close to contact. It was in Tongyong, the port city. I had to go out at night to get medicine for Wonha. She was hemorrhaging badly. Just as I was returning to our lodgings, I saw Samgyoo, Inho, and others of the old gang leave a nearby inn. We left the town early and headed west to Mokpo, where she died. The war came while I was in Pusan. By now Kwak's connections with Rhee had surfaced, as he got appointed head of an intelligence wing in his government. But the war kept everybody busy and I was left in relative safety, until in Pusan I took off for America, a country I had been conditioned to hate.

* * *

The sun had risen above the ironwoods of Pupukea, shining on my bed through the window. What a nightmare! I tried to get up, ashamed of my sloth. My arms and legs, in bandages, hurt. Mr. Kealoha came in with a deed of transfer making me owner of a hillside lot in Kahaluu.

"It isn't much now, nothing but rock and thistle, as you know," he said. "But you will make something of it. You are free to go to your own property as soon as you feel strong enough."

Nothing would dissuade this Hawaiian gentleman from making me this gift. He had a strain of royal blood in his veins and lived by a code of fairness unique to the native islanders. To refuse beyond what modesty required was to insult him, or worse, condemn him to the eternal vagabondage of the ingrate spirit in the nether world of Hawaiian theology. Eventually I learned to justify the acquisition as a just payment for my years of free labor.

Roasting in the sun, I dug out rocks and boulders, some the size of a house, and battled the tough, exuberant weeds that would, if left alone, easily engulf a paved city. I sometimes doubted whether Mr. Kealoha had done me a favor at all, but five years of backbreaking, unremitting work, from dawn till long after sunset, began to pay off. Alas, I was a man of estate, a man of means, and these immigrant Koreans came to me for handouts.

A squall, sudden and gusty as usual, forced me to leave the lanai only to run into Deacon Cho, who smiled broadly, revealing all the gold of his molars. Somehow I didn't mind him at all. His officiousness, his vanity, his snakiness, all seemed more cute than diabolical, a perfect fit in the total design of nature. I smiled back to him cordially.

"Where have you been, Grandfather?" he said, grabbing my hand. "We are organizing a Committee for Re-Immigration to the United Fatherland and we want you to be on it. You will, won't you?"

No Korean party was complete unless something grand was organized, to which everybody clapped and swore eternal allegiance. Of course nobody remembered a thing about it the next morning and it was bad manners even to bring it up. Deacon Cho was a well-mannered Korean and so was everybody else at Shim's.

"Of course," I said cheerily, without the least reservation.

The Water Tower

Seething with rage, John Bay stomped from the customs
area. As if acting on a sure tip that he was a dope smuggler or
espionage agent, the Saudi officials had subjected him to the
worst indignities, breaking open his luggage, inspecting the
most personal crannies of his body. The opaque glass door
with the restricted-area sign on the opposite side opened to let
him out. A figure stepped off the wall of waiting people, almost
bumping into him.

"Wonsok!" the man said, calling his former Korean name.
It was his friend Tago Byun.

"Let me take that," Tago offered, grabbing at John's suitcase.

"No, it's light," John said, jerking it back but quickly
regretting his churlishness. Tago had taken him by surprise.
Somehow John had not expected to be met by the head of the
Seven Star Middle East Builders at Riyadh Airport, several
hours' drive from Buraydah, their current job site.

"Over ten years, hasn't it been?" Tago said, leading the
way to his parked car.

"Just about," John said.

"You don't look changed a bit," Tago said. "America must
treat you right."

"You look fit, too," John said perfunctorily. "Saudi Arabia
must agree with you."

John shot a furtive glance at Tago, hoping the insincerity
or malice of his remark had gone unnoticed. His friend's
paunch was gone and so was the oiliness of face that John
remembered. But it was something other than fitness. The
man's stretched skin and protruding bones gave him a
haggard look, though the deep tan camouflaged it.

"Yes, the world's best sanatorium, with year-round sun that

169

burns up all germs," Tago said.

"Is it always this hot?" asked John, wiping his neck under his shirt.

The air-conditioner of the Cadillac huffed, pumping in hot air.

"This is cool by local standards," Tago said. "It gets to 150 degrees shortly after the meridian. So how was the flight?"

"Okay," John said, looking at the bleak desert scenery dancing in the heat and haze, suppressing his irritation at being reminded of the sadism of the Saudi customs. "So what's been the problem?"

"What problem?" Tago said, laughing hollowly.

John looked at Tago askance. What was that urgent telephone entreaty if it wasn't a mayday?

"Come on," John said snappishly. "You wouldn't have hauled me all the way here if there wasn't an engineering crisis of some sort. Tell me all about it and let's get it over with."

"Everything's been wrong," Tago said, after an aborted attempt at bluffing. "The supervisor has been at us, faulting everything we do. Now he's sent this ultimatum."

Under the impressive colored letterhead, Cagle and Manson, Engineering, Inc., London, the missive declared: "I have repeatedly asked for a meeting, both orally and several times in writing, which you have consistently ignored. I am not sending any more notices. Unless you appear for a conference at my office at nine Monday morning and we work out an understanding, not only your present contract but all other pending ones with his majesty's government will be voided." It was signed George Winthrop, Engineer, MA, Ph.D., PE, CSE, HMU, etc., etc.

"That's tomorrow," John said.

"Yes," Tago answered dully.

"Why haven't you met him?"

"To hear the same old rubbish? He's out to wreck me, insisting on impossible conditions."

"A title-conscious Englishman, eh?"

"That's the name of the game. The Arabs are too fat and dumb to do anything themselves, so they specialize in the art of manipulating their foreign servitors by pitting one against another. They hire a Swede to draw the plans, an Englishman to supervise, and a dirt cheap Korean to do the job. Doesn't it stand to reason to make coterminous the contracts for both supervisor and contractor, because the supervisor can supervise only what the contractor performs? Not with the devious Arabs. The supervisor's contract is open-ended, and he gets paid by the day as long as the job lasts, but the contractor has a deadline. He must complete the job by that date or he pays a heavy penalty unheard of anywhere else in the world, like one per cent per day. Naturally, the engineer punk wants to prolong his paid vacation. It pays him to make the job run over."

"Why take on jobs here of all places?" John asked.

Tago took a while answering the simple question, as if addressing a profound metaphysical issue.

"Because in this recession this is the only place left in the world to pick up a few dollars. Korean goods are not selling too well on the international market. All we can do is dump our labor."

"What's the total value of the job?"

"One hundred and fifty million dollars for each of the three towers."

"What was the next lowest bid?"

"Three hundred and twenty-five."

Heat danced in waves, blurring the two-lane concrete road, hot as fire brick. John was on edge, anticipating the imminent blowout of the tires. But the greater danger lay with the Arab drivers who roared past as if the highway was meant for one-way traffic, their way.

"Look out!" John yelled in horror, bracing his hands and knees against the dashboard. A Ferrarri had jumped into view from the other side of the hill and zoomed head-on towards them. Slamming on the breaks, Tago jerked the steering wheel to one side, sending the Cadillac screeching and plowing into the sand. The Arab in the Ferrarri went his way merrily, not even turning his head.

"That bastard was on our side of the road," John protested, throwing his weight at the door jammed up against the sand outside.

"Ya," grunted Tago, pushing open his side door. "But the cops would never see it that way, nor the judge. A foreigner had better watch out here. Once I parked in a marked parking stall on the street. An Arab came along and banged my car, but you know what he said? He said it was all my fault and I had to pay for the damage to his car."

"You're kidding."

"I'm not. He had a point, though. I shouldn't have parked where he was going. He told me to pay $500 or he'd call the cops."

"*He* call the cops?"

"I ended up giving him $200 and drove off. You see if the cops come, they just put you in the can, no questions asked. A foreigner in trouble with an Arab is automatically guilty, until proven otherwise. You rot in their jail without food or water until your case comes to a hearing days and days afterwards, if at all."

"Where is the consul of one's country?"

"How do you get in touch with the consul if you are physically cut off from the world, locked up? Your friends and family may go to the Saudi police and only get the famous Arabian runaround. They don't, or pretend not to, speak English, and after gesticulating and trying a dozen different languages, all you get is a blank stare and a shrug to the next desk or office."

Tago walked to the back of the car and from the trunk took out a shovel and traction mats. Apparently he was prepared for such events. Fortunately, the sand was easy to dig and after a few minutes of puffing they put the car back on the road.

From slightly higher ground, they could see the highway stretching out like an arrow, intersecting with another in the distance to form a big cross astride the expanse of shimmering white. As they neared the intersection, traffic was slowing down. Tago brought the Cadillac to a standstill at the end of a long line. The light, hung over the intersection half a mile ahead, had changed to green twice but there was no sign of forward movement.

"Is there an accident?"

"No, they're waiting for the cross traffic to stop."

"Didn't they stop when the light turned red on their side?"

"Oh, that. No Arab observes the lights. They just come to an intersection, look left and right, if they're considerate, then zoom across. So once the traffic in one direction gets going, the cross current has to stop and wait for its turn, which may take a long time. Meanwhile, the lights may change five or six times. The longest I've had to wait was 31 cycles. Let's hope this doesn't break the record."

"Why do they have the lights at all?"

"Just for looks. You see the highway planners are foreigners, and the Arabs who approve them have been abroad and seen the traffic lights. So they leave them in."

They were within the city limits of Buraydah with a population of about 70,000. The construction site was on the other side of town. The two other future job sites were located further south near Abha. The entire citizenry of Buraydah had poured out and headed for the square in front of the City Hall, where thousands already were packed around a high dais.

"Is it some kind of national holiday?" John asked, watcing the veiled faces, strange physiognomies, gaits, heavy

172

unwashed coats and head wrappings, shouts and laughter, un-intelligible babble and cackle, not minding for the moment what seemed an interminable wait.

"You may say that," Tago said. "It's a flogging day."

"Flogging!" John exclaimed. He had heard that the Arabs still administered corporal punishment like amputation of hands against thieves. But public flogging seemed ludicrous in this day and age.

"It's a Frenchman, a tourist, that is to be thrashed publicly. On his bare rump. Buraydah is the sixth largest city in Saudi Arabia but probably the most conservative. Every woman must wear a veil and there is no exception to the rule. In Riyadh, the capital, foreigners are exempt from this rule, but not in Buraydah. Foreign women must comply with the law. Either out of ignorance or in contempt, the French couple, hotel owners in France on a sightseeing tour, came riding into town, the wife sitting primly in the front seat, her face not covered."

"But why is the man to be whipped?"

"There's Arab chivalry for you. The offender is considered the man who does not keep his women under proper control. So he is punished. All the Arabs are coming to see the exposed backside of a white man. The news has gotten around. It should be quite a sight. I think the Arab sheiks hold on to their power because they have the knack for providing exactly the kind of entertainment their benighted countrymen want."

"Is the Frenchman taking it like that?"

"He's screaming his head off but what can he do? The wife is in custody until her infraction is expiated by her husband. Even if the French consul knew about it, he would probably do nothing, especially since his government is anxious to wangle Saudi contracts."

The swing gate led into a barbed-wire fence compound, built around a huge circular pit, about 500 feet in diameter and 50 feet deep, except in some sections where digging was still under way in solid rock. On this footing a cylinder 200 feet in diameter and 600 feet in height would rise to support a globe 500 feet in diameter. Only the lower half of the globe was to be for water storage, while the remaining space was divided into three floors. The first was to house the elevator, water pump, air conditioning, and other electrical and mechanical units. The second would have a 1,000-seat restaurant and bar, and the top floor, at the pole of the sphere, would be a lookout room completely of glass. What one would look out on in the middle of the desert was a mystery to John. Maybe the stars at night. Weren't the Arabs the astronomers of the Middle Ages?

"Didn't you make a soil test before digging?" John asked.

"No. The site was fixed in the specs and we had to build it there, no matter what. That was our first row with Winthrop."

"You've been busting the rock with those?" John asked, indicating the backhoes with hydraulic Horams rigged at their booms.

"Yes," Tago said. "We tried to blast with dynamite, but the Arabs have a thing about earthquakes. According to them, even a firecracker might start one. So we had to chip away, eating up all our time."

Parked by the backhoes were giant Caterpillar 977 loaders on tracks, equipped with formidable rippers in the rear, which looked curiously dwarfed by the enormity of the excavation. At the end of a Poclain crane a cable dangled above a bucket half-filled with rocks. The men were at lunch in a long equipment storage shed, slapped together out of plywood and two-by-fours. Glancing at the glassed-in cab of the crane in the sun, John ran his eye over the diners, certain that he could pick out its operator, the one with broiled meat curling off his cheeks. But they all looked sooty, dried up, hard as coal and indestructible. Teeth flashing, lips smacking and slurping, they ate their rice, kimchee, and soy sauce soup with sullen intensity. What struck him was the total absence of spoons and chopsticks, let alone forks and knives. The men dipped their fingers into bowls and jars for any solid pieces they couldn't suck up or clamp up with their lips.

Out in the sun on the sand, about ten feet from the shed, lay a four-by-eight foot sheet of metal, its zinc-plated surface gleaming iridescently. A man dashed out with a container full of eggs. With one hand he picked up an egg, dug thumb and finger on opposite sides, and broke the shell in two neat halves. The contents flopped on the sheet metal and began sizzling. In the time it took him to walk around the rectangular space, rows of white circles with yellow centers streaked the length of the sheet. The cook was now dancing around the rectangle, sprinkling salt and crushed sesame seed. From under his arm he produced a broad wooden paddle which he proceeded to use as a spatula.

"It sure saves on the heating bill," Tago said.

There is the secret of the Korean contractor's ability to bid low, John mused. They have workers who eat nothing but rice and pickled cabbage, and an occasional egg as a treat, then go into the furnace to work fifteen hours or more for pay that an average American worker would refuse for an hour.

The executive suite was at the end of an army-style

quonset. The interior was exquisitely paneled and well insulated; the air-conditioning was effective, though a bit noisy, and the contrast with the outside was chilling. Tago led John to a carpeted room with a private toilet and shower. The white sheets of the twin bed seemed particularly tempting after the 25-hour flight.

"Very nice," John said, trying the faucets of the shower which spluttered with instant reaction.

"It's no Waldorf Astoria, but we try our best for our VIP's," Tago said.

A regular *jongshik* course of rice, broiled beef and steamed fish was laid out for two in Tago's office. Sipping champagne, John unbelievingly fingered the chopsticks.

"You noticed," Tago said. "The tradition started from the first days of Saudi expeditions. The men, peaceable fellows ordinarily, were prone to losing their tempers over nothing at mealtime and flew at each other with anything that came to hand. Naturally sharp objects did the most damage. So it's been mandatory for all Korean contractors in the Middle East: No chopsticks or spoons. I guess it was from being cooped up for months on the compound, with no drink or women to relieve them. Did you know these Arabs don't permit prostitution? They have an interesting substitute, though. It's free, too. They have certain days of the month set aside to employ female prisoners for the purpose. On those long-looked-for days the male population of the region turns out in force at break of dawn and lines up for a turn. Unfortunately, foreigners are not allowed in the line. For them and for those improvident Arabs who don't get to have a turn at the prison, they have trained mares. For ten bucks one can have a go at the mares, either standing up or sitting on specially designed chairs."

"While somebody holds up the tail, I bet," John sneered.

"You think I am joking? My men swear..."

"Don't bother," John cut him short, having little taste for this Korean-Arabian strain of smut. "I believe you. I can believe anything in this country."

John and Tago went to Winthrop. His secretary made them wait in the anteroom while he pondered the serious breach of protocol—Tago turning up against his expectations with a bodyguard or something to crowd his peace. John was told to write out his credentials, so much irrelevant dross for getting accomplished the job at hand, before they were admitted into the Englishman's audience. Even with them in the office the pompous little man sat behind his huge desk poring over John's half-page scrawl through his thick glasses, scorn written on his pinched face. His highness was not at all im-

175

pressed: anybody other than British and Cambridge was so much surplus weight to the already-burdened earth.

"Under no circumstances," he began enunciating with oracular gravity, "would I condone deviation from the specifications. Mixing or pouring concrete at 180 degrees in midday is out of the question. The concrete will not react chemically. Even at 4 a.m. the earth temperature here is around 120 degrees, still too high to give the concrete the specified strength."

"What do you suggest, then?" John asked.

"I don't know," Winthrop said blandly. "That's your problem. I can only say that the cement has to be mixed at the optimal temperature of 75 degrees, not a degree higher, or lower, for that matter. The specified 5,000 p.s.i. is essential in this earthquake-prone zone."

"You are no doubt acquainted with the recent articles in the *Journal of the American Concrete Institute* about mixing at excessive temperature using potassium compounds?" John put the question as tactfully as possible.

Winthrop stared at him, as if he had uttered some unspeakable obscenity.

"I don't hold with unorthodox American experiments," he said slowly. "The old and tried is the way to go, which incidentally accords with the specifications."

That left no room for further discussion. John rose and led his friend out of the room, leaving Winthrop to exult in his glory.

The interview had a devastating effect on Tago. John wondered how one could change so drastically in half an hour. The man seemed to have visibly shrunk, his clothes hanging loose around him, like a popped balloon.

"We'll give that son of a bitch his 75 degrees," John said. "A 20-ton capacity ice machine is what we need to chill the water with."

Tago showed no reaction and passively followed John, eyes not focusing, arms and legs moving mechanically. John took the Cadillac's wheel and drove back to the camp in silence, glancing now and then at the pathetic sight of his companion slumped in the corner. John had only himself to blame for the mess he was in. As if the consultantship had been an offer of the Nobel Prize or some singular honor, he had jumped and come running at the first call from Tago. To his chagrin, John had to admit, the real motive for his alacrity had been petty revenge. He had gloated that Seven Star was tottering, like so many upstart fortunes in post-War Korea, that Tycoon Tago, heir to Seven Star, would tumble and bite the dust, while he,

John Bay, was the rising star. He had dropped everything and flown over not so much to help as to triumph over his old friend and rival in distress. Triumph over this overgrown child, wilting like some tender shoot at first breath of frost? John felt mortified at the complexes that still rankled, the grudges that still festered inside him against his fellow Koreans after seeing the continents and oceans, long after he thought he had put the accidents of his upbringing in their proper perspective.

Particularly galling was his vindictiveness toward Tago as successful romantic rival: it had no basis in fact. It was he himself who had brought Ayran to one of the fabulous New Year's Eve parties at the Byun residence in Seoul. A nice-looking girl from an impoverished aristocratic background in the country, like John's, she should not have been so cruelly exposed to the megaton radioactivity of wealth. Smitten with guilt for deflowering her and frustrated at not being able to marry her at once because of his uncertain prospects, he had secretly desired to be rid of her, to be freed from the burden. He still vividly remembered the startled look on her face when he introduced her to Tago as a distant cousin, hinting at her availability. Soon afterwards John was offered a full scholarship for his doctorate in engineering at the University of Hawaii and left Korea without even looking her up; paperwork for his passport and visa had indeed kept him on the run up to the very minute of his departure but he had been all too glad of the excuse to spare himself the embarrassing goodbye and empty promises. Almost immediately he was apprised of Ayran's marriage to Tago.

After Americanizing his name when he took the oath of allegiance for his naturalization, John had resolved, quite gratuitously and irrationally, never to have anything to do with his compatriots, consistently avoiding them in Honolulu and skipping newspaper articles with any reference to Korea. His former professor had to steer him to the ad in the *New York Times* about the contest for the design of the US-Korea Centennial Tower to commemorate the 100th anniversary of diplomatic relations between the two countries. The ad was in other major newspapers throughout the world, and the award money, jointly offered by the two governments, was a princely sum, far in excess of the usual architect's fee. By winning the contest John had attained instant fame and acclaim.

Polar Supply was the largest refrigeration supply company in Riyadh. Ted Bundy, an American, was the proprietor, in a strangely hobbled sense. The firm's ownership was 51 per cent

Arab and 49 per cent American. No foreigner was allowed to do business in Saudi Arabia, unless he had an Arab partner with a majority vote. So the American had to find an Arab, who took no risk, put up no money, and did no work. Bundy told John that only Carrier built to order such giant-capacity ice machines at a cost of maybe a couple of million dollars. The transportation, another half million with insurance, would take seven months, as it had to come by ship. Only military transport planes had large enough freight bays.

"You have contacts at the Pentagon?" Bundy asked.

"Don't be absurd," John said.

"That's the only way to do business in this hellhole, my friend," Bundy said. "How do you think we survive at all without Uncle Sam's armed foot in visual range of these hooligans? Now and then he kicks them in the ass with it, hard, just to remind them."

A call to the Carrier office in Pittsburgh, Pa. confirmed the gloomiest projections. John took the bad news to Tago, who seemed to have gotten over his semicomatosity somewhat, though he still looked drained and crumpled.

"We have until the end of the year to finish," Tago said listlessly, like a chant. "Six months. After that, after New Year's Eve..."

Tago broke off, his eyes briefly meeting John's before they slid off to some distant object. Could he be thinking of the New Year's Eve parties at his ancestral mansion atop the headland parting the two branches of the Han—with their concert bands, dances, fireworks, food, resplendent guests? Could he be thinking of the particular New Year's Eve party to which John had brought Ayran? Neither of them had discussed Ayran or any other personal matter, however trivial, as if afraid that one might lead to another, and ultimately to the taboo: Ayran. After New Year's Eve, John knew, they would be slapped with a fine of one per cent per day. That was one million and a half. John shuddered at the barbarity of the stipulation.

"But surely they must understand unavoidable circumstances like war, earthquake, storm, or other calamities. Any court will."

Instantly, John reproached himself for the emptiness of his reassurances. He had had sufficient evidence that it was not *any* court that they had there; it was the worst jury-rigged affair in the world. The contract was written in Arabic. Translations in the Western languages might be attached, but in case of doubt or dispute one had to go by the original Arabic, which was notoriously lacking in precise technical terminology. One term for a bolt could serve for a hundred dif-

178

ferent things, ranging from nails to screws, bushings, nuts, and washers. So the intepretation was extremely flexible. Besides, who could read Arabic except the Arabs? And they were the types to give flexibility even to the most rigid mathematical symbols. No foreigner, especially those from the poorer countries like Korea, had a chance in an Arab court.

"We'll have to rig up a freezer big enough to handle the problem," John said.

Tago's eyes flashed with a glint of hope but quickly resumed their dull focuslessness.

"Can you do it?" Tago asked weakly.

"The engineering principle is simple enough," John went on. "I need a compressor, delivering at least a thousand horsepower, run by a V-belt on a diesel engine. Then I need some tanks, tubings of different sizes, ammonia. Maybe Ted Bundy has most of what we need. If not, we should be prepared to go shopping to Marseilles, London, wherever planes fly."

Tago nodded without enthusiasm.

"Don't you believe I can do it?" John said sharply, annoyed at his friend's progressive disintegration. "I need welders, ironsmiths, pipefitters."

"You can have everything here," Tago said absently.

John had never built a refrigeration system before, but there was no alternative. Cylinders of ammonia were bought at Al Madinah from a bankrupt Dutchman who had imported them for soap and toiletry manufacture, but had to close down because his Arab drone, a Bedouin, had disappeared into the trackless sand with his band of camel riders. The diesel-driven piston-type air compressor came from the harbor master at Az Zahran who was replacing it with an electric model. Made by General Motors in 1935, its valves were still good but had to be modified by new channels and ventricles for the suction and discharge of the refrigerant. The hairpin bends of the tubings for the condensing and evaporating coils were tricky, as they could easily kink and ruin the whole unit. Often a tubing of the required size couldn't be obtained and the next larger size had to be used, crimped the whole length.

Even after the tubing sizes and lengths seemed to be correctly proportioned according to the best calculations he could make, freezing did not occur. After a series of refittings and resizings with negative results, he had to start from scratch, doing away with the handbook-recommended ratios and computations, and going by gut feeling. A succession of elongations in the capillary showed a hint of frosting around the evaporator. More radical overhauls and readjustments had to be made throughout the system, checking against a table of dimensions to avoid repetitions, though under the circumstances the margin of error was so large that he felt like he was groping and fumbling in the dark.

Days went by with the whole compound anxiously watching his every move and expression for an encouraging sign. The pressure of such mass expectancy was unnerving. To them he was the great engineer from America come to deliver them from the impending peril. He simply couldn't disappoint them and worked feverishly night and day. One morning, exhausted, in desperation, John unthinkingly crimped one section of tubing with vandalistic abandon. The system coughed, kicked, and caught, quickly achieving an operational level of freezing.

Ice trays punched out of sheet metal with gallon size cups were shoved on shelves surrounding the cooling coils. No attempt was made to automate the emptying process. Men were detailed inside the freezing compartment to pull out the trays with an overhung hoist and tip them over to shake the chunks of ice into a collection bin which was carried out full by a forklift. At first the ice stuck to the metal and wouldn't shake loose, but a polyethylene coating solved the problem. The ice detail turned out to be the most popular duty among the men and had to be scheduled in short shifts to be fair to all. Everybody wanted to escape into the arctics, though in a few minutes they froze unless protected by heavy overalls, hoods, gloves, and boots.

Trucks brought water from an oasis forty miles away and filled a tank dug in the ground. The water in the tank was heated to near boiling by afternoon sun, then cooled slowly overnight. Even at 3 a.m. it was still above 120 degrees, and the ice dumped in it melted quickly away. The chilled water supplied a spray-nozzled hose mounted on a truck that circled the crater, dousing the installed rebars and adjacent ground. Hot steam shot up, filling the pit like a Turkish bath. Another pipeline fed the mixer. The hot cement and gravel hissed and crackled like wood on fire. The ready mix was pumped down a chute to where it was needed. The ice machine, motors, and pumps clanked on, working through the entire stock of cement, sand, and gravel, after finishing only half the foundation. New orders for cement and gravel had not arrived. Sand was no problem but gravel had to come from the quarries in the north, and cement from the port of Az Zahran.

John did not mind the hiatus, which he devoted to building the formwork for the superstructure, especially the globe. The initial plywood mold, held together by wires and beams, had been worked out by Tago's engineers but rejected by

Winthrop for not reflecting the semicircular bulging caused by the rotating sun and for not allowing enough post-tension in the lower sections of the globe, where the thickness of the slab was over four feet. Winthrop's suggestion was to order a plastic form made by a West German firm, in which John found out Cagle and Manson had some stock interests. The estimated cost was $10 million.

According to John's analysis, the West German engineers were no miracle workers. After careful calculation of the bulging quotient and post-stress, the Germans used strong polystyrene instead of plywood. The plastic naturally gave the product a seamless finish, dispensing with post-cure sandblasting, but it did not accomplish anything mechanically or structurally superior. John had to prepare a 300-page thesis, with detailed drawings and calculations, showing that the Korean workers could make the form with the given allowances for distortion using plywood.

From his office in the executive suite, where lately he was the sole occupant, John saw through the window the gravel trucks finally drive in one afternoon, most of them only half loaded.

"No unloading before you pay," said the Arab driver leading the convoy.

Haygoon Koo, the field manager who seemed to have taken over all the day-to-day decisions, offered to pay for ten yards per truck.

"It is twenty yards," the Arab said.

"How can it be? The maximum load is 15 yards. Look. The GVW, 20 yards, is factory stamped on the body of the truck. That's GVW. You have to deduct five yards tare for the vehicle weight and you get 10. And they're not even full."

"It is 20 yards. That's what my paper says."

"But..."

One of the Korean workers nudged at Koo's elbow and whispered, "Don't antagonize these guys. They'll never deliver another load and we need gravel."

Koo changed his tone, apologized for his error, and paid the Arab off. John thought he had seen everything, but this seemed to top them all. He felt he had to leave right away before he lost his sanity. Besides, there was another pressing reason for his departure. The Governor's office had called from Honolulu about the groundbreaking ceremony for the Centennial Tower in a week's time. Both countries, represented by cabinet-rank officials, would give John letters of appreciation for his award-winning design, as well as presenting him the check. The choice of Hawaii as the site for the tower was to

honor its distinguished role in Korea's struggle for independence from Japan.

"Where is Tago?" John asked Koo, suddenly remembering
that he had not seen him around for some time.

"He said he was flying to Morocco, sir," Koo said.

"Whatever for?"

"Seven Star is building the Marrakech airfield. It's been a
big money loser."

Losing money seemed to be the theme of Seven Star. All
those fat Arab sheiks must smell from miles away the Santa
from Korea who kept cramming dollar bills into their already-
brimming pockets.

"Why didn't he tell me?" John demanded.

"Perhaps he didn't want to disturb you in the middle of your
work."

"I'm here to be disturbed and consulted," John thundered at
Koo, who cringed submissively.

To leave him in the lurch like that! This latest stunt of
Tago's was inexcusable. It was desertion in the face of fire,
perfidy in the highest degree. But soon his anger gave way to
pity for the rich kid destroyed in the wilds of real life. That he
should have felt competitive, jealous, nay inferior, to such a
babe in the woods! From another point of view, Tago's disap-
pearance was opportune. His own departure could now be
hurried up. He'd leave this very minute. His conscience was
clear. In fact, he had performed above and beyond what was
called for in the consultantship. Besides, the rest of the work
was more or less routine, just sticking to the plans and work
schedule. The Abha towers would be a repetition of Buraydah
and go without a hitch if the experience here were stream-
lined, though of course there was no such thing as replication
in construction. Even the simplest job was new and original,
with its space-time variables and unpredictables.

"Where are the cement trucks?" John asked.

"Swallowed up in the desert sand, sir," Koo said. "The Bel-
gian customs broker at Az Zahran says the trucks left after
being pressure-loaded at the silos on the docks a week ago,
enough time for three round trips between here and there. But
they are not here. We can't check their whereabouts. There is
no highway patrol, no radio, no telephone."

John had just started packing when he heard a knock on his
door. It was Koo, reporting the arrival of the cement trucks.

"What held them up?" John asked.

"They had a flat," Koo said.

"They all had a flat?"

"One flat or ten flats makes no difference to them. They all wait together."

"At least they could have sent half of the good trucks on, instead of all of them keeping company."

"Try to argue with the Arabs, sir," Koo said mournfully.

"You can start mixing now," John said, slamming down the lid of his suitcase.

"Sir, can you possibly reconsider waiting a few more days until the boss returns? Maybe we'll run into problems we can't handle..."

"You won't," John said, stepping out of the room. "I have a date in Honolulu that I must keep."

"Yes, we know. Of course you must be there. Congratulations, sir."

* * *

Staring into the clear Hawaiian sky, John lay in a half slumber on the veranda of his upper Manoa home built on stilts sprouting from the rock of the near-vertical slope. The tall ironwoods, sighing and swaying in the trade winds, ringed the railing like deferential courtiers. The setting sun hovered beyond Punahou Ridge, casting a veil of soft twilight over the valley. From their wooded perches birds sent up throaty even-songs. It was good to be back home. Nothing would induce him to leave it again, ever.

The telephone jangled, breaking the quiet of early dusk in the woods.

"Yes?" John said.

"Mr. John Bay?" queried the Korean-accented operator. "Long distance call from Seoul, Korea."

"I am he," John said, still trying to shake the cobwebs from his eyelids. He could hear the operator telling her client to go ahead in Korean.

"Hello," a woman's voice said, Ayran's. "I know you've just returned from Saudi Arabia but could you go back?"

"Well," John mumbled. "I've had a bellyful of Saudi Arabia and I have other engagements here. What's up anyway?"

"Tago is dead," she said hurriedly.

Strangely, the news did not surprise him, as if he had anticipated it all along.

"When did it happen?"

"They found his body two days ago."

"I thought he was in Morocco."

"That's what he told everybody. He had never left Saudi Arabia. His body was found in the sand near the Buraydah compound."

183

"It must have been an accident," John said, though he knew it to be otherwise.

"It doesn't matter," Ayran said curtly, as if disdaining his condolences. "There is no insurance or other complications to worry about."

"Is his funeral to be there?"

"No. His body has been flown home. I called to discuss something else. Seven Star needs somebody to tidy up its Middle East ventures, if it is not to be wiped out. He took on the Buraydah job to get the 20 per cent advance, $30 million, which he needed to service a government loan for the botched Morocco job. The next payment was due last week, which was to have been paid with another 20 per cent advance at the halfway point of the Buraydah tower. The payment never came. I guess the job didn't go too well."

"He never mentioned the interim payment or what it would be used for. We were just trying to beat the year-end deadline."

"The government has started foreclosure proceedings but there is still a chance of saving the situation, if payment is made soon. I've talked to the Minister of Commerce and Industry. Can you take charge, for *our* son's sake?"

"*Our* son?"

"Don't tell me you didn't know all this time. I sent you a photograph of him when he was six."

That must have been during the period when he threw away all mail from Korea unopened. It was some time before he digested the full import of the revelation.

"You mean you haven't suspected it?"

"Never. Why didn't you tell me then?"

"Would it have changed anything?"

"No," John replied. It was no time for dissembling or playing games. "Do you have any other children?"

"No."

"How old is he now?"

"Ten. And remarkably like you."

"Did Tago know?" John asked with a tremor in his voice.

"Only recently. The Seoul papers had a big write-up about you with your photographs in them. Yonday's framed birthday picture happened to be on the desk next to the newspaper photograph of yours. The resemblance suddenly penetrated Tago. He never asked me, but he knew. The realization must have been shattering. He had loved his son very much. You see, he didn't have to go to Saudi Arabia. His field managers would have done as good a job as he, or as bad. He just had to get away."

John called American Airlines and booked a passage to Riyadh leaving Honolulu in two hours.

The Grateful Korean

Battered by the raging sea, the 25-ton tuna boat *Sea Warrior* rolled and pitched, now riding a crest, then plunging awash into a bottomless valley, to be disgorged, miraculously afloat, in the next swell. With the alternator down, the engine batteries had run dry. All the lights were dead. The rudder had seized five points to port. The bilge pump had stopped and slush seeped through the shaft case, relentlessly filling the engine room, already up to the oil filter can. The radio was out. Harry Song had signaled Mayday just before it went completely dead and thought he had heard the Coast Guard, but it could have been just static on the waning power. Electricity was out. They were on a dead vessel whose heartbeat had stopped. Lightning flashed, zigzagging eerily the doom of his boat and crew across the pitch dark, crazed sea.

Harry grabbed the wheelbox as the floor dropped from under him, the sea crashing through the broken windshield and flooding abaft, wrenching the cabin door off its hinges. Next moment he was on his back, the gravity pulling at his numbed arms around the wheelbox, the profile of the figurehead, Lady with the Flowing Mane, above him. The boat was plummeting stern foremost down a suction chute to the miry floor of the ocean. Then, after a shuddering hesitation, the vessel shot up with the abruptness of a missile fired from a submarine, dizzily weightless, salt spray lashing the exposed hull.

Strangely, before the certainty and imminence of death, Harry felt the immobilizing shock of fear wear off, his mind re-engage with calm determination, his perception sharpen. Quickly he took stock of the cabin, a shambles. Inho Kim, his engineer, thin face pinched tightly, nose bleeding, eyes almost tearful, hung on to a bunk post helplessly. His feet vainly tried to clamp down on the engine room hatch.

"We are finished," sobbed Yong Ha, his boatswain, choking with salt water and clambering from under the lower bunk. With another tilt of the floor, he collapsed against the bulkhead, yelping sharply like a puppy being kicked, his hands groping in midair. Those hands could not be fingerprinted, to the amazement and annoyance of the Immigration Service when Harry had taken him down for his lost green card, the skin having been worn smooth by constant handling of the lines.

"Try the transmitter again," Harry yelled to Sam Chay, who was clinging to the sink in the galley under the battery-operated location transmitter overhead. His face, tanned coffee black, was drained of blood, eyes under the bushy brows hollow and unseeing. The floor twisted and Sam's legs foxtrotted away from under him, his hands and chin vised on the edge of the sink.

"It's dropped on the floor. It's no good," Sam said, gagging, his permanently hoarse voice an inaudible rasp. He had ruined his voice from shouting his wares, knitted T-shirts, one of his business ventures and failures, in different country market places of Korea.

"Pick it up," Harry shouted.

"Okay," Sam gasped. Wriggling his torso and legs across the length of the galley passageway, he managed to scissor the transmitter between his feet and push it to the space below the sink. Between gyrations of the floor, with split-second timing, he let go of the sink, picked the radio up, and put it on the sink. The boat pitched forward.

As another broadside slammer sent the boat drunkenly reeling and bobbing, Harry dashed to Sam's side and snatched the transmitter. He clasped Sam by the waist. The transmitter fell on his feet, lighting a thousand matches before his eyes, his whole left side going numb. Suppressing a scream, Harry took hold of the gadget again and flipped the switch on and off, praying it would work. There was a weak prolonged static, a sputter, then nothing. The battery had shorted out in the salt water. Why hadn't Sam, a no-good loafer he should have fired a long time ago, picked it up sooner? Harry could have thrown it at Sam's head but checked the impulse, noticing the scar down his cheek. Sam was the one who, when his cousin's lumber business went under in Korea, had stood up to and checked the unpaid workers who were storming the management building, smashing everything in their path.

Another torrent of water through the windshield sent Inho sprawling on all fours to the rear of the galley. The engine room hatch came off and floated down the passage, stopping briefly at Sam's feet before floating back toward the opening where the water cascaded into the engine room. Detaching himself from the sink, Sam flopped down on top of the square hatch, frantically jiggling it to fit on the opening.

"It won't make any difference," Harry said, nevertheless kneeling beside Sam to bear down on the hatch.

The moisture-charged air held the barometric level at the 900's. The whole Pacific, the greatest misnomer, boiled and churned. Or could it be that the storm front was focused on the *Sea Warrior*? Was it some kind of divine retribution for his avarice? The only way to beat the Japanese middlemen at their game of price rigging was to turn up with a shipload of fish when the supply was really scarce, as during a long storm. The local Japanese appetite for sashimi, fresh ahi fillets, was no respecter of weather and would not stand for manipulation, even when Japanese-inspired. If greed had driven him, then at least he had put his life on the line, unlike the middlemen who got fat sitting in air-conditioned offices, playing golf, entertaining their pretty secretaries. Nor did Harry feel guilty about the plight of his crew. They were no children. With luck they could each make three or four thousand dollars for only a few days' work and they knew it. He had the best profit-sharing record on the dock and didn't have to use persuasion. They had come running when he put out to sea. If they drowned, would their families sue? Perhaps, the ingrates. They quickly forgot what he had done to settle them in Hawaii, to give them hope, even a measure of prosperity. Let them sue all they wanted. Who cared? He would be dead along with them. Death pays all debts, even multiple deaths. He was sure of that. Or was he? Does one death really pay for more than one, say four?

* * *

Coming to the U.S., to Hawaii in particular, had been like being born again. He could start all over. Gone was his despairing helplessness, the prostrating feeling of guilt, of being trapped in perpetual unremitting penance. The new country had opened her arms wide to receive him, a cornucopia of men and things, customs and languages, finding their common denominator in seminudism, informality, pidgin, bagong and kimchee, a high threshold for indifference, if not tolerance or acceptance, which motivated him to tireless work, boldness, originality. In the rough types that were his neighbors and customers, whose dissoluteness, improvidence, violence,

physical, tangible code of an eye for an eye, a tooth for a tooth
revolted the more genteel and better established inhabitants of
the island, he saw beauty, purity, simplicity as befitted the
lawful heirs of Oceania, and shared their nostalgia for the
past. Even their gormandism and indolence, their shapeless
corpulence, were symbolic of their nobility and largeness of
spirit, their freedom from petty calculation and discipline. With
the eagerness and fondness of a child he listened to their
stories of woe, of domestic squabbles, unemployment, trivial
and sordid injustice, which wove into the grandeur of the
underlying epic of a fallen tribe of giants. He gave credit freely
and never turned to check on shoplifters. Soon he had half
a dozen willing unpaid assistants, burly fellows, working as
his stockman, delivery boy, or even cashier. The opposite of
prudence had rewarded him with success. The short holiday he
had intended for his children and himself, midway between
Korea and the U.S. mainland—after all Hawaii was a world-
famous resort, the stopover would not cost anything extra, and
they might never have a chance to come back—had turned out
to be his permanent residence. He'd never regretted it.

Then he had plunged zestfully into the fishing business,
not knowing a hook from a line, and in three short years he
owned four longliners, each valued at $200,000, despite the
machinations of the established Japanese fishing interests
to keep newcomers like him out. Recently he had taken his
worst beating from the dealers. The pre-Christmas storm had
forced his boats to be tied up at Pier 17. They would soon miss
the critical New Year market, when every Japanese had to
have sashimi for good luck. Though it was customary to space
out boat departures to avoid in-house competition, he was
forced to launch them at the same time, as soon as there was a
respite in the weather. All four of them arrived, loaded to the
deck, on New Year's Eve. But the other boat owners had done
the same thing and there was a glut which was promptly
exploited by the wily dealers. What would have fetched $5 a
pound, to retail for $15, went for under a dollar. A big year-end
bonus the dealers had worked out for themselves, a neat trick!
The demand was still there, seasonally quadrupled, but
because they had control of the outlets and storage, the few of
them could fix it up to knock off all the independent operators
like him. He almost dumped the whole catch rather than play
into their hands. But he had been through the Korean War;
food was sacred.

Sure he had his share of reverses and close calls, but he
still remained the enchanted mariner. The sea had her moods
and tempers, terrible and devastating, but she could be gentle

and giving, more munificently so than one's own mother. If only his real mother had been alive to see him at the helm of his *Sea Warrior*, the flag ship of his little fleet! And his father, too.

The memory still returned with the vividness of a nightmare from which he had just awakened. He had been hiding in a cave behind the village to avoid conscription into the People's Army, which had overrun all of the Korean peninsula except for a small pocket of resistance where MacArthur's army was locked in. It had been a miracle for Harry to escape the tightly roadblocked, cordoned-off streets of Seoul where he was a law student. Every mile of the rural roads had checkpoints and patrols. His native village turned out to be deadlier than the impersonal hostility of Seoul. His family had been landowners for generations, the benefactors to whom the whole country had flocked for help, praising their goodness. At the first arrival of Red Army contingents all those who had sworn eternal allegiance became strangers, accusers, arrogant masters. Only through a tenuous connection with the head of the County People's Committee, formerly a sharecropper whom Harry's father had helped to release from jail, the old couple's lives had been spared so far. But Harry was a different matter. To show their contrition for past sins and loyalty to the new order, his parents were to report his arrival or whereabouts immediately. They were even tortured. The couple managed to send food and clothing to Harry themselves, eluding the surveillance. They had nobody to trust with the task. Even his father took turns, coming the long, hard way up the hill, though his knee tendons had been severed by his torturers. Then Harry did not receive supplies for days. There was a limit to survival on a diet of wild berries and roots. He had to go down to the village to investigate and forage. An axe stood in his mother's neck and another in his father's skull, maggots swarming the decomposing bodies. Nobody had bothered to bury them.

He roamed up and down the countryside, convinced of his parenticide, refusing to return to his place of birth to face those ingrates and murderers who, now that the South Korean regime had been restored with U.S. support, had reverted to adulation of the old order and condemnation of Communist banditry. Even when his immigration to the U.S. was confirmed, he had sent an agent to sell off his patrimony. During his peregrinations, he had stumbled into Moonhee's village. At the gateway of what looked like the biggest house, he saw a four-year-old boy wallowing in his own waste, his movements clumsy and uncoordinated, his language an unmodulated

monosyllable, saliva drooling from his slack lips, his face
muscles contorted in a fixed half-smile or grimace. Only his
eyes moved without impediment. Harry picked him up, washed
him in the nearby ditch, and took him inside. Two women put
down their flails on the mat in the courtyard where they had
been thrashing rice and came over. The younger woman
almost snatched the child away from Harry, embraced him
tenderly, and took him into a room. The older woman apologized for her daughter-in-law's behavior and thanked him,
noting that he had been the first person ever to pick the child
up.
    "Why shouldn't I?" he said. "He's a good boy."
    "You're kidding," she said, her eyes yearning to hear other-
wise.
    "I'm not," he said sincerely. "I like him. His eyes are gentle
and full of expression."
    A blush of happiness suffused her face.
    "What's his name?"
    "No Name," she said.
    "You mean you haven't named him yet?"
    "Yes and no. With the war and all, we didn't think of
naming him. Then people started taunting him and calling
him No Name, and when the last census was taken, we just
reported it as No Name."
    She insisted on his staying for dinner. Then he was staying
through the next day and the next, helping them with the
heavy farm labor. The older master Jon, a landowner and
aristocrat like Harry's own father, had been murdered by the
Communists. The son, Moonhee's husband and No Name's
father, had been drafted into the People's Army and never returned. It had been over two years since the war's end, but
neither mother nor wife had any doubt about his eventual safe
return. It was pitiful but touching. What was wrong with an
illusion that kept people going? Harry encouraged them in this
belief. There was something deeply moving about Moonhee's
marriage to No Name's father, Kyongsoo. They were both
musicians, Moonhee a pianist and Kyongsoo a composer, both
going to the Seoul Conservatory of Music. Moonhee's father
had been a pastor, and she had played the organ in his
church. Kyongsoo had been going to this church and singing
in the choir three times a week, every Sunday and Wednesday
for five years, before he worked up enough courage to ask her
to a concert. They both got jobs as music teachers at the same
high school, and even after their marriage they remained an
affectionate, considerate couple, loving each other deeply. That
sort of love was meant to last forever, and Harry respected

190

and honored her feelings, as if her husband was in the same house or in the next village on a short trip. Nor did he detect from her any sign of even passing interest in him as a male. His position in the Jon family was undefined and untenable. He had to move on, but a strange reluctance or inertia deprived him of the will to act, and even in the third year he still found himself in the Jon household. In the meantime he and No Name had grown really close, the child preferring him to either of his kin.

Then, one frosty morning shortly after the rice harvest, a commotion outside woke him. A crowd of villagers lined the courtyard, looking on. In the center, surrounded by scattered clothing and other personal effects, was Moonhee on her knees, hugging No Name and weeping.

"Mother, I swear it's false," she wailed. "No Name is your true grandson. I never knew Mr. Song before that day when he first came to this house. You were there yourself."

"Don't lie, you slut," Grandma Jon spat. "I have it on the best authority. You and this Song were lovers. You cheated my son into marrying you to cover up the fattening of your stomach by your lover. No Name has none of our Jon blood. There hasn't been such deformity in the Jon gene. The retard is his, your lover's and yours."

Harry stepped out into the courtyard, outraged, to vindicate Moonhee's honor. Seeing No Name escape from Moonhee's arms and lumbering about, excited by all the strange faces, his soiled diaper squeezing out, Harry ran to him.

"See how he cares for him!" the old lady Jon screamed. "The ugly little monster disgusts everybody, but look how his father cannot hug and kiss enough of him!"

The crowd jeered, hissed, and spat.

"Get out of the village before we put sticks and stones on you," they yelled.

So began their marriage, and Harry had been forced into a blessing for which he would have willingly sold the whole world. The birth of their first child, a girl, was duly recorded and so was that of their two other children. Each time Harry insisted on entering No Name as their first child, but she refused for some reason. So No Name had no legal status. Over twenty, his language was still monosyllabic and his diaper had to be changed. But now there had developed an embarrassing pattern in his behavior. With unerring regularity he zeroed in on any female in his ambience. His mother was no exception, nor his sister. He was no rapist or physical menace exactly; in fact, he could barely outrun a two-year-old child. He would sidle up, unnoticed, close to the object of his quest, position himself so his groin touched the object's thigh, and rub once or twice, which was apparently all it took to make him stand in orgastic rigor, a sickening grimace on his face. Harry tried to teach him masturbation a few times but had to give it up as a lost cause. Like his anal tract, this outlet was beyond No Name's control. But even that did not diminish Harry's love for him, which seemed to run deeper than that for his own flesh and blood. No Name's disturbing habits made no difference. In fact, they served to remind Harry constantly of the human condition, making No Name his greatest moral teacher. He did not mind the social exclusion his family suffered on account of No Name and would not hear of committing him to an institution. Too bad about the other children if they withered and wilted under the stress of ostracism. They should learn to live with it. That was what life was all about. You didn't go around amputating your nose because it was not as useful as an elephant's trunk.

The immigrant visas had come through, and the matter of No Name's legal status surfaced again. No amount of proving or pleading would change the U.S. consul's attitude. Even if No Name was their real child, the U.S. law prohibited the entry of physical or mental deficients, he said. Further insistence on the inclusion of No Name might result in the cancellation of the whole package. When Harry returned home to announce his decision to forgo the immigration, he could not find Moonhee or No Name. The children were no help either, having come home to an empty house after school. After three months of futile search the police officially closed the case. Then a messenger came from Boogongni, from Grandma Jon. She was dying and had a matter of mutual interest to discuss with him.

There is a certain venerability in longevity, in the sheer persistence of the physical body against the odds. In her case this was enhanced by an indefinable extra quality. Her lined, gutted bronze-brown face, like the mossy bark of old pine, radiated an air of dignity, tranquility, even beatitude.

"I've heard you have three children," she said, smiling the benign smile that had so endeared her to him at their first encounter.

"Four, Ma'am," Harry corrected.

"Of course," she acquiesced. A cloud of pain crossed her face and she closed her eyes. After a barely audible sigh, she opened her eyes.

"My conscience is clear," she said. "That was the only way I knew of making her leave with you to find your happiness together. I didn't want to see her remain a widow for the rest of her

192

life and lose a good man like you. She was such a thoroughly good, loyal creature that nothing else would have moved her. And you would have moved on, sooner or later. Maybe sooner. There had been gossip, some pressure, though you probably didn't know about it. Back to the present..."

There was a long hiatus before she resumed and disclosed the awful fate of Moonhee and No Name, who had turned up a few months ago begging her to bury them. Before Lady Jon could do anything about it, Moonhee had thrust a stilletto in her son's heart, then quickly stabbed another in her own.

"I know you will bury me next to them," Lady Jon said, gulping her last breath. "We are all together at last, all the Jons. I feel fulfilled..."

* * *

"Why did you do it, Moonhee, why?" Harry groaned as he woke from his coma. He was told he had gotten trapped in the engine room, trying to pull Inho from it. The Coast Guard tug had arrived and towed the stricken vessel, submerged to the top deck, to Honolulu. All the crew had been saved. But his sense of relief was quickly dashed by what he heard next. There had been three Coast Guard fatalities. Responding to the first Mayday at 2 a.m. a helicopter had been dispatched to the approximate spot twenty-five miles north of Maui. The radio signals from the vessel went dead and the helicopter, braving the worst weather this side of the Pacific, had to fly low and close with the vessel in zero visibility, in the howling, blinding storm. Getting caught in an updraft of air, the helicopter had crashed into the side of a nearby mountain, but not before radioing the exact position of the *Sea Warrior* to the nearest tug.

Harry was gripped with the same intensity of guilt as at the deaths of his parents, Moonhee, and No Name. Three Coast Guard lives and a whole helicopter lost just to save his miserable vessel and crew! Including his own, the fishing vessels worked by Korean fishermen had been notorious for their inadequacy of equipment and safety standards, and their failure and breakdown rate at sea had the dubious distinction of being the highest in the Honolulu Harbor. After a rescue, the Coast Guard crew greeted the Koreans off, "See you next week." The Koreans cheerily waved back, then joked among themselves, "Private lifeguard." The enormity of such insensitivity had always revolted Harry, and now he saw himself as one of those grinning ingrates who took the life-saving work of the Coast Guard for granted. Harry went to the University of

Hawaii and engaged the services of a Dr. William Smith, Professor of Korean in the East Asian Literature Department, at the rate of $85 per hour to compose a letter to the Coast Guard Commandant, 14th District.

"I am mortified," the letter read, "to learn that no appropriate expression of thanks and condolences has been made. As one of the immediate beneficiaries of the sacrifice and heroism, I myself have just recovered from a coma and only now heard of the tragedy...I beg you to oblige me with a list of the names and addresses of the families of the dead, so I might write them individually."

"Dear Sir," the Rear Admiral wrote back. "We thank you for your expression of concern. We will continue to protect lives and property at sea, willingly accepting sacrifices in the line of duty...."

Did the Admiral think Harry had written with the mercenary motive of ensuring the goodwill of the Coast Guard so they would come to the rescue of him and other Koreans in spite of what had happened? Indeed there was talk among the fishermen that the Coast Guard might wise up and not come to the aid of Koreans any more. In fact, Harry had almost gotten into a fist fight with another Korean boat captain who accused him of ruining the image of the Korean fisherman, as if there had been one to ruin.

"Dear Admiral," Harry wrote back. "I happen to own four longline boats, each about the same value. I have decided to deed over one vessel to each of the surviving families and to sell the last one and put the proceeds in trust for my children's education, they being as much victims of the tragedy as the others. From now on I will have nothing to do with the sea."

His offer had made a front-page story in the papers, both local and national, and correspondent after correspondent came to his door for their version of the grateful Korean. With this fame came offers of jobs, titles and positions, both remunerative and honorary. Then jealous tongues, especially those of his own countrymen, began wagging. The whole thing was a calculated publicity stunt, they sniggered. The Korean boat owners were angry with him for maligning their fishing operations and threatened to sue him for libel.

* * *

When the door bell rang at the gate, he was in the backyard digging. He told Steve, his older son, to send away whoever it might be; he was not interviewing any more reporters. Steve came back after a while.

"She's no reporter, Dad," Steve said behind him.

"I'm not seeing No Reporter, either," he said gruffly, his back still turned, grappling with a rock.

"She's Mrs. Thompson," Steve said.

"Makes no difference," he panted, straightening his back as he hefted the 200-pound silicate from its wedge in the dirt.

"Jesus, the widow!" he exclaimed, suddenly remembering and dropping the rock a quarter inch from his toes.

"I am she." He heard a deep, velvety alto.

Was this to be the vendetta, the avenging Fury herself, in person? Slowly he turned, eyes closed, expecting the report of a revolver or the pain of the stilletto as it sliced through his aorta. The stilletto! Moonhee! He opened his eyes and came face to face with a tall, beautiful woman, elegantly dressed, her blonde hair interspersed with gray, her high nose with slightly flaring nostrils, her chaste yet strangely sensuous lips, her light brown eyes speckled with dots of blue. No, she wasn't Moonhee as he remembered her, but who knows. In her death she might have had the good sense to be reborn Caucasian, the passport to eligibility.

"I've been so looking forward to meeting you," she said, extending her hand.

"My hands are soiled, Ma'am," he said, retreating a little and shooting a glance of anger at Steve who stood on, arms akimbo, a smirk on his knowing face.

"I have written to you," he said, affecting formality. "I am still very sorry for Commander Thompson's loss, of course."

"I'm not here to discuss the dead," Joan Thompson said. "Not that I don't miss Donald. I still can't get over his not being around, but life must go on."

Ah, this damnable efficiency and practicality of Americans. His Moonhee would have lived a widow ten years or twenty.

"What can I do for you, Ma'am," Harry asked, feeling vaguely defeated.

"Can't we sit down somewhere?" Joan said.

"Of course. Let's go into the house."

"Good. You see I have this boat, a well-equipped longliner. In fact, I have two more, owned by my partners as the result of your munificence. Unfortunately, we know nothing about boats or fishing and need another partner to run the business for them."

"You're talking to the wrong man, then. I have no interest in the sea."

"I don't think you're being honest. Once a mariner, forever a mariner, as the saying goes. The country needs men like you to work the sea. Our seas are fished to exhaustion by other nations, while we sit back, landlocked, doing nothing, occassionally passing ineffectual, irrelevant moral statements, which nobody listens to anyway, about endangered species. Honolulu should be the base for an outreaching global fishing industry of our own. Like the whalers that used to sail the seven seas. That's why my partners and I have come up with the capital to buy more boats, to really go into fishing big. In fact, I represent substantial sums of money, millions of dollars, from many other sources. We want you to build and operate the tuna industry on a meaningful scale, first to match and then to outstrip the Japanese and Russian pirates. How about it? Look upon it as a patriotic duty and do it, just as Donald and the others did theirs."

The elegant, eloquent Joan Thompson stayed on for dinner and then for breakfast the next morning. That afternoon, Harry was down at Pier 17 asking about Inho Kim, Yong Ha, and Sam Chay. Were they working? Would they like to be?